"Treads the fine line between nostalgic creepiness harking back to the classics and modern pacing, with believable characters you really care about. Not to be missed!"

Paul Kane, bestselling and award-winning author of *Sherlock Homes and* *Arcana*

SUCH PRETTY THINGS

LISA HEATHFIELD

TITAN BOOKS

Such Pretty Things
Print edition ISBN: 9781789095623
E-book edition ISBN: 9781789095630

Published by Titan Books
A division of Titan Publishing Group Ltd
144 Southwark Street, London SE1 0UP
www.titanbooks.com

First edition: April 2021
10 9 8 7 6 5 4 3 2 1

A CIP catalogue record for this title is available from the British Library.

Printed and bound in Great Britain by CPI Group Ltd, Croydon CR0 4YY.

To Lucy Howe – for bringing extra sunshine to the world

1

Clara sees the trees sticky with sunlight. She can taste heat on the roof of her mouth, her tongue sitting close to her throat as she breathes in. She doesn't mean to open the car window, knowing only that her fingers find the handle slippery as she turns it.

'Keep it closed,' her father says, his voice marred with the same slick of tar that's been there since her mother's accident.

'It's too hot,' she says. *Can't you tell*, she wants to add.

She feels his eyes watching her in the rear-view mirror, looking from her to the road, to her brother, to the road. Beside her, Stephen traces his finger on the glass, whispering something only he can hear.

'What are you doing, Stevie?' she asks, using the material of her dress to brush the crease at the back of her knee.

'It's an antler,' he replies.

'You saw a deer?'

'It was on the road,' he says.

Clara doesn't remember the animal, although she's sure she would have seen it if it had been there. There's been nothing to do for hours but stare out as the world changed; the streets she's always known – the close-knit houses, the lamp-posts, the bus stop – disappearing behind them until the homes and shops were replaced by endless, endless fields and trees. She hasn't even been able to draw, the jagged lines of her pencil in her sketchbook making her ill.

'Stop kicking my seat, Stephen,' their father says.

'I'm bored.' Stephen's scowl is instant, exaggerated, his feet a steady pendulum beating a rhythm that Clara knows must grate between their father's teeth.

Her father takes his left hand from the steering wheel and wipes his palm across the back of his neck. The speckled line of dirt on the fold in his collar makes her suddenly, crushingly sad; if the fire hadn't happened, then their mother would have washed it. She'd have been able to stand in the kitchen, pressing the iron flat onto the shirt. Clara thinks of the heat in the hospital room, the starched bed-linen, the tubes unceremoniously pushed into her mother. The degradation of lying motionless as strangers prodded her skin.

'You must do as you're told when you're with them,' their father says. He grips the steering wheel again, Clara feeling his tension in her own shoulders, a subtle grasp of fingers that aren't there. 'It's good of them to take you on.'

He'd told them only yesterday, how he couldn't keep working and look after them. How someone had to pay the bills. *Your aunt and uncle have the time and the space. I don't know who else to ask.*

Stephen's tantrum. Their home filled by their father's resulting bellow, the echo of which Clara still feels deep in her core.

'I don't want to stay with people I don't know,' Stephen says.

'They're not just people. They're family.'

Who we haven't even met, Clara nearly says.

She looks out of the window as their car breaks free from the trees, at a marshy stretch where the grass slides into darkened dips and purple thistles rise up in hazy clusters. Beyond that, there's the silent roar of mountains, their outline picked out in thick, grey ink.

'See those, Stevie?' she says. 'They'll be ours to explore.'

He forgets his anger. 'Did mummy go there?'

'Maybe.' But it's impossible for Clara to grasp, their mother as a child, her footsteps running in and out of the heather.

Their father steers the car from the road, stops in front of a gate. On a post, the name Ballechin is written in faded blue paint, yet there's no sign of the house from here. The children watch as he gets out, arches his back with his arms above his head before he opens the gate, pushing it far enough so that it catches in the long grass. He brushes his hands together as he gets back in.

'Let's go and meet them.'

It's a narrow drive and their father curses as he steers around ruts that threaten to scratch the vehicle. On either side there are thick branches with early blackberries twisting and looping among them.

'Can we pick some?' Clara asks.

'We can't,' her father replies. 'They'll be waiting.'

Clara catches glimpses of brick between the trees, sees the elbow of a window's edge through parted leaves. From here, she can tell that Ballechin isn't a small house and as it steps out from behind the shadows of the pines, she loves it immediately – the window frames with glass cut neatly into separate squares, the curved porch supporting a honeysuckle, surrounding a front door made of dark wood. Roof tiles slant down, holding two tall chimneys and a pair of round windows nestled so far back that they're almost impossible to see.

Gravel crunches under the car's wheels before it stops and, as their father turns off the engine, silence takes over the air.

'Did mummy really live here?' Stephen asks.

'Yes.' Their father laughs and Clara notices how his shoulders relax, as though the strings that have been forcing them up have been cut.

'What's that?' Stephen is pointing to a small footprint of grass with a stone column at its centre. It's no higher than Clara's waist, with a metal fin balanced on the top. Part of her wants to lick the metal, to taste it on her tongue.

'It's a sundial,' their father says. 'Although I doubt it works very well, surrounded by so many trees.'

'It tells the time,' Clara tells Stephen, but already he's looking elsewhere, at a vegetable patch that runs away around the corner of the house.

'There she is.' Their father's seat rubs quietly as he turns to his children and they all look to the woman standing on the front doorstep with an apron tied tight around her waist, the red poppies on it smothered by the folds of the material. 'Come on,' her father says, pushing up the middle of his spectacles. 'We can't keep your aunt waiting.'

Stephen scrambles from the car, the blur of his eight-year-old self already rushing towards Ballechin, his arms reaching forward. Clara wants to follow him, but for a moment she finds it difficult to move, instead watching the flower bed nestled along the length of the house, where fuchsia bushes reach high enough to touch the windows. She feels a need to pop the red buds between her fingers.

'Clara?' It's her father's voice, bent slightly with irritation. She picks up her satchel, puts it over her shoulder and gets out of the car, to see Stephen standing close to their aunt. Clara ambles over the gravel to them, struck by the mismatched smells of honeysuckle and soap.

'They're beautiful,' Auntie says. She crouches as though to hug Stephen, but his wide eyes make her hesitate and embarrassment settles among them all. Their father's cough breaks through it.

'That's kind of you,' he says, his hand on Clara's shoulder.

Auntie seems to struggle with the right thing to do and her smile begins to falter with the effort.

'Do you have any luggage?'

'The suitcase is in the boot.' And their father steps away from them to return to the car.

Clara looks towards the vegetable patch, where the runner beans overstretch their bamboo sticks, slumped leaves interspersed with almost glowing orange flowers. She'd like to go and sit among the plants, to draw a picture of their stillness.

'I've brought my toys.' Stephen stands so close to Auntie that his fingers brush against the material of her skirt.

'We'll find space for your things.' She watches them in a way that Clara has never seen before, as though she and Stephen are some sort of miracle standing on her doorstep. The feeling slips under her skin and she thinks that perhaps she can be happy here.

'I'm Clara,' she says, almost laughing at her desire to curtsey.

'Clara,' Auntie echoes. 'And how old are you?'

'I was fourteen two weeks ago.'

'Of course,' Auntie says. 'And here's Stephen.'

'Does anyone else live here?' he asks, and Clara knows he's hoping somehow for other children, secret cousins to appear behind the windows.

'Only my husband, Warren,' Auntie says. 'We're so happy you're coming to stay.'

'How long can we be here?' Stephen asks.

'I've already told you,' their father tells him. 'A few weeks. Perhaps a bit longer.'

Clara only realises she's biting her nail when she takes her finger from her mouth, reaching over to squeeze her brother's hand.

'It'll be fun,' she tells him.

As Auntie stares at them again, Clara studies her face, but she can't find any trace of their mother. Perhaps that's a good thing. It'll be easier to stay here if she can pretend that there never even was a fire.

'So,' their father says, suitcase in his hand. 'Shall we go in?'

Auntie looks over at him. 'You're staying?'

Clara knows that his laugh is nervous. 'Only for a breather before I drive back.'

'I was worried for a moment that I hadn't made up a room for you.' Auntie smiles, relief and warmth on her face. 'Would you like a cup of tea?'

'I wouldn't say no.'

Clara has a sudden desire to hold her father's hand, but he just winks at her as Auntie turns from them and starts to walk through the door.

'This way.'

And so they follow.

Inside the house it's surprisingly dark, the daylight not quite reaching far enough, the heat left behind. There's a bright rug, though, a large circle and Clara likes the way that it's threaded with neat lines of colours. It reminds her of the sun, with Auntie treading around the edge of it as though it might scald her.

'We'll take off our shoes here,' she says, slipping her feet from her own. Stephen looks up at Clara, confused, but when she takes off her shoes, he copies. Auntie straightens the soles into a row.

'I like your house,' Stephen says, shifting his weight from one foot to the other.

'Thank you,' Auntie replies.

It's a big hallway with wide stairs in front of them, the ceiling reaching far above. The only piece of furniture is a small table pushed against the wall, a black telephone sitting alone on the top of it. Of the four doors, the only one open is to the right of the staircase, showing Clara a glimpse of a dining room painted dark green, with a table and straight-backed chairs.

Her eyes follow the curve of the banisters as they go up, the balusters carved so finely they look like they could snap.

'Can we explore?' Stephen asks.

'In time,' their father says.

Clara runs her hands over the skirt of her dress. Just this morning she was in her own home, sounds from the street filtering into every corner, her friend Nancy helping her pack. Their conversations overlapping and clutching together at the idea of so much distance soon to be between them.

'Should I leave their suitcase here?' their father asks. Auntie looks around, as if there might be somewhere better than the empty space of floor.

'I suppose so. Yes. And I'll bring some tea.' She steps towards the door on the left, pushing it open. 'If you could all wait in here, I won't be long.'

Musty air seeps from the room and even though Clara holds her hand over her mouth, the smell is still there. Stephen doesn't seem to notice it, running towards the dust motes hanging in the filtered sunlight.

'Look,' he says, turning to scatter the fragments.

'This is a cosy room,' their father says.

The one sofa has its back to the tall window and there's a dark red armchair next to an unlit fire. Opposite is a wooden chair with a woollen blanket folded neatly across it. Clara wonders if they might sit here in the evenings and whether she'll be allowed to choose one of the stories from the shelf that sits snug in the wall. She steps towards it and runs her finger along the books' spines, imagining taking the one from her satchel and slotting it alongside them.

'Any interesting ones?' her father asks, standing next to her now.

'They look a bit old,' Clara tells him.

He pulls one out, just a bit. 'They'll keep you busy on rainy days.'

'I'm sitting here,' Stephen says, running to the red chair and jumping into it, the leather squeaking as he settles into its arms.

'Move up,' Clara tells him, but there's not enough room for the two of them, so she shifts him onto her lap. She can tell that he doesn't really want to sit like this, would prefer instead to feel like a little king with his fingers splayed wide on the arms of the chair and it gives Clara a piercing rush of love that he chooses to stay with her. She's aware that he tiptoes around her sadness, that she's no longer the sister who makes him laugh by strapping pans to her feet. How that girl is lost somewhere in their mother's blood-soaked bandages.

Their father sits on the sofa, perched too close to the edge as he looks out of the window. 'You really are in the middle of nowhere up here. You'll have fun discovering everything.'

'Is there definitely a garden?' Stephen asks.

'There is. Your mother talked about it a lot.'

Clara listens for echoes of her mother's childhood voice, but hears only the ticking of the clock on the mantelpiece.

The door opens and Auntie comes in, the slight clatter of the tray betraying the shake in her hands.

'Oh,' she says, as she puts it down on the low table in front of them. 'Two of you in one chair.'

Stephen tries to move from Clara's lap, but she holds onto him.

'We'll be careful not to spill it,' she says, as Auntie stands straight again, a glass of squash in each hand.

'I'm sure you'll be fine.' She nods. 'I bought this especially for you.'

Stephen pushes clumsily against his sister, a shock of loneliness brushing past her as he frees himself to sit instead on the sofa next to their father.

'I've been thirsty for hours,' he says.

Clara smells the orange first and can tell that it's been made too strong; the first mouthful sticks sweetness to the top of her mouth, the liquid thick as she swallows.

'Is Warren here?' their father asks, taking his tea from Auntie.

'He'll be home later.'

There's the quiet again. Clara sits as still as she can to listen to the silence.

'How is Jane?' Auntie asks.

Their father rubs his thumb across the china cup he's holding. 'As good as can be expected.'

'She's still asleep,' Stephen says and the clock ticks on as Clara remembers the months their mother has been lying unmoving. 'Do you have a kite?'

'A kite?'

'To fly in the garden,' Stephen says.

'No. No, we don't have a kite.'

'I'm sure there are plenty of other things for you to play with,' their father says.

'Yes.' Auntie nods. 'We have toys.' Clara watches as she pulls her smile back into place, that same sense of wonder in her eyes as she looks at them.

'It's a big house for just you and Uncle Warren,' she says.

'Yes. I suppose it is.'

Stephen wriggles about on the sofa, the liquid dangerously close to spilling.

'Finish your drink, Stevie,' Clara says. And he does, his mouth smiling at her through the glass.

'Do you ever want to move away?' their father asks.

Auntie looks confused. 'Why would I?'

Clara thinks that her aunt is somehow offended, but she can't see how. There's still so much about the adult world that she doesn't understand. She feels the line of her age drawn on the earth as she teeters along it, falling at times into the side of childhood and at others slipping into the strange mist of growing-up.

Her father takes a bigger gulp of his tea and Clara wonders if it's scalded his throat.

'Have you got children?' Stephen asks.

'No,' Auntie replies. 'We were never that lucky.'

'Well now you have two,' their father says with forced cheeriness. 'Temporary ones at least.'

'We've been looking forward to it.'

Clara glances up at Auntie when she can, looking for clues of their mother. There are mannerisms, if nothing else, an understated elegance in the way she holds herself. Clara would like to draw her, to find more similarities. For now, she just tries to copy her posture, with her back straight, her own lips barely brushing the rim of her glass.

'Things must have been difficult for you,' Auntie says, directing the question to their father. 'You have to keep working after all. You can't just stop.'

Their father nods. 'It will be easier with the children out of the way.'

His blunt words sting Clara and it's only a kind, knowing smile from Auntie that comforts her.

No one says anything more as they finish their drinks, the sound of Stephen's heels kicking against the base of the sofa. As soon as their father puts his empty cup onto the saucer, he presses his hands on his knees and stands up, brushing imaginary specks from his arm.

'Right. I suppose I ought to get going,' he says. 'It's a long drive back and I'd like to make it before dark.'

'Of course,' Auntie says, standing too, redoing the bow at the back of her apron. 'We'll say goodbye, then.'

Clara sees in Stephen's eyes a brief flash of fear, of impending homesickness. 'We'll be very happy here,' she says as she picks up her satchel, proud that she's reassuring all of them gathered in the room.

'I'm sure you will be,' their father says, as they follow Auntie into the hallway.

At the front door, he's slow to put on his shoes again and they watch as he ties each lace.

'Will you visit us?' Stephen asks.

'I'll try to come next week.'

'It's a bit far to travel for a short visit,' Auntie says.

'Jane will want me to see the children,' he tells her.

Clara feels fierce tears pushing at her throat, thinking there's so much she wants to, and should, say.

'Are you leaving us now?' Stephen asks.

'Yes.' Their father nods. He takes his spectacles from his face and blows on them, cleaning them on his sleeve before he puts them back on again.

'Give mummy a kiss from me,' Clara manages.

'I will. And you look after your brother.'

'We'll telephone you if we need anything,' Auntie tells him.

'Good.' He straightens up, his jaw tight.

Clara thinks that he'll kiss her, but he doesn't, only squeezing her shoulder before he strides back across the gravel and gets into his car, pulling the door towards him, closing himself from them.

The three of them watch from the front step as the vehicle turns, the engine splitting the clean air. They watch as it disappears around the corner of the drive and they stay like this until they can no longer hear even its whisper on the air.

Clara reaches down for Stephen's hand and he takes it willingly. She believes they'll be fine here, but still needs his little soul by her side to steady her.

'So,' Auntie says. 'It's just us now.' She clasps her hands in front of her chest like a child.

'Can we see our bedroom?' Stephen asks, as he runs back inside the house.

Clara picks up their suitcase from the hallway, before they follow their aunt up the stairs. This close she can see that the varnished balusters are carved with weaving corn too delicate to touch, so she keeps nearer to the wall with its paper of faded flowers.

'We stay on the carpet running down the middle,' Auntie says, without glancing back.

Clara is disappointed with herself, even though the rules contradict each other – how there's a rug downstairs to avoid, yet here she must keep away from the floorboards. But when Auntie stops and turns to look at them, Clara is relieved to see the kindness of her smile.

'Would you like me to carry that?' she asks, holding out a hand.

'No. I'm fine.' Clara's answer seems to stall Auntie, flustering the air around her. 'Thank you.'

'You must be tired,' Auntie says.

'It was ages in the car,' Stephen tells her.

'It certainly was.' Auntie laughs lightly.

'Clara was sick coming up through the mountains,' Stephen says. 'Daddy had to stop so she could upchuck in the bushes.'

Clara drops the suitcase, hoping it'll hit his foot, but it misses and lands loudly on the floor. Auntie tries to keep smiling as she studies the skin on Clara's lips.

'I think you should have a bit of a wash, then,' she says, her voice forced bright. 'Don't you?'

The air is clammy at the top of the stairs, where the wallpaper has given way to wooden panelling and the damp of the surrounding hills has had hundreds of years to seep inside. Above each of the five closed doors hangs a dried posy of flowers, clusters of pale, crisp petals tied with faded ribbons. Clara feels her mother's fingers on the flowers, sees her pick them to arrange in the shed back home, hears the shattering crackle as the blaze destroys them too.

'Look, Clara.' Stephen is pulling her sleeve, dragging her back to Ballechin. 'We're high up.' The smell of smoke drifts away as she peers with him over the banister into the hallway, to the table with the telephone, the colourful rug below.

'Don't lean too far,' Auntie says, encouraging them away and through the door on the right at the top of the stairs. It's a bathroom, with the day squeezing through the frosted window, leaving patches of sunlight on the walls. The bath is bigger than their one at home and Clara likes the tiles with blue dots that blur when she stares too much.

'This is a strange basin,' Stephen says. It sits balanced on a short, wooden cupboard and, without asking, he opens the small doors.

Auntie has a hand stretched out as though she needs to stop him, but when she doesn't Clara realises that Ballechin is a place where Stephen can be himself, that he'll be happy and hopefully his regression to tantrums will be a thing of the past.

'Hold your hands under here,' Auntie tells her, before she turns the tap to drop water onto the girl's fingers. Auntie's knuckles remind Clara of button mushrooms that have been left out of the fridge, withered and hard. 'Good. And a bit of soap,' Auntie says, as she rubs Clara's palms to make sure that all grains of vomit have disappeared. 'That's better.'

Clara feels full of gratitude. For so many weeks now, since the fire that almost killed their mother, she's been thrust into the role of carer, somehow at times even for their father, fumbling through her enforced responsibilities. Yet now she's being looked after again, and the shock of it threatens the ache of tears in her throat as she shakes her hands free of water and grasps Stephen's shoulder.

'Ow,' Stephen says, squinting up at his sister. 'What's wrong?'

'Nothing.'

Auntie gathers Clara's hands in a towel, looking closely at the fingernails.

'You bite them,' she says.

'I'm trying to stop.'

Auntie smiles at her. 'It can take time.' And she starts to pat the fingers dry, each in turn, standing close enough for her skirt to touch Clara's own.

Maybe she even loves us, Clara wonders, as Auntie blows on the backs of her hands before she hangs the towel straight on its rail. *Because we're not strangers exactly, we're family.*

'My friend, Nancy, said she'll buy me a sherbet fountain every week for a month if I manage it.'

'That's kind of her,' Auntie says, reaching for Stephen's hands. 'Your turn.'

'But I wasn't sick,' he says.

'Your hands will still be dirty from the journey.'

'Can I see my bedroom next?' Stephen asks, as he holds his hands under the flow of water and lets Auntie dry his skin.

'Yes,' Auntie says. 'You'll be sharing.'

Clara tries not to show her disappointment. She's never had a room to herself and she was hoping that here at least she'd have her own place in which to hide.

'Is it big?' Stephen asks.

'Big enough for the two of you.' Auntie laughs. It's an unusual sound, here in the light-speckled bathroom.

'Your house is so big,' Stephen says.

'That's why we need to fill it with children,' she says, tapping him on his shoulder gently. 'Follow me, then.'

Out on the landing again, Clara notices for the first time that the knotty grains of the wood wall are only painted to look that way. Up close, she can see the brushstrokes, the different shades of brown. She wants to lick her finger and rub at it to see if it smears, but she senses that Auntie wouldn't approve, so she clutches the suitcase handle instead.

Ahead of them, at the end of the short corridor, is a window looking out over trees. On the sill sit three ancient-looking dolls, two girls and a boy, and even from here Clara can see the fine detail of their clothes, their lifelike eyes painted onto porcelain skin. She knows she's too old to play with them and that her friends would definitely tease her if they knew, but she has a desperate urge to go and pick them up, to be a child again.

'I'm afraid that they're not for touching,' Auntie says, following Clara's gaze. 'Even though they're such pretty things.'

'I don't even want to,' Stephen says.

'Warren and I thought that you'd like the east room. You get the morning sun, so it's nice and warm.' Clara sees the slight pleading in her eyes as she opens the third door along. Cooped-up air greets them, before Auntie blinks and walks inside.

There are two beds next to each other, with plumped pillows and matching patchwork counterpanes. They're similar to one that Clara tried to make at school, with Nancy talking more than sewing as they squinted and pulled thread, lining up the hexagonal patterns. Clara had found the niggling material difficult to pinch and control, but she wishes now that she could have finished it.

Between the beds is a tiny table with a toadstool lamp. The red curve with white spots has been partly cut away to show a family of rabbits in their kitchen in a burrow and Clara isn't surprised when Stephen rushes towards it, kneeling down to peer inside.

'I thought you'd like that.' Auntie laughs and he looks back at her, his face lit up with happiness. Clara wants to ask him to stay still so that she can capture it in a drawing, but he stands and the moment is gone.

The shining wooden floor of this east room holds two rectangular rugs, one for each child. White curtains are hooked back from the window with little red bows. Tucked close to the glass, almost hidden under the curtain's hem, is a dead fly with its legs held together in prayer. The blue wardrobe in the corner. The little chest of drawers with a vase of flowers placed carefully in the middle.

'They're harebells,' Auntie says when she sees Clara looking. 'I picked them for you this morning.'

'Thank you.' Clara finds it difficult to know how else to reply. The room is so pretty that it disintegrates her disappointment of not being on her own. She just wishes that Nancy were here to see it and envisions her friend spinning wide-eyed circles between the beds.

'And look what's here,' Auntie says, closing the door slightly to show a desk behind it, with two notebooks sitting side-by-side, two new pencils sharpened to a point. Clara wants to pick up one and smell the lead tucked inside. Instead, she turns to the bricked-up fireplace with orange tiles surrounding it and the mantelpiece above, with an ornament of a boy sitting on a rock. His face has been worn thin, his nose hollow and the colour in his eyes rubbed away.

'What's that?' Stephen asks, reluctantly pointing to it.

'He was mine when I was your age,' Auntie says. 'I thought you might like him.'

'Oh,' is all Stephen says, frowning at the faded grey of the little boy's trousers, the chips of china scratched from his arms.

On the wall above the beds there's a round clock in the middle of two identical paintings – perfect sunsets above perfect hills, each one encased in a heavy gilded frame.

'They're difficult to dust,' Auntie says, nodding towards them, 'but they're worth it. Do you think?'

'Yes,' Clara replies. Stephen leans his head to see them from a different angle and Clara hopes he won't say that he'd prefer it if they were motor cars, or at least a train.

'I made you clothes.' Auntie sounds like an excited child as she turns the handle on the wardrobe door and opens it. Inside, there's a row of hanging dresses and little hanging suits. There's a smell too, like dogs' skin, and Clara tries to cover her nose and mouth without Auntie noticing. 'They're all yours. I hope that you like them.'

Stephen is touching his suits, each in turn. 'I'll look just like daddy.'

'I think you should change before tea,' Auntie says. 'We might as well start as we mean to go on.'

'I'm comfortable as I am,' Clara says. She knows she won't like the high necks of lace and the hems that will skim her ankles. 'Thank you, though,' she remembers.

Auntie stares straight ahead and Clara can almost see her mind stuttering behind her pale-blue eyes.

'Maybe tomorrow, then,' she eventually says, and Clara feels a shade of guilt as Auntie's shoulders sink with the stone-weight of disappointment. 'I'll leave you to settle in for a bit, then.' She's twisting her hands awkwardly, her fingers brushing again and again against the apron. She's picking the poppies, Clara thinks. 'I'll call for you when tea is ready.' And their aunt hurries out, a beetle scurrying away.

'Have you seen the garden? The grass is in lines.' Stephen rushes over to try to push up the window, but it wants to keep the stuffy heat trapped inside.

Clara smells the harebells, disappointed at their weak scent, before she goes to stand beside her brother and stare out. It seems more like a park than a garden, big enough to hold a hundred children, with a hedge drawing a neat line across the middle.

In the centre of the lawn is a circular flower bed filled with white flowers.

'It looks like the moon,' she says.

There's a rose-walk leading to an opening in the hedge; beyond that more lawn, before a forest and the steep rise of the mountains. Clara is amazed that she's here. Before, there were the four of them, but somehow that time has been swept away and life's unpredictable current has led her to a house in the hills. She puts her finger on the glass and follows where the garden has been mowed, leaving a faint smear that disappears like fog as soon as she lifts her hand away.

'It must take hours. Do you think they'd let me do it?' Stephen asks.

'I'm sure they would.' There's a memory, somewhere, for Clara. Only a few months ago, Stephen jumping in their father's carefully placed grass shavings. Clara's thoughts echo now with the sound of her brother's tears from behind their locked bedroom door.

'Clara?' Stephen's voice cuts through the green-smeared skin, the whiskers of their father's moustache.

'Yes?'

'I like this room,' he says, jumping onto the bed, his joy infectious. 'And she's nice, even though she's a bit old.'

Clara puts her fingers to her lips. 'She wants to look after us, when she didn't have to. We're lucky.'

'She must have one of those gold hearts,' Stephen says.

'Yes, she must.' Clara is suddenly overwhelmed by gratitude for her aunt, for letting her feel safe, cocooned from the horror that came before.

'Can we unpack?' Stephen asks, but before he's even finished the sentence, he's racing towards the suitcase and is dragging it across the room.

Clara puts her satchel on her pillow before she helps him lift the suitcase onto his bed, and together they unclasp it and the top springs open. Inside it's so jumbled with toys that Clara doesn't know where to look.

'When did you put these in?' She'd been the one to pack the bag, the last one to close it.

'I swapped some things,' he says, as he reaches past all of the toys to pull out his Walrus. He puts his nose to its fur and inhales deeply.

'Where are the clothes I packed for you?'

'There wasn't enough room for everything.'

'You can't only wear the clothes you've got on.'

'I've got new ones now.' And he looks towards the wardrobe.

Clara wants to tell him that the suits will turn him into a stranger, that she doesn't want him to wear them, but she keeps quiet, worrying that it'll only burst this new layer of happiness he's building around him. Instead, she sits on the other bed and stares out of the window, sees how in the distance the hills rise steeply to touch the white sky. Closer to the garden there are so many trees watching back. They can see only her head and shoulders through the glass, but for some reason Clara doesn't like them knowing that she's here.

So she lies down, curls tight into a foetus. Sometimes she does this, rucks up the sheets around her, resettling herself in her mother's stomach again. Even when her mother was better, she liked to pretend she could hear the gentle thud of her mother's heart. Clara lies like this and if Stephen really looked, he'd see freckles of tears, perfect circles balanced in the corner of her closed eyes. She's glad to be in this house, she knows she is, but the tears escape to slide across her nose and slip down her cheek.

* * *

*D*ownstairs, *Auntie pushes open the wooden door to the kitchen, to where the cast-iron stove waits for her. Above it, the shelf is laid with brass pans that gleam in their order of size. There's only one small window in here; she sometimes thinks that the room reminds her of a womb, before that thought shrivels up inside her.*

She hears the children in their bedroom and thinks of the boy with his earnest expression, the girl with her nervous smile. They're really here, in her house and the thought makes her heart ache with happiness. It's exactly as she'd hoped it would feel.

Yet her euphoria fades slightly when she hears their suitcase being dragged across the floor. It took her hours to polish, her knees bruised to the bone, but still she kept dipping her cloth in the tub, rubbing it frantically across the wooden boards.

'Don't they know?' she wonders. 'How long it took?'

She thinks she will go up there and remind them to be careful, but suddenly the little boy laughs. It's a sound she can barely remember and it covers her, smothers her, tipping her towards a place she's forgotten ever existed.

'Pull yourself together,' she chides herself.

Hanging on the end of the shelf is a tube of twisted garlic. She notices immediately that a piece of its translucent skin has come loose, but is calm as she snaps it off, the dry rustle comforting her. She lifts the bin and pops it in, before washing her hands in the deep white sink.

What to cook? She's planned a stew, but now she's met the children she's not so sure. What would they prefer? The children. She has to stand still and concentrate on her breathing, slow down the need to cry and laugh and shout all at once. Instead, she just screws up her fists in glee and stamps her feet excitedly, where no one can see.

'They'll like the fish,' she says out loud. It's a good dish, peppered with herbs she's spent the summer drying, hanging in the larder where their smell masks that of Warren's muddy boots.

The fish has been resting in her fridge in a pot of brine, as her husband likes, the salt sinking even into the wide, round eyes. She worries that the juice is already strong and possibly a taste that they're not used to.

'In time,' she says.

She pulls the two pieces of fish from the tangy water and places them on the wide chopping board. She chooses the right knife, the one she uses only for this, and slices clean along the length of one of the bodies. She can smell the sea from it.

'Did you swallow the ocean?' she asks, even though she knows that it can't reply.

Auntie scrapes the mess from inside it, scooping it up, dropping it into a bag and into the bin, soaping her hands and drying them on the towel hanging from its hook on the wall.

She likes the sound of the fish frying, the sight of them turning from wet pink to white. They shrink so slightly, yet enough for her to see. She hums as she melts butter into the silver scales.

She never thought she could be this happy.

2

There's a gentle knock on the children's door. Stephen stops, his hand still on the wooden fire engine as the door opens. Auntie stands in her stockinged feet, her apron, her blouse.

'Hello,' Stephen says.

'Are you settling in?' Auntie asks, looking into the room.

'We've been unpacking,' Stephen says, swinging back for her to see. There's chaos on the floor, toys strewn across the bed.

'It's a bit of a mess already.' Auntie tries to make her voice light, but Clara can tell that the toys scattered around the room are taking up too much space.

'Oh,' Stephen says looking around. 'Is it?'

They sit still amid the awkward silence.

'I came to tell you that Warren's home, so I'll be serving tea soon. You can wash your hands and come down.'

'Thank you,' Clara says, hoping that the affection in her voice is enough to make Auntie happy.

* * *

From the bathroom, the children go out onto the landing and hear voices drifting up to greet them. Clara peers over the banisters to the hallway below, and though she can see neither Auntie nor Uncle Warren, she's surprised by the hard beat of nerves in her heart. She glances towards the dolls on the sill, hoping for them to give her courage, but they don't even look at her.

The children stop at the bottom of the stairs and see their shoes pushed neatly against the wall, in line with Auntie's. Clara hadn't noticed the coat-stand before, hiding behind the open door when they arrived, but it's there now standing like a tree, a long, brown coat hanging from one of its branches.

'There you are.' Auntie comes out of a room. Excitement spills from her eyes, onto her hands, to the end of every fingertip. 'Come this way.' She's holding out her hand to them and winces slightly as they step straight through the middle of the circular rug to get to her.

'This is our dining room.' Auntie smiles, opening another door.

It's the green room that Clara saw into before and now she can see how large it is. She tries to ignore the lingering scent of old people as she looks at the long table in the centre, set with four of everything – four leather place mats, knives, forks and spoons and sparkling glasses filled with water. Behind it, windows stretch all the way from the floor to almost the ceiling, proudly showing the garden beyond. In the corner a lifelike little boy sits on a chair, his stitched leather skin sewn to make a face, hands, feet, waxy and pale. He wears a white shirt under his small blue suit, arms hanging by his sides as his button eyes stare at Clara.

She needs to get Stephen's attention. If he sees the boy, they can make fun of it together, before it can slip any seeds of unease into her. But her brother is looking only at the tear-drop icicles hanging from the glass chandelier and the light falling around it.

Auntie goes to stand by his side. 'It was my great-grandmother's,' she says. 'Rumour has it that it came all the way from Scandinavia.' She looks down at him as he nods enthusiastically. 'I used to like looking at it when I was your age, trying to spot colours that no one else could see. I think it steals them from the room,' she says, pointing to the walls, the yellow curtains, a tapestry of flowers hanging from a hook.

'So it was here when our mother was a child?' Clara asks.

'Yes,' Auntie says. 'Yes, it was.'

'Mummy's with the doctors.' Stephen's innocence lingers in the air until Auntie coughs.

'Shall we sit? Stephen, you go here.' She pulls out the chair for him, before he can choose somewhere else. 'And Clara.' She points to the chair opposite, the one with its back to the window, the one too close to the motionless boy.

'Can't I sit next to Stephen?' she asks.

There's an odd, lurching silence.

'No,' Auntie says. 'This is your place.'

And Clara now sees two tiny pieces of card on the table, each folded down the middle. When she settles in her seat, she realises that the one in front of her place mat has her name painted on it, with pink ribbon laced around the letters, underneath carefully drawn silver shoes. The room seems to fall completely still as she looks at it.

'Did you do this for me?' she asks.

'Yes.' Auntie swallows.

Stephen picks up his own card.

'Look, Clara,' he says, turning it so that Clara can see the precious painting on it – of a miniature boat, the sea against the red wood.

'It's beautiful,' Clara says and Auntie beams as she leaves the room.

'It's cold in here,' Stephen says.

'Maybe she'll light the fire for us,' Clara tells him.

A shelf clock stands on the mantelpiece above the empty grate, between two gilt-framed photographs. Caught behind one is the face of Auntie. She's trying to smile, but it looks more like an apology, her eyebrows arched, her lips barely raised. She was younger then and Clara wonders that if she could touch her cheek, how smooth it would feel.

The second picture fills her with a jolt of unease. A man with a thick beard and heavy-lidded eyes stares straight towards her. Their father has told them so little about Uncle Warren – barely more than his name – and on the way to Ballechin Clara had filled in the gaps with reasons for the secrecy. She'd built him as the hero of the story, but now she can't picture this man running away with Auntie to live in the hills.

'Have you seen that funny thing?' Stephen asks, pointing to the silent boy watching them, just as the door swings open and Auntie comes back in clutching four plates. They make a soft sound as she puts them on the table, one in each of their places.

'I won't be long,' she says, scuttling out again. Clara knows she should offer to help, as she'd never expect their mother to serve them food on her own. But this woman isn't their mother.

She looks over to where Stephen sits opposite, where he concentrates on making himself go cross-eyed.

'You'll give yourself a headache.' She laughs, so he pulls at his lips with his fingers and waggles his tongue.

Clara is thirsty, but she doesn't like the thought of touching the glass of water, not with the unpleasant smell that sits like mist in the room. Perhaps she can lean over and lap at the liquid with her tongue, but that seems even worse – such an intimate part of her body exposed to the air. She tries not to think as she lifts the water, gulping it.

'You're not meant to drink it yet,' Stephen tells her, but she just shrugs at him. She'd like to throw some of the water up into the chandelier, watch it drip down and see if it drags with it the colours that only Auntie sees.

She puts down the glass instantly when the door swings open again.

In one hand Auntie carries a bowl of corn-coloured potatoes and in the other a ceramic pot with thin wisps of steam pushing out of two small holes in the lid. The oven gloves are big enough to protect her hands from the hot handles and she lowers them slowly onto the mat in the middle of the table. Pride sweeps over her face as she takes off the lid and the smell of fish swims into the air.

'I thought I'd make my best dish on your first night,' Auntie says. 'Fish stew.' Just the sound of it is enough to flip Clara's stomach. 'Pass me your plate, Stephen.' And she starts to ladle out what looks to Clara like lumps of gristle in oily sauce.

'Not too much for me,' she says quickly, as she passes her own plate. Auntie pauses, her smile suddenly stuck. 'I'm still not feeling too good from the drive.' Clara hopes that she has the right look on her face – that of gratitude mixed with reluctance.

'Of course,' Auntie says. 'It's not easy the first time you come up here. It's a challenging road. We can get cut off for days if a tree comes down, or weeks if it snows heavily.'

'That would be exciting,' Stephen says. 'We'd have to be survivors.'

'Help yourself to potatoes,' Auntie says, as she sits down. Stephen reaches for them, but as soon as he picks them up Clara knows that his wrist isn't strong enough to hold them and the bowl tips down, potatoes rolling onto the table.

For a moment, they all stop and stare.

'I'm sorry,' Stephen says. Clara can tell that he's about to cry, so she jumps from her chair and starts picking them up, dropping them hot back into the bowl. She licks her fingers at the tips of melted butter and sits back down.

'It's ruined,' Auntie whispers.

'They're fine,' Clara says.

'We can't eat them now.' Auntie is bent over slightly, leaning one hand heavily on the table. She takes a cloth from the pocket of her apron and starts to rub at a patch where the potatoes' heat has bubbled the varnish.

'We can still eat them,' Clara says. 'Mummy always tells us that a bit of dirt makes you stronger.'

Auntie's eyes widen as she picks up the potato bowl. 'I'll get some bread,' she says. Clara expects her to stomp from the room, but she doesn't. Instead, she just stoops a bit as she leaves them, looking sad enough for sympathy to sneak into Clara.

'You must be more careful,' she tells Stephen.

'I'm sorry.'

'And you mustn't cry,' Clara says. 'We have to look happy for her. She's helping out a lot by having us here.'

Stephen is smiling by the time Auntie comes back in carrying a board laden with thick chunks of straight-cut bread, putting a slice on the edge of each of the plates.

Clara had wanted potatoes, but she doesn't say. And she'd prefer to have butter on her bread, but she doesn't say that either. Because she can see clearly the tear-stained lines in the whites of Auntie's eyes and she knows that, somehow, they've failed her.

'Break it over your stew,' Auntie says, before crumbs have a chance to spill from Clara's fingers. She does as she's told, peeling off a corner of her slice and balancing the rest on the side of the plate. She dunks the bread into the stew, releasing more steam that makes bile rise in her throat. It becomes the smoke that choked their mother and she has to blink it out of her eyes, to stop it reaching into her.

She drops the bread into the fish sauce, watching it bubble and sink under the surface, before she quickly breaks another piece and stuffs it dry into her mouth.

Stephen happily eats the stew, barely chewing between each spoonful.

'Where's Uncle Warren?' he asks. The fourth place sits empty.

'He's in the garden,' Auntie says.

'This late?' Clara doesn't like the thought of a stranger out there, even more so if it's the man who scowls down at her from the mantelpiece.

Auntie finishes her mouthful before she speaks. 'He likes to work hard.'

'Will he eat supper with us?'

'He'll have to eat later now.'

'Daddy sometimes does that too,' Stephen says.

'We will meet him tonight, though?' Clara asks, dreading it, but needing to have the moment of greeting behind them.

'Not tonight,' Auntie says. 'I have to be honest and say that he's not as keen as I am that you're here. He's not used to children.'

They all turn at the faint tapping at the window.

'Is that him?' Clara tries to keep her voice above a whisper.

Auntie smiles. 'I'll have to cut back the fuchsia. The wind sometimes comes rattling across the lawns and catches the buds.' She spoons up another mouthful and takes care to chew properly.

'When Jane was younger, her favourite flowers were bluebells. Does she still like them?'

Such a small question, but it's unwieldy for Clara. She thought she loved her mother more than life, yet she doesn't know this simple thing.

'Yes,' she lies, 'they're her favourite,' as beneath the table she pinches hard the skin of her thumb.

Stephen suddenly screams and drops his spoon. Splashes of stew splay out across the table.

'What is it?' Clara asks, stunned.

'There's an eye.' Stephen stares in horror at his plate.

'An eye?' Clara hesitates. She doesn't want to look over, to see something shiny and round blinking through the fish sauce.

Auntie seems too shocked to move, seeing the spilt food. 'There's only one. It means that you're lucky.'

'I don't like it,' Stephen says, moving far back in his chair.

'I got it wrong,' Auntie says, moving now to sweep a cloth around Stephen's plate. And for a hideous moment, Clara thinks that Auntie might cry.

'No,' she tries to reassure her. 'Everything is right.'

Auntie scoops up the eye into her spoon and Clara doesn't look away in time. The image of it sitting there burns into her mind, the blind circle held in the curved metal. It feels like she swallows it, clearly pressing against her throat as it goes down. She listens to Stephen chewing, wonders how he can already be eating again, when Auntie comes back in.

'This is nicer than mummy's food,' he says, and it's enough to thaw Auntie.

'I'm glad,' she says, before she looks at Clara. 'But you don't like it?'

'I'm allergic to fish,' Clara tells her, the lie slipping warm into the room.

'Allergic to fish?' Auntie is taken aback. 'No one told me.'

'Daddy must've forgotten.'

Auntie looks at the table. 'But that means the meal isn't perfect.'

'I'm sure it's very nice, though,' Clara says, trying to make the lie less painful.

Stephen gulps down her dishonesty with every mouthful of his stew.

'She gets awfully sick,' he suddenly offers. 'It makes her go red and shake.' He starts to giggle, wiping his nose on the back of his hand. Auntie takes a tissue from her left sleeve and passes it to him. He has to take it, and it makes his laughter stop. Clara knows he won't want to touch its crumpled smell of perfume, and he drops it onto the table as though it's hot. The air suddenly ripples icy around them.

'The bread is delicious, though,' Clara says, wanting Auntie to know that she does like her. 'Did you make it yourself?'

Auntie barely nods. 'Every day,' she says. 'I make a new loaf every day.'

'Mummy tried to teach me once, but mine just stayed flat,' Clara says. 'It was like a rock. We nearly broke our teeth on it.'

The memory should make Clara happy, but it only hurts.

Stephen finishes his stew noisily, sweeping up the last smear with the end of his crust, unaware of the creeping disappointment seeping among them all.

Clara needs the meal to be over. She's relieved when Auntie's plate is empty, watches as she puts down her cutlery gently enough not to make a sound.

'I think we'll save any pudding until tomorrow,' Auntie says.

'You've made pudding?' Stephen asks.

'Plum pie,' Auntie says. 'But it'll keep.'

'Couldn't we eat a bit now?' Stephen asks. 'I've finished my stew.'

Clara would love some too; her stomach is still scratchy with hunger.

'No,' Auntie says, as she stares out of the window. 'You can't have pudding if you haven't eaten your first course. We'll have to save it for tomorrow.'

'Clara,' Stephen says, sulking back in his chair and even crossing his arms heavily across his chest, but Clara knows she can't eat the congealing food in front of her.

'We can help clear away,' she offers as Auntie stands up and starts to stack the plates, Clara's one on the top, the lumps of fish still sitting heavy in the cold juice.

'I'll be fine to do it on my own,' Auntie says. 'You go back to your room and play.' She lifts the pile of china, cutlery sticking out like an unbalanced spider. 'Or you could tidy it.' And she hurries once more from them.

A giggle cracks from Stephen's lips. Clara watches as the laughing holds tight around his waist and shakes him.

'Shh,' Clara says, as he tumbles helpless to the floor. 'She'll hear you.' But the laughter pelts headlong into her, a wave that she can't stop even when Auntie is in the doorway again, confusion sculpting her to stone.

'Stop it,' Auntie utters, but the sound of her makes Stephen squeal louder. Clara waits for Auntie to march across the room, lift up her brother by his trousers and slap him hard across the legs. But instead she stumbles towards the table, picks up the casserole dish. 'Stop it,' she mutters again, 'Warren won't like it,' before Clara sees her disappear out of the door.

Stephen tries to speak, but the laughter is too sharp in him. And his eyes too filled with tears to see the stuffed boy at the edge on his chair, glowering at them with a mouth sewn shut in disapproval.

When they finally calm down, Clara feels sadness stalk in and muffle her mouth with a heavy hand. Because this house might be big and beautiful, but she misses the powder-scent of her mother, the sound of her walking through the front door. And there's something else now too – Uncle Warren doesn't want them here.

When a sob falls from Stephen, Clara jumps up and runs around the table to put her arms around his little body curled on the floor. He feels so small, so unlike the whirlwind of light who normally shakes the room. It's as though he's fragmented and Clara wonders if she can keep him whole.

'I want to go home,' Stephen whispers.

'It won't be for long, Bean. And we'll be so happy here,' Clara tells him. 'You'll see.'

But he grinds his forehead into his knees and doesn't answer.

* * *

It feels strange for the children to walk up the stairs on their own. Clara keeps her arms close to her sides, but Stephen drags his fingers along the wallpaper. She tries not to draw in the smell around them, the earth creeping up through the bricks leaving a trail of damp.

She doesn't want to go into the bedroom, not yet. Instead, she tiptoes down the short corridor to the window at the end.

'What are you doing?' Stephen whispers, staying close to her side.

'I just want to see them.'

The three dolls sit close together, their lips puckered and painted, staring straight ahead. The boy in the middle is wearing a jacket so small that his arms are forced out straight from his sides, as though he's reaching for the girls' hands to hold. Clara touches the felt of his trousers, but it sends an unpleasant flicker down her backbone, as though she's slipped cotton-wool between her teeth.

She can tell from the glass eyes that the dolls will be the type to blink if you tip them, so she reaches out to the ruffled lace of the girl nearest her, the dress thick with age.

'Auntie said not to,' Stephen says.

'I'll be careful.'

Clara picks up the doll, strokes the buckle of her shoe and wishes she could take it off, just to put it back on again. She holds the girl's belly and moves her forward, watching the eyes click open and shut.

'You're too old to play with it,' Stephen tells her. Clara knows what he really wants to say – that he's frightened what will happen if they get caught. She remembers that they're not sure where Uncle Warren is; maybe he came into the house and perhaps he's behind one of these doors. She puts the doll on the windowsill, careful to arrange the tiny fingers with their pink varnished nails on the ruffled lap, reluctant to leave her there as they rush back towards their room.

When Clara opens the door she almost expects everything to have disappeared and that they'll be stepping into the sky, but it's just as they left it. There are the two beds, the two rugs, the hanging curtains and the wardrobe filled with clothes.

Stephen goes straight to where his Walrus is waiting on the pillow. He holds it to his face and takes a large breath.

'Allergic to fish,' he giggles, his eyes peeping up over Walrus's tusk.

'It was grundy,' she whispers, sitting on the other bed, unsettled by the unfamiliarity of it. 'How could you eat it?'

He shrugs. 'I was hungry.'

'If I had nothing else on earth to eat, I wouldn't eat that.'

Clara feels so tired, but she doesn't want to lie down and have her skin touch the bed.

'Shall we go and play in the garden?' Stephen asks. Clara looks over her shoulder at the darkness creeping over the top of the mountain, edging closer to the window.

'It's too late now. We'll go tomorrow.'

'Are there wolves out there?'

'Only foxes, daddy said. Nice ones, though.'

She stares out at the shapes of the trees in the distance, straight lines like rooted soldiers, spiking to a point. There are the neat bushes, cut exact on top. And empty fruit trees. She wonders if apples sit wrapped in newspaper in boxes in a shed somewhere.

Footsteps are coming up the stairs again, sounding heavier than Auntie's, stopping abruptly just outside their bedroom door. Then nothing. Stephen squeezes his fingers into the eyes of his Walrus as he looks at his sister.

'Hello?' Clara says.

There's a light knock, before the door opens and Auntie is standing with the false light of the hallway behind her. Clara is relieved to see that she's smiling.

'I made you nightclothes,' she says, holding her hands out straight, a nightdress and pyjamas folded neatly in her palms. Clara takes them from her, the material unexpectedly scratchy against her skin, before she puts them on the bed.

'Thank you,' she says.

She wonders how long they must have taken to make. In school she struggles through her sewing classes, unable to ever make things look pretty. She wants to tell Auntie about the girls who sometimes laugh at her, but finds the admission stuck on her tongue.

'Are you ready to do your teeth?' Auntie asks.

'Yes.' How remarkable to have a mother's care again, after so many months of absence. 'Where's your toothbrush, Stephen?'

'I've brought new ones for you,' Auntie hurries on. 'They're waiting in the bathroom.'

'Leave Walrus here,' Clara says, pulling up Stephen by the hand.

Auntie glances over and sees the precious animal's fur engraved with years of dirt. 'Is that yours?' she asks.

'Yes,' Stephen says, as he puts Walrus on the bed, half-perched against the pillow so that the animal almost folds in the middle. They follow Auntie, just one step behind, back into the bathroom that Clara likes. This time, there are two toothbrushes sticking up out of a mug, a thick tube of toothpaste nestled next to them.

'Here they are.' Auntie beams, as if she's giving them sweets. Stephen is still holding Clara's hand and they watch as the tube is squeezed, and stubby worms are curled first onto one set of bristles and then the other. Clara thinks Auntie will pass them the brushes, but instead she hovers one near Stephen's mouth.

'Open wide.'

'He can do it himself,' Clara tells her.

'I can help,' she says.

Clara senses that there's desperation hidden in Auntie, so she nods at Stephen and he opens his mouth for her.

Auntie starts to brush his front teeth, but his lips get in the way. The toothpaste buckles slightly, almost falling to the floor. She brushes quickly, turning the paste to foam, reaching into the crevasses.

'We don't want your teeth to fall out,' she says, concentrating so hard. 'Ready to spit?' She puts her arm around Stephen's shoulder and holds him to her. He nods and she fills the blue mug almost to the brim and he swirls and spits white water into the sink as Auntie looks away.

Clara picks up the other toothbrush before Auntie has a chance and she puts it into her own mouth, scrubbing back and forth. She doesn't like the taste of the toothpaste, the mint so strong it melts into her gums. In the mirror, she watches as her brother's face is patted dry with a towel. He looks blissfully up at Auntie and Clara feels split between a creeping jealousy and deep contentment. She spits her own foamy mouthful into the sink and watches it slide towards the plughole, turning on the tap to make it disappear.

'I think you should have a bath.' Auntie touches the two towels she's folded over the rail on the wall.

'No, we're fine thank you,' Clara says, wiping her mouth with the back of her hand.

'But you need to.'

'We can have one tomorrow.'

Auntie takes a few quick breaths. 'Right,' she says. Her voice is forced, upbeat, but it's smeared with panic. 'You must have your medicine, though.'

'What medicine?'

'Malt treacle. It's good for children.'

'Our mother doesn't give it to us at home.' Clara's words seem to stall Auntie.

'Well a mother should.'

The judgement is swift enough to only graze Clara's sense of loyalty and she can't place her feelings before Auntie turns a tiny key in a mirrored cabinet on the wall. She takes from it a large, brown bottle and from the pocket of her apron, a spoon. She unscrews the lid, perches it on the sink and begins to pour the thick, mucous liquid. When the spoon is filled, she twists it, tipping back the bottle to stop any from sliding down the neck.

'This is for you,' she says to Clara, holding it so close to her lips that there's no choice other than to open her mouth.

The taste is sweet and delicious, but it feels like a dead slug.

'Is it nice?' Stephen asks her.

Clara clenches her teeth as she swallows it. 'You'll like it,' she says, desperate to drink from the tap.

Stephen takes his spoonful willingly. 'Can I have more?' he asks.

'One's enough for now,' Auntie says as she rinses the spoon, shakes it dry and pops it back in her apron. When the brown bottle is replaced in the cabinet, she turns to them, her expression achingly proud.

'I suppose it's bedtime, then.'

'Already?' Stephen says.

'You need a good night's sleep.' Auntie reaches out to ruffle his hair. 'It's a big day tomorrow.'

'Where are we going?'

'It's our first full day together.'

'Oh. Just that,' Stephen says and she drops her hands from him.

'Come on, then,' she says, her voice still light as she leads them back along the corridor. Clara peers over the banister, knowing that Uncle Warren must be somewhere downstairs. The thought both terrifies and fascinates her, like the need to twist a loose tooth. She wants to see him; she wants him to stay away.

Auntie hesitates in the bedroom doorway, before she manages to tread among the toys scattered across the floor. When she gets to the window, she pulls the curtains closed, holding onto the material for a moment, before she turns to them.

Clara and Stephen stand staring at her.

'Would you like me to read a bedtime story?'

'No, we're fine,' Clara says before Stephen can reply. She sees disappointment crawl up Auntie, but she wants her to leave them alone. The sadness of the hospital, the drive here, the need to do everything right, all thread together to weigh heavily on Clara. And she wants to have her brother to herself.

'Shall I turn off the light for you?' Auntie asks.

'No. We'll need to get changed first,' Clara says. 'Then I'll do it.'

'Oh. Of course.' She's clearly reluctant to leave, but she must know she can't stay, so she walks back across the cluttered room, careful not to touch anything. Passing the mantelpiece, she doesn't seem to notice that the haggard china boy has been pushed so close to the edge that he might fall.

'I'll come and get you in the morning. For breakfast.'

'That would be nice.'

'Will Uncle Warren be there then?' Stephen asks.

'Good night,' Auntie says, as though he hasn't even spoken.

'Good night,' Clara replies. She doesn't like to see Auntie sad, knowing only too well the relentless scraping of loneliness, and she doesn't want her mother's sister to feel it too.

When the door is closed the children wait, looking at each other, listening for Auntie's footsteps that don't come. She's standing on the other side of the door and Clara guesses why.

She turns to Stephen. 'It's a lovely house,' she says loudly, making herself go cross-eyed as she screws up her nose at him. 'She's very nice, too.'

'Yes, I like her,' he says, his voice even louder than Clara's. She waves her hands at him, telling him to quiet. He starts to giggle, so she throws him onto the bed, smothering the sound into the pillow, feeling her own laughter pinching at her.

She listens until she hears Auntie tiptoe away, across the polished wood of the landing. As soon as the sound disappears, Clara goes to the china boy and pokes his side to move him to safety.

'We mustn't play with this, Bean,' she says. 'It's very precious to her and we can't break it.'

'I didn't touch it.'

Clara is aware that behind Stephen's denial there's the faint rumbling of a tantrum and she's too tired to find the pieces to diffuse it.

'Someone else must have, then.'

She wipes her finger clean on her dress, yet a feeling remains on the tip of her skin. A coldness that doesn't seem to want to shift.

Stephen has already picked up his new pyjamas.

'She made them for me.' His face is awash with awe.

'You don't have to wear them.'

'They're mine,' he says.

He's pulling off his clothes from home, eager to shed them onto the floor. Clara helps him, wanting to share his excitement. She should love her nightdress too, with its carefully sewn collar and sleeves. But she leaves it where it is, folded, lifeless.

* * *

Clara knows that she has to get into the bed. She doesn't understand why she's reluctant; when she does sit on the mattress, it's better than her wasp-thin one at home. The sheets are cold as she likes, but she doesn't want them touching her. They smell wrong and whichever way she moves she can't get away from it.

'You need to turn off the light,' she tells Stephen. 'You're closest.' He's lying on his back, his hands clutching at the top of the blanket, his Walrus tucked in the crook of his arm.

'I don't want to,' he says.

'You have to.'

'I don't want to walk back to bed in the dark.' He stares up at the ceiling, at the triangular, brown lightshade that hangs down.

'I'll put on the lamp, then.' Clara moves onto her side to find the lead that runs down the back of the small bedside table. When she presses the switch, the toadstool glows.

'It's pretty,' Stephen says. Inside it, one rabbit sits on a chair, another stands by the sink with paws disappearing into tiny ceramic bubbles. Stephen stares at them and he doesn't move.

'I'll do it,' Clara says, shoving back the sheet and blanket. The rug feels gritty under her bare toes and she steps quickly from it and across the wooden floor, flicking off the switch and darting back in the cobwebby dusk.

'It makes patterns,' Stephen says, pointing to the ceiling. Clara sees how the toadstool's shadow is warped, smudging down the tops of the walls. It scares her a bit, but she doesn't want to turn it off and invite the night in.

She feels so heavy all of a sudden, as though too many feelings are smothering her, trying to force her into the mattress. She knows how lucky they are to be here, how there was no alternative, but there's an unfairness to it all – life has pushed them down a path and left them in a house with two strangers and unfamiliar air breathing around them.

She knows she has to be strong for Stephen, but she can't stop the sob that escapes her.

'Clara?'

She is frightening him, but even clenching her teeth together can't stop it.

'I'm all right,' she tries to say. She hears her brother scramble out from his bed, patter the two steps between them, wriggle himself and his Walrus under the sheet. First his toes, then his knees, before he slides his whole little body in next to her.

'I thought you liked it here,' he says, wiping the tears from her cheek. She curls herself up and holds on tight to him, the coarse feel of his new pyjamas foreign to her.

'I do,' she says. 'I just miss mummy.'

'I'll look after you.' But this makes her cry even more. Her hair is sticking wet to her face and he tries to brush it back. 'She won't make fish stew again.' He giggles and it's enough to change her, even to make her laugh.

'I'm glad I've got you, Stevie,' she tells him, and he grins and closes his eyes.

In time, Stephen falls asleep. Clara wishes she could leave this room and follow him into that darkness. Instead, she lies staring at the outline of the white curtains and thinks of the blue ones in the hospital. She imagines herself sitting next to her mother, looking onto her closed eyelids and willing them to open. In her mind, Clara reaches with her fingers and prises the lids apart. She stares into her mother's milk-mottled eyes, but knows they can't see back.

She pulls the lids closed again and tries to stop her heart from beating so hard, tries to remind herself that she's safe and her mother is in the best possible place.

It's in the quiet of this unfamiliar room that Clara hears the faint sound of something roll across the floor. It seems tiny, like a marble, and Clara thinks that perhaps Stephen isn't asleep, that he's awake and playing somewhere.

'Stevie?'

She moves her leg just slightly and it brushes a limb of her brother, so she knows that he's beside her. There's the sound of the marble near the door, maybe on the landing, not in here at all. Clara feels stuck between night and day; perhaps she's the one who's been asleep. She listens again, but the marble has gone.

She distracts herself by wondering where Auntie is. She takes her mind down the stairs and finds her in the room with the books, sitting on the sofa with the green woollen blanket across her lap. Clara thinks that if she went to her now, Auntie would look up and make space for her under the blanket. Perhaps she'd even hug her and hush her sadness. Clara is tempted to go, to know a mother's love again, but the thought of stumbling upon Uncle Warren stops her. She doesn't want to meet him, for the first time, in the darkness on the stairs.

* * *

*A*untie is where Clara had imagined, but she's sat across from the sofa in the old wooden chair, next to an unlit fire. On the table beside her is a cooling mug of chrysanthemum tea, the petals plucked in the summer, dried through the winter and strained through boiling water to create a drink that reminds Auntie of the past.

She threads a needle, ties a knot and begins to sew. Now that she's finally met the children, she knows what colours they would suit. This material reminds her of a summer sky, just before nighttime arrives – the deepest blue. She's making a shirt for the boy and she's chosen the most beautiful buttons that look like the eye in a peacock's tail.

Auntie reluctantly admits that she feels differently towards the girl, as she'd feared she might. She suspects a wildness in her, struggling to get out. Clara is courteous, as she'd hoped, but Auntie feels it's just a sheen, that there's irritability lurking.

Yet sewing clothes for her boy swims such serenity into Auntie that she thinks the clocks must have stopped ticking, the clouds stopped moving. She had believed, over all these years, that her time would come and now it's here. They are her children – if only for a few weeks – but as Jane's seen no improvement for months who's to say it won't be longer? Surely, as their sole carer now, it means that she is their mother. Doesn't it? Auntie grasps the moment and never wants to let it go.

Outside, there are familiar noises, the silence rattled by the throaty sound of a fox, a scavenging screech. They add a layer to Auntie's comfort as she pushes the needle through the material, finding a sense of peace in the rub of the thread as she guides it through the button's eye.

3

Clara wakes before Stephen. The bed is too hot, but she doesn't move. Instead, she keeps her nose nuzzled close to his hair and breathes in the smell of him. Bits of the new day find their way around the curtain and mingle with the lamplight, faint enough for Clara to know that the light isn't far behind. She looks for spider-webs in the corners of the ceiling, but can't find any – it's just the flat, bone white paint. There are noises somewhere in the house, muffled movements and the sound of pans on surfaces.

Clara feels the suffocating strangeness of this place and she knows she needs to get out. She moves her legs from the bed and the cold in the room touches her. The rug under her feet is old enough to hold the dry skin of forgotten people and she jumps back from it, shocking Stephen awake.

'What's wrong?' He sits up quickly and she sees the brief seconds of remembrance on his face. That this is where they are.

'Let's go and explore the garden,' she says.

'Now?' He hooks the sticky sleep from his eye and Clara slaps his hand away as he puts it towards his mouth.

'I've never seen a garden so big. I want to see what it's like.' She pulls him from the bed and steps over the rug. 'Put this on.' She pushes his blue jumper over his head, squeezes his sleepy arms through the sleeves and pulls it to his waist, covering the pyjama top that Auntie made.

'You'll be cold in your nightie,' he says.

'I've got my cardigan.' Clara slips it on, picks up her satchel from the floor and takes Stephen's hand, before she opens the bedroom door.

The house has been waiting in the night, standing just here, breathing its stale breath. Clara grips her hand over her nose, not wanting to inhale the smell. She's aware of the dolls on the windowsill watching and glances over to where they sit at the end of the corridor. The boy has moved. He's on the end now, facing away from the girls, focused on a door they haven't been through. Clara is tempted to go to him, to see what he sees, but Stephen is pulling her and so she runs with him down the stairs, a hushed blur of clothes and fresh skin.

She helps him put on his shoes, as the last remnants of sleep fall from him. There's an excitement in her that she hadn't expected, and droplets of guilt too. The motionless body of their mother, the reason why they're here. The handle on the front door feels warm as she twists it quickly and they're out in the air, the tight grey sky already humid. For a moment, Clara is stunned to stillness by birdsong, the delicate sound of it encircling her with its endless questions.

Stephen crouches, soldier-like.

'Don't be a scaredy-cat.' Clara laughs. 'We're allowed to be out here. It's ours now.' She deliberately keeps her back straight as they go left around the edge of the house. Next to them now is the vegetable patch that Clara noticed when they arrived, with its neat rows of hard, turned earth, pockets of giant courgette leaves, twists of tall runner beans and squat spinach with the dense smell of soil packed beneath them. At its edge stands a wooden bird table: a pole with a flat tray and a miniature house on the top with just one round window.

'Look,' Clara whispers, pulling her brother to a stop. Their eyes rest on a bird perched pecking there, its vulnerable wings curled close to its body. The children barely move, only the wind lifting a lock of Clara's hair and rearranging it on her cheek. 'It's a robin.'

'I know that,' Stephen says. 'It's got red bits.'

Clara is relieved that his scowl is fleeting, hoping that his tantrums will be kept at bay in the wide expanse of Auntie's home. He remains entirely still, as they watch the gentle tapping of the robin's beak into the sprinkle of seeds.

'I could keep it as a pet.' Stephen steps forward and it's enough to startle the bird, instinct making it fly before it even knows the danger.

'You won't be able to catch it.' Clara carries on walking. 'Besides, it belongs in the sky.'

'You could draw it,' Stephen tells her.

'Maybe.' Clara knows that she'd want to be on her own, though she wouldn't want to leave Stephen alone.

At the back of the house they come to the top of the garden, but from here it looks different, as though it's swallowed the rest of the world. The lawn stretches its back away from them, sloping towards the hedge, with the flower bed like an eye at its centre. The walled part of the garden is further away than it seemed, the bricks stacked higher, the mountains hunched behind the thick spread of trees beyond.

Clara's chest feels compressed, imagining their mother as a child just out of sight.

'Where shall we go first?' Stephen's voice drops into the silence.

Clara doesn't trust herself to speak as they walk from the patio and down the stone steps. She feels the curve of other people's feet worn into them, her own shoes fitting snug. She crouches down to touch the grass, hoping there'll be dew clinging to it, but it's dry and coarse.

They stop when they get to the circular flower bed and Clara drifts her hands through the white-topped plants, sure that they're the fairy lace her mother named on one of their rambles through fields near their house. They'd return home on these afternoons, bunches of wildflowers in their hands, to find Stephen a ball of fury at being excluded.

Clara catches the stem of a flower, snapping it and tucking it into her hair.

'Does it look nice?' she asks, but Stephen only screws up his nose as he pulls her by the hand over the rest of the lawn, until they're standing by the rose-walk. Here, the flowers are full globes, their sweet smell sticking to the children as they follow the short path to the arch in the hedge. They step through and into the shade.

The birdsong is so vivid that Clara pauses to listen, wishing she could catch the sound of it on paper. What picture could she draw to convey something she'll never be able to see? Lifting the flap of her satchel, she touches the corner of her sketchbook, thinking maybe her fingers will trap the memory there.

The grass to the right of them ends in a stack of large rocks pushed close to a fruitless apple tree; everywhere else it borders a forest.

'Can we go there?' Stephen asks, pointing to where the trees near the front stand apart from each other, letting daylight in.

'We could find a path through them and go up the hills,' Clara thinks aloud.

'They're mountains,' Stephen corrects her.

'Come on then,' she says. They could get lost and stay out there, survive in the wild like Stephen had hoped.

Clara looks back as they move away from the hedge and sees the house appearing again, first the chimneys, then the roof, the tips of the windows. She wants to work out which is their bedroom and what the other windows might be, imagining Nancy running along the floorboards, sneaking into rooms and pulling Clara inside. The thought of her friend not being here grips her enough to momentarily forget the birds.

'A swing,' Stephen shouts, running to a yew tree that Clara hadn't even noticed. Tied to a branch is a slab of wood attached to two thick lines of rope, each slick with mildew and knotted at the top. 'Did Uncle Warren make it for us?'

'I think it's been here a long time.' Clara sees her mother's childhood fingers clutching tight to the weather-beaten rope. Maybe it was new then, hung especially for her.

A memory tiptoes in from behind the trees: Clara's father nailing planks into the high branches, his hammer taken from its place in the shed.

'Clara?' Stephen is sitting on the swing. 'Will you push me?' She reaches out, her thoughts scorching the ropes as she pulls them up through the horror of that hospital bed, as high as her arms will reach and, as Stephen screams, she lets go.

He kicks his legs towards the leaves at the top and suddenly he's laughing, the sound thrown loud into the air. Clara feels his joy race across the lawn and imagines it touching the windows, finding the one she's sure Auntie is behind.

She steps forwards and backwards with the rhythm of the swing, only realising when she looks down that there are newly fallen rose petals scattered around her feet. Between each push she bends down to gather some, slipping her thumb into the smooth cup of each segment. Last summer, their mother had shown her how to make perfume by soaking fresh rose heads in water. The result had been disappointing, smelling of mouldy roots, and she hadn't minded when Stephen kicked it into the flower bed, but it was followed with a sharp slap from their mother's hand. It's not a thought she wants to keep, so instead Clara looks for where the petals have fallen from. She turns all the way around, but they must have drifted here from the rose-walk by the hedge.

'A cat!' Stephen shouts, slipping and scuffing his feet on the grass. Clara barely has time to pull on the ropes, before he jumps down.

'Go quieter.' She touches his arm. 'You don't want to scare it away.'

They creep behind the animal, gloom now playing against their skin as they step across the invisible line into the forest. The cat doesn't notice them; it is too focused on a squirrel burrowing its snout into the tangled earth. For a moment, the children watch. The cat's tension as it prepares itself, pulling back on its motion, a quiver in its hind legs.

It pounces before Clara can shout. Its claws grip the squirrel's back. The animal slips free, but the split-second is too short before the cat clamps its mouth into the fur-soaked flesh.

'No!' Clara screams, startling the cat, but still it gnaws into the animal's neck. The squirrel's eyes are wide in panic as it looks to them, flicking its tail, its body a writhing mess. 'Stop it.' Clara runs forward, but the cat darts away, dragging the animal with it, teeth deep through muscle and already nestled into bone. The last thing Clara sees is the blood and she knows it's too late.

She stops running, suddenly aware that she's further into the forest, where overhead the trees' leaves make a cold ceiling to hide the sun. She waits, listening. Brushing her hair from her face, she feels the fairy lace still clasped there, small patches of it crumbling into her fingers. There's no sound from the cat and so Clara hurries back to where her brother stands on his own, his body framed by trees, behind him the hedge and the tips of the house.

'Did you get it?' he asks.

'No. It was too quick.'

'I want to see it,' Stephen says. 'Can we go and find it?'

'We won't be able to. It'll be long gone.'

'Is it dead?'

'Yes. I think it probably is.' Death has crept so close to them and Clara doesn't want it here. For too many months she's been transfixed on the knowledge that a heart can stop beating, the stain of the end stalking her thoughts. She puts her arms around her brother, kisses the top of his head and tries to rock him, but he pushes her away.

'I don't need that,' he says. 'I want to explore some more.'

She follows him as he runs back under the arch in the hedge, through the rose-walk, spilling onto the top lawn. The house looks at them, glass eyes pockmarked into it.

'Let's go there.' Clara pulls Stephen across the grass to the high wall where she wants to hide.

The bricks look much older than she expected and she runs her hand along all the cuts and dents that make them so imperfect, plucking at a pimple of a weed to pull it free, its roots letting go with ease. It doesn't take long to find a door and she only has to turn the metal handle before they slip inside.

They're greeted by knotted knee-high grass and stalks of wild plants almost as tall as Stephen. Along one wall is a pungent cluster of yellow chrysanthemums, so crammed together that they're fighting to breathe.

'This is wicked,' Stephen says, his shoulders rising close to his ears. 'I'm a pirate.' He's searching for something, as Clara leans to press her palm onto the top of a thistle. The pain is almost imperceptible, and she's tempted to pluck it and press it into her forehead to see if it can puncture her thoughts.

Stephen has found a stick and he swipes at the brambles to make a path. Clara pulls the sleeves of her cardigan over her hands, shy of the nettles wanting to sting her.

A bird flies up and over them and Stephen shoots it with his gunfire.

'I got it between the eyes,' he says, but the bird doesn't realise and disappears out of sight.

Clara picks up a crack of branch and begins to strike at the weeds too, at the tiny specks of blue petals. She moves away from Stephen, making her own path, enjoying the crunch of broken stems and the release of dark-smelling earth by her feet. Her stick hits something hard. She pokes at it, but it won't budge, so she bends down and pushes back the leaves with her arms. There's a tiny stone cross, sticking up from the ground.

'Stephen,' she calls, as she hears him trampling away.

She flattens the wild plants so that she can see it clearly, but that's all there is. Just the cross – no name, no date, no words. She's seen a grave before and remembers how her mind stopped short of letting her think what was really beneath her feet. But there's something so intimate about this cross that she wishes she could pick it up and place it in her mother's hand. It'd remind her of what would remain if she slips away from this world. It might make her mother fight harder to stay. Clara won't cry; she can't cry when Ballechin is such a happy place.

She wanders on and soon stumbles on another cross. 'Stephen,' she calls, louder this time, standing up to see him, wiping the heat from the back of her neck. 'Come and look at these.'

'What is it?' he asks, struggling to run towards her.

'Crosses. Two of them. I think it's their pets.' Clara is fascinated now, even though she doesn't want to think of a buried dog, its soft ears and wet nose filled with earth.

Stephen slashes at more weeds with his stick, trying to make a new path, but instead he hits something hard and Clara knows straight away that it's another cross. She bends low as she rips up chunks of overgrown grass, clearing space for the little graveyard to grow. There are three more and she quickly finds them. Five in all. Five little bodies beneath her feet.

'I think we should go back now,' she says, a wisp of fear touching her.

'To the house?'

'Yes.' And she pulls him by his wrist, following the path through the weeds.

'Just because of the dead things?' he asks, yanking his arm away. 'You drip.'

'No. Because if Auntie finds we're gone then she'll be worried about us.'

'You're no fun,' he says as he stamps past her. He wants to stay fighting off hidden pirates in the tangle of brambles, but instead he has to stand by the heavy door in the brick wall, waiting for his sister to open it, just as it starts to rain.

* * *

As soon as they step into the hallway, they hear Auntie's voice.

'Where have you been?' she asks. They look up to see her on the landing. 'You should have been in your room.'

'We went into the garden,' Stephen says.

'But it's before breakfast.'

Stephen starts to giggle, but Clara tugs at his hand as Auntie scuttles down the stairs towards them, blinking quickly.

'We just wanted to explore,' Clara says, taking the fairy lace from behind her ear and tucking it into her palm.

'But it's wet outside.'

'It's still warm. Besides, we like it in the rain.'

'In your nightclothes.'

'They'll be fine,' Clara tells her. 'It's only a bit of water. We'll go and get dressed for breakfast if you'd like.'

She's about to step forward when Auntie grabs at her clumsily.

'Don't go on the rug. You're filthy.'

Stephen looks up at Auntie, his hair painted wet on his forehead.

'We found your pet graveyard.' He steps towards Auntie and holds out his hand, but her whole body stiffens.

'You went behind the wall,' she says.

'Yes. I was a pirate.'

'Stevie,' Clara says, knowing that he can't sense the quiet panic pulsing in Auntie.

'Don't ever go there again,' Auntie says.

'But we could make it nice for you,' Stephen says. 'I'd like to go back.'

'You need to go to your room now. I'll run you a hot bath. Stephen, you can get in first and then Clara.'

'I don't want one,' Stephen says and he runs up the stairs.

'But you're cold,' Auntie calls.

'He's not,' Clara tells her, unsure how to make things better. 'We don't mind being cold, it's so lovely here.' She follows the trace of her brother, careful not to run and careful to keep to the strip of carpet that leads her up the stairs.

In the bedroom, Stephen is standing by the window. Clara closes the door before she speaks.

'That was rude of you,' she says. 'She's trying her best for us and we're lucky to be here.'

'I'm sorry,' he says quietly.

'We promised daddy we'd be good.'

'Do you think she likes us?' Stephen asks.

'I hope she does,' Clara replies.

She finds her sketchbook and opens her hand to reveal the fairy lace. The separate stalks are already wilting and loose crumbs of petals fall as she tucks the flower into the back page.

'I'll wear one of my suits,' Stephen says, already opening the door to the wardrobe. 'That'll make her happy.' He pulls the dark green one from its hanger.

'You'll look like a clump of moss.' Clara laughs.

'There's a waistcoat,' he exclaims, as he peels back the jacket. And there is, underneath, a beautifully made waistcoat lined in purple, with matching buttons. Clara watches as he carefully twists them out through their holes, before he takes off his pyjama top and puts on the waistcoat. It's a bit too small but he doesn't seem to mind, breathing in dramatically to make it fit.

'Will you do up the buttons?' he asks.

'You'll need a shirt,' she says, trying to distract herself from the unsettling feeling whispering inside her.

She doesn't find any in the wardrobe, so she tries the chest of drawers. They're more awkward to open than the one she has at home, but she pulls it enough to see a row of neatly folded vests and underwear, on one side for her and the other for Stephen. She doesn't want to touch them and when she pushes the drawer it catches so she has to shove it, rocking the whole thing on its legs.

In the next drawer she finds the shirts, white ones with starched collars.

'This one?' Clara drags out the top shirt, then helps Stephen put it on. 'There,' she says. 'Chrome-plated.' She puts the waistcoat over the top and fixes the purple buttons, before she picks up the green suit jacket from the floor. She'd prefer her brother not to wear it, but his face has a genuine glimmer of excitement as he pushes his arms into it and shuffles to the mirror inside of the wardrobe door. He beams.

'Not so good with pyjama bottoms, though.' Clara stands behind him and leans down to rest her chin on his head, and for a moment she just watches them both, before he wriggles away.

Stephen concentrates hard as he puts on the trousers. He looks so different, Clara thinks. The little suit has turned her brother into a stranger, just like their father has become. She wants to reach out and grab him back to her.

'Are you going to wear something from the wardrobe?' he asks.

'They're not really my thing,' she replies, walking back to where she threw her clothes on the floor last night.

'But she made them for you,' he says, speaking to her reflection.

'I don't like them.'

'You'd look pretty.'

'Pretty awful.' And she's out of her nightclothes and into her own dress before he says any more.

There are footsteps on the stairs, brisk ones this time, and then the waiting silence of someone on the other side of the bedroom door. Clara counts to eight before the knock comes.

'We've got to go to her,' Stephen whispers, his hand half over his mouth.

'What if it's Uncle Warren?'

The tapping comes again, before the door opens and Auntie

71

is here. There's hope on her face, but it folds away instantly when she sees Clara.

'You're not wearing your clothes,' she says.

'I'm wearing my suit,' Stephen says, stepping towards her.

Auntie doesn't blink. 'It fits,' she murmurs. 'You look just right.'

'It's a bit small.' He holds his arms out straight to prove it and they all see the cuffs ride slightly up his wrists.

'I can make a bigger one,' she says, as she glances past Clara into the room.

'We'll tidy it later,' Clara offers, and Auntie's eyes finally brighten again.

'I've made breakfast,' she says.

'We'll come down.'

But Auntie doesn't move. 'Did you sleep well in here?' she asks.

'Yes,' Clara lies, noticing the tinge of relief in Auntie's eyes. 'The lamp was nice. Stephen liked the shadows, didn't you, Stevie?'

He nods, picking up his Walrus to burrow his nose into its back. He places it on his pillow so that it looks towards the tiny ceramic rabbits.

'Come on, then,' Auntie says. 'Follow me.' And before she turns away she has a smile that makes her whole face shine. Clara nearly rushes forward to hug her. Auntie may not be what she expected, even what she hoped, but she likes her and she wants desperately to know the devotion of a mother again.

Stephen holds his head straight and keeps his hand on the banister all the way to the bottom. The only sound Auntie makes is her stockinged feet on the carpet. Wisps of her hair have escaped to mingle with the tie at the neck of her apron.

The dining-room door is open and Auntie ushers them towards it.

'You can sit in the same places as last night.' Her voice is tinged with an excitement that she's clearly trying to suppress. 'I'll be with you in a moment.'

Stephen rushes in and Clara follows. Everything still feels so unfamiliar, a world she's stepped into by mistake and can't quite find her way back from. Already the table is laid: two teaspoons, two glasses of milk, two napkins that Auntie has folded into exact triangles. The little boy with his stitched skin is no longer in here, the small chair in the corner empty, yet Clara senses that he's still watching as she sits down.

Next to her place mat is a small pile of salt, its tail trailing towards the edge of the table.

'Look what's been spilt,' she whispers to her brother.

He peers over at the white grains.

'She might think it was you.'

Clara draws the tip of her finger through it, making a letter C, before she sweeps the salt into her hand.

'Now what do I do with it?' She knows her laughter is close to the surface.

'Put it on the floor.'

She sprinkles it like Stephen suggests, scattering it in a wide arc so that the evidence doesn't clump at her feet, just as Auntie walks in holding a glass of milk. In her other hand, sitting in the palm, is a small white pill.

'This is for you, Clara.'

'What is it?'

'Your sulphur tablet.' Auntie's voice is quieter, as though it's a secret for them to share. 'For your skin.'

Clara instinctively touches her cheek. Her fingertips feel the raised spots that she wishes could disappear. Nancy's face has never had a blemish, but for a while now Clara has been riddled with white and red marks that make her want to bury her face in a pillow for the day. She'd foolishly hoped that Auntie hadn't noticed them and embarrassment swarms her, suffocating any comfort about being mothered.

'Thank you,' she says, her hand brushing Auntie's as she picks up the solid white circle. The pill is hard against her throat as she swallows it with the milk.

She doesn't look at Stephen as they wait for Auntie to bring in the breakfast, watching in silence as Auntie unloads a tray, placing a plate with neat-cut toast in front of each of them. A boiled egg balanced in a plain pink eggcup that has ingrained stains creeping up the side. She takes a knife from the tray and cuts the top clean off Clara's egg, scooping pulpy white from the skull, leaving it to sit in the teaspoon. Clara hasn't had anyone help her with her food for years.

Auntie does the same for Stephen and he beams up at her.

'I love them like this,' he says, picking up a slice of his toast and stabbing it into the crumbling yellow. 'Oh. It's not runny.'

Clara's own egg is slightly more successful, with wet yolk touching the edge of her toast, but Auntie has already been cut by Stephen's disappointment.

'I could make another one.' Although she seems to regret saying it. 'As long as you finish this one first.'

'Yes please,' Stephen says, jabbing at his dried yolk with a spoon.

'We're not allowed to have two eggs,' Clara reminds him. He looks up as he chews.

'That was mummy's rules,' he says.

'And you're here now,' Auntie intervenes proudly. 'And as I'm your mother for the moment I think two eggs is a grand idea.'

Clara sits slightly stunned as Auntie rushes from the room. There are new emotions inside her that she can't even name and she grasps at reasons, flailing to find a fragment of control. Now Stephen doesn't look at her, instead concentrating on curving his spoon around the inside of his eggshell, catching every last bit of white.

'When she brings it in, you'd better not eat it,' she tells him.

'I'll have to. She's cooking it for me.'

And it's there, bleakly, the realisation that there's someone else fighting for her brother's affections.

'But I said you could only have one.'

'You're not my mother.'

Clara stares at him, willing her tears to stay away.

Breathe. Count to ten.

'I'm sorry,' Stephen says. 'I didn't mean it.' He looks so small to his sister, the back of the chair looming above his head. 'I'll go and tell her I don't want it.'

'No. I will,' Clara says, overtaken by a snap of triumph as she stands up and goes out of the room.

She can hear singing as she pushes open the kitchen door. Her presence shocks Auntie enough to jolt the pan she's holding, splashing boiling water over her thumb.

'What's wrong?' she asks. 'Is Stephen all right?'

'He doesn't want two eggs,' Clara says. But her feelings of victory disappear when she sees that Auntie must have been working hard, the butter dish on the side next to a stack of clean, dried plates.

'Oh,' Auntie says, looking down at the egg in the pan, distorted by the bubbling water. She steps towards the sink, turns on the tap and holds her thumb under the running cold, numbing the spread of heat on her skin.

'It's not that he doesn't like them,' Clara says. 'It's just that it's not good for him.' She wants to leave the kitchen now, with its unpainted walls and window too small to let any warmth in.

'I've never heard that.' Auntie turns off the tap, picks up the pan and starts to tip the boiled water into the sink, catching the half-cooked egg in a spoon. 'But I wouldn't want to hurt him.'

It's a sense of shame that Clara feels, reluctantly pushing through.

'I'm sure Stephen could have two today,' she says. 'Just for once.'

'But I've poured away the water now,' Auntie says.

'Another day, then.' Clara speaks as lightly as she can. 'Do you have chickens?' She points to a basket of eggs, smooth hills nestled together, some sand-coloured, some almost white.

'Yes.' But Auntie seems lost in her own home.

'Maybe Stephen could help you collect them? He'd love that.'

They both turn as the door opens.

'I don't like being in there on my own,' Stephens says, coming quickly to hold Clara's hand. The quiet walls have unsettled him. The gaping fireplace, the unfamiliar pictures. 'Can we see the toys?' he asks Auntie, and her face brightens.

'Yes,' she says. 'Yes, you can.' She folds the cloth and puts it into the pocket of her apron, before tucking her loose hair behind her ears. 'Warren was worried about having toys in the rooms up here,' she tells them. 'So I cleared the basement for you.'

'There's a basement?' The word comes to Clara smothered with cobwebs. When she'd been sleeping last night she hadn't known there was a cavernous hole waiting underneath the house.

'Come and see.' Auntie puts out her hand for Stephen, but he's already holding onto Clara. She recoils slightly from the rejection, yet keeps a wide smile.

They follow her around the edge of the rug in the hallway, to a door under the stairs. Clara hadn't noticed it before, its ribs disguised by the wood surrounding it. Behind it there are steep steps leading to darkness.

'The light is halfway down,' Auntie says. 'I've no idea why.' It's the first time that they've heard her laugh and it's encouraging for

Clara. 'If you keep open the door, I'll find my way.'

Auntie's feet are faint on the steps, her hand steady on the wall as she sweeps her fingers down to find the switch. It clicks bright light, enough for Clara to see the stairs ending in a room. Auntie looks back at them, her face eager.

'Warren decorated it for you. I thought you'd like yellow.' She turns and is at the bottom step now.

'It's just a room,' Clara urges Stephen, trying to convince herself too. 'It's the same as a room upstairs.' She leads him, one step at a time, into a place that smells of new paint dried over decades of damp.

In the middle of the basement is a table, and on the table is a train track. Auntie watches them expectantly.

'Is it ours?' Stephen's eyes are wide.

'Yes.' She nods. 'It's yours now.'

'Did Uncle Warren make it for us?' Stephen steps towards the track, seeing how it travels over a bridge, around corners. There's a tunnel, a station and the smallest people with circles of plastic at their feet to help them stand.

'It was my brother's,' Auntie says. 'When we were young.'

'Does he mind that we're using it?' Stephen asks.

'Our mother doesn't have a brother,' Clara says. 'We would know.'

Auntie tips her head slightly to the side. 'Edwyn died when he was seven.'

'Oh,' Stephen says.

Clara looks at Auntie. 'Mummy had a brother?'

'Yes.'

Clara has the strangest sensation that she's no longer in her body, that she's in a new place she doesn't want to be.

'Does daddy know?' she asks.

'I couldn't say.' Auntie glances around the room, when Clara wants her to look directly in her eyes, to tell about this brother who lived at Ballechin too. A brother who died.

'Look.' Auntie's fingers are suddenly fiddly with energy. 'You put this here.' She leans over to take the train from where it rests in the centre. The same train that her brother must have held, by the same trees that he must have touched. But now he's gone.

'I like its colour,' Stephen says. 'Our father would call it bottle green.'

Clara thinks of their father alone in his study, the hours he'd spent away from them all. Did he know about the tiny boy locked in a coffin somewhere? For a moment Clara feels herself in the same box, struggling to breathe.

'This is how you start it,' Auntie carries on. 'The switch is here.' On the back wall of the station a tiny black square juts out. 'You have to put the carriage slowly onto the track.' She pauses for a second. 'You must be very careful, Stephen.'

'I will be.'

Auntie lowers it, and when she's sure it's in position she lets it free from her fingers. The train pulls away, running faster and faster. There's only the clattering thud, over and over as it builds up speed past the miniature trees, the tiny lamp-posts.

'See?' Auntie presses a button on the station platform, as she points across the table to where the inside of the tunnel lights up.

Clara watches as Stephen runs around, following the train when it races past the painted pond with ducks. She wonders what Edwyn looked like, whether he played with their mother. If his fingers had touched the same piece of track she's looking at now. When the train is struggling slightly up the bridge it's Stephen, not Edwyn, who goes to help it with a push.

'No,' Auntie shouts too loudly. 'Don't do that.'

Clara's nerves jolt, but Stephen doesn't seem to mind. It's so peculiar to her that she's here, in the basement of this house. She tries to visualise herself sitting on the train racing back home, to a time when their mother was well. But still she's standing here, feeling Stephen somehow drifting from her.

Auntie plays like a child, as excited as Stephen as they move the plastic people around, placing some by the pond, others hidden among the trees.

'They're poachers,' Stephen says, even though the man he holds has a briefcase in his hand and a smart hat on his head.

Auntie laughs, a girl-like giggle that seems to sew her and Stephen even closer.

Clara wants to ignore the jealousy that's tapping at her. She has to like this woman, to remember everything that she's doing for them. She touches the closest wall and the yellow paint becomes dust on her fingertips. She needs to wipe it off, but doesn't want it on her dress.

'How did he die?' she hears Stephen ask. 'Your brother.'

When there's a silence, Clara looks over her shoulder.

'He fell into the grain on the farm.'

'The grain?'

'We weren't allowed in the building, we were told not to, but he went anyway. The machines were off, but the vat of grain was full. Edwyn was always fascinated by anything.' Auntie's voice is almost a shadow. 'And he fell.'

'And then he died?' Clara is struggling to understand the horror of it, the helpless grabbing of air as the little boy was sucked down, his mouth and nose filling with dusty granules.

'Yes.' Her voice reaches around them.

'He couldn't breathe,' Stephen says.

'He suffocated.' Auntie looks down at the train still struggling on, even without Edwyn's eyes to watch it.

The street lights start to dim, slowly turning off.

'Look,' Auntie says, her smile suddenly extraordinary. 'It's daytime. Listen.'

The children both stand so still that Clara thinks the dead brother will speak from somewhere. That he might emerge from the walls and whisper in her ear. But it's birdsong they hear. The high-pitched morning sound, squeezed from tiny speakers they can't even see.

Clara needs to get out of this room. The basement is pressing in on her, as the grains pressed onto Edwyn's face.

'I'm going back upstairs,' she says, even though she doesn't want to go anywhere in the house alone. 'Are you coming?' she asks Stephen, but he hesitates, and she knows he won't join her.

Auntie touches another button and the tiny street lights start to glow again.

'It's boring down here,' Clara says, watching to see Auntie falter. She feels childish, but she needs to tempt Stephen to come with her.

'Can't you stay with us for a bit?' Stephen asks, but already he's distracted, watching the train as it chugs into the lit tunnel again.

'I'll see you later,' Clara says, hoping that he'll follow her. She saunters up the steps, giving him enough time to change his mind.

Halfway up, she flicks off the light switch.

'Clara.' Auntie's voice drifts upwards.

'Clara?' Stephen sounds frightened, so she flicks it on again, puddling the cellar with light.

'Sorry,' she says, waiting to give him one more chance to follow. But he doesn't.

At the top, in the hallway, she's alone and regretting it. This house is still unfamiliar to her, filling her with a feeling that she's in a room with glass walls, where she can see the world outside, but doesn't know how to touch it. She can still hear the whirring clack of the train, but she can't go back down. There are the four doors leading from the hallway. Clara knows what's behind three of them.

Which one shall I choose, mummy?

There's silence.

That one.

It's the only door that Clara hasn't been through. She pushes it open, but it's almost dark inside and she hesitates, waiting for her eyes to adjust, for the shapes in the room to appear. They're little more than silhouettes, but the light from behind her is enough to lead her around the edge of the room, where she reaches for the curtains and pulls them apart just a bit. For a moment she's unwilling to let go of the material, wanting her mother's childhood fingers to meet her there. When she feels nothing, a part of her catches light and starts to burn.

She turns away from the window and sees that there's a doll's house on the table next to her, the front of it painted with tiny bricks, the roof made of wooden tiles stacked one overlapping the other. Clara thinks of the hours that she and Nancy could have spent playing with it when they were younger and the temptation now is too strong as she pushes the stiff front door. She has to bend low to look in, seeing only a miniature woven rug, the bottom two stairs. Standing straighter, she touches a top window and peers through. But it's not enough and so Clara unhooks the latch and pulls the front wide open to see inside. It's perfect. The tiny staircase runs up through the middle, disappearing onto a landing. There are the rooms, the smallest blanket on the arm of the sofa, a radio the size of a postage stamp.

And there's one boy, sitting alone in the kitchen. He has the same white shirt and green suit as Stephen, the same brown hair. He stares at the wall, his smile fixed. Clara pictures him standing on tiptoes to look into a vat of grain, she sees him lean too far and topple, but as he falls she reaches out her hands and catches him. She's saved him.

'I'll look after you,' she whispers, before she puts him into her pocket, his stiff arms by his sides, his limbs pressing against the fabric of her dress as she closes the front of the house.

When she glances back into the room, she sees in the darkness of the corner a carved wooden rocking horse, a red bow around its neck. *Was it yours, mummy?* Clara moves towards it and this close she sees how its eyes look wet, so real that she doesn't want to touch them. Instead, she runs her hand through the mane and lets it fall like water from her fingers. She pushes the horse slightly and it creaks, swinging back before whispering to a stop. She wants to hear her mother's childhood voice. *Did you play in here with Edwyn before he died?* Clara thinks of this secret brother flickering in death, yet their mother never told them. Their mother, trapped in the blazing shed. Trapped now in bandages that stick tight to her melting skin.

Clara pinches a piece of the horse's hair and pulls until it comes free, dropping it onto the floor before she grabs another knot in her fist and yanks it. She lets it float from her fingers, stamping on it, twisting it into the red-flecked rug with her heel. With each shred of the horse's mane she hears her father's voice telling her that her mother locked herself in, that she wanted to die. But Clara doesn't believe it; she'll never believe it.

Anger's fire is in her now, but she doesn't know where to put it.

She hits the horse hard, wanting it to break, and when it doesn't she screams so violently that she hopes the bricks in the walls will shatter.

The door slams open.

'What is it?' Auntie is breathless, terrified. 'Are you hurt? Clara?' She runs straight to her, but doesn't hug her.

'Clara?' Stephen stands in the doorway. He's never seen his sister like this and it startles him to stillness.

She hears him, though, his voice bringing the room back to focus, regret clinging to her as she feels the horse's mane under her feet.

'Stephen?' Her arms reach out for him, but still he doesn't move.

'What happened?' he whispers.

'What's wrong with her?' Auntie asks, staggered to see the destruction, the wounds in the horse's head, bald patches of wood peppered with tiny holes. 'What have you done?'

'I didn't mean to,' Clara says, frightened by the cold creeping over Auntie.

'Warren made it,' she says, bending down to scoop up the lifeless hair. 'It's been waiting here for years.'

'I'm sorry, I didn't mean to,' Clara says. 'I miss my mother.'

Auntie looks confused. 'But I can be your mother.'

'You can't be!' Clara's sudden shout shocks them all.

Auntie looks dazed. 'You're not meant to behave like this,' she says.

'It's all right, Clara,' Stephen says, but he doesn't go to her.

'No, it's not,' Auntie says. 'She destroyed the horse.'

Clara feels rage clawing its way into her again. 'It's ugly in any case. And Stephen didn't even like your train track,' she lies, the floodgates open. 'We hate it here.' She doesn't recognise her voice, so dripped in vitriol.

'Go to your room,' Auntie mutters, keeping her focus away from the mutilated horse.

'Come on,' Clara says to Stephen, taking his reluctant hand tight in hers. The pain on Auntie's face is so stark that Clara thinks she may as well have seared the horse right through her chest. 'We're going.'

But Stephen won't move. 'I'm sorry,' he says quietly. 'I really like it here. I really do.' Until Clara pulls him with her and they push past Auntie and run up the stairs.

On the landing, Clara stops. The boy who had been in the dining room, the one with the stitched leather skin, is sitting on the floor, his head held straight by the banisters as he watches them.

'Why's he there?' Clara almost expects the thread between the boy's lips to stretch apart, a gentle voice able to answer.

'Because she thinks we'll like him,' Stephen says.

'Well I don't,' Clara retorts, still entrenched in complex fury.

'She does things to make us happy and you're ruining it all.'

Inside the bedroom they stare at each other, the thought of the horse's ripped mane and weeping eyes hanging between them.

'It was sort of an accident,' Clara says. 'It just happened.'

'A bald horse,' Stephen says, before laughter suddenly bubbles up. As though a button has been pressed, one where they're wired together, they shriek into their palms slapped over their mouths. Clara topples forward onto the bed and turns onto her back like a beached beetle, holding her anger in her stomach as she lets her laughter into the room.

'I'm not doing very well,' she attempts to say, as Stephen dives next to her, stuffing his face into his pillow until the material becomes wet with his giggles. When he lifts back his head, his laughter explodes.

Clara knows that the sound isn't real happiness, but it will seep under the door and wind down the stairs to twist towards Auntie. She sees it pinning her to the spot and she tries hard to stop, but the laughing comes until she's squeezed dry.

Stephen is suddenly quiet beside her. He thinks for a while, before he speaks.

'I really like the train track.'

'Oh, Stevie.' Clara feels guilt, amongst it all. An acidic feeling that battles for space in her cramped emotions. 'It wasn't my fault.' Yet she knows deep down that it was.

'There were birds singing and the street lights went on and off.'

'She'll let you play with it again.'

'Will she?'

'Of course she will.' She turns on her side to face him. He's so small, yet Clara feels tired under the weight of looking after him. Here, in this house, she's been given the gift of someone to share the burden, but now she thinks she's destroyed it all.

'She might send us away. Daddy says he can't look after us if we go back home. We won't have anywhere else.'

Clara wants to reassure him, but she doesn't know if she can.

'I'm sorry I did that to the horse,' she says.

'Why did you?'

'I don't know.' It seems nonsensical now, that she'd wanted to destroy it, as if ripping out the mane would somehow pull her own pain from inside her. 'We need to make it better. We have to make her know we're sorry.'

'Yes,' Stephen says. 'Now?'

But Clara is fearful that laughter might pop from him again and shatter Auntie completely.

'Soon.' She feels the doll in her pocket pressing into her, so she takes it and slips it under her pillow before Stephen can see. When she turns onto her back next to her brother, they both stare up at the freshly painted ceiling, the unending whiteness of it. Clara searches for answers, but there are none.

* * *

Beneath them, Auntie waits for so long, wondering that if she doesn't move then life will disappear and maybe she can start again. But the walls around her remain. The ruined rocking horse is by her side. Warren had made it for their first-born, for the baby whose voice she'd never heard, the silent boy who'd slithered from her weeks too early before her husband had even carved the horse's eyes.

And the next time, filled with hope, she'd watched Warren finish sandpapering the mouth and chipping the teeth, while her own hands had rested on her stomach swelling steady again beneath her apron, waiting to feel her little one kick.

The door is still there, waiting for her to step towards it and turn the handle and push it open. She goes to it, bringing the rest of the house back to her.

She puts on her gardening shoes and gardening coat, wraps a scarf around her head to block out the weather and the noise, before she steps outside towards her vegetable patch to pick the last of the rhubarb, cradling it in her arms as she walks back to the house.

In the kitchen she strips the pink stalks from their leaves and cuts them into squares. It calms her, the way that the knife slices through to make neat lines – cubes that match, barely a millimetre out of place. She puts them flat into the pot, sprinkles brown sugar in a thin layer over their top. And the smallest spoon of water, just so that they won't stick and char.

The fruit's sweet cooking smell heals her breathing and she stands, her face hanging over the steam, letting it in. She thinks of the two children upstairs and imagines her womb growing them, forming their fingers, their toes, their hair. She changes them to become the children in her mind, so that they want to be by her side. She'll sit on her son's bed to read him stories and then rock him to sleep until he's too heavy for her arms.

She forgets to make them their lunch. There's a kitchen to clean, surfaces to wipe and taps to polish. She takes everything out of the fridge and lines the butter, the cheese, the milk along the floor so that she can scrub the cold shelves. Then she runs a dry cloth over them, pressing hard enough to soak up the drops. It's one of her favourite things, putting everything back in order. There's a place for it all, a pattern that she's familiar with and that she needs to keep.

For hours, she wipes the children from her mind, rinsing them away, until they're only flecks drifting somewhere in her memory, stubborn specks that she can't quite bleach completely.

Auntie only remembers them when she goes into the larder and sees the cake sitting there, decorated with iced flowers. The shock is genuine. How could they have slipped from her unnoticed after years of yearning? She throws her cloth onto the side, not even bothering to hang it up and finds herself running up the stairs, terrified that she'll find them huddled like skeletons.

She opens the door without knocking. But the room is empty.

4

Outside, Clara has found them somewhere to hide from the rain, a shed with only three sides, the fourth looking out over the vegetable patch. She sits with Stephen against the back wall, the wooden planks pressing into her spine. The garden forks and spades leaning beside them have dried mud where the metal meets the handle and Clara reaches over to crumble some of it free.

From here, Clara can see how the earth creeps so close to the house that it almost slides inside. The rain can't touch them, but Clara watches as it batters the courgette plants that push up from the ground. There are no birds on the bird table, but a string with something hanging from it sways from its miniature roof.

'Do you think Uncle Warren is in the garden?' Stephen asks.

'He'll be at work,' Clara says, though she's far from sure. She tries to see all the way down the lawn, beyond the hedge, but it's impossible from here.

'I'm hungry,' Stephen complains. Clara understands, but her own cramping stomach spills intolerance into her.

'There's nothing I can do about it,' she snaps. The smell of summer dust is taking her dangerously close to their garden back home.

'It's your fault she didn't give us lunch.'

'It wasn't,' she says. 'She just forgot.' Clara stares out across the garden, to where patches of puddles sit on the terrace and on the grass. She'd like to stamp on them with her bare feet and concentrates on the idea of that instead, the sensation of the surface of each puddle breaking apart.

'Shall we go and say sorry?' Stephen suggests.

'We should've done it earlier. Now it'll look like we're only saying it to get food.'

'But we are.'

'Our mother would never have done that,' Clara says. 'She never would have left us without any lunch.'

'We must have made her very angry,' Stephen says.

'It's no reason to starve children.'

'We're not starving.'

'Why are you sticking up for her?'

'I'm not.'

'I bet she won't let you play with that train track again.' Clara regrets it as soon as she's said it. She sounds like her younger self, when she could be mean, and now Stephen looks so sad that she has to make it better. 'How about we have a courgette duel?'

'A what?'

'Come on, Bean.' Clara jumps up, runs out into the rain, right into the middle of the vegetable patch. She grips a courgette stalk tight in her hand, looking at the lines and paths of the leaf's palm, ignoring how it tries to scratch her before she shreds it so that its veins are exposed to the air. She tries to forget the hunger biting at her as she reaches for the root, pulling with both hands. Stephen watches, hesitating at the edge, when a sudden pop breaks the stalk free and throws Clara hard to the ground.

Stephen tramples across the vegetable patch to get to her, his shoes slapping against onion stalks and grinding the shoots of winter kale.

'Did that hurt?' he asks.

'A bit,' she says.

'As much as this?' He laughs, snatching the thick courgette stem from her and jabbing it into her side. She scrambles to her feet, yanking up another stalk and swiping at her brother.

'We need umbrellas,' he says, so they pause as Clara picks a giant leaf for him. She holds it over his head and the rain thuds onto it, dripping in rivulets down the side.

'Better?' Clara asks him. He kneels down, scrabbles in the earth with his hands until they're covered in mud, drags them across the ridge of his nose and over his face.

'I'm a warrior child,' he says.

'She'll flip her lid.'

'I'll do yours.' And she lets Stephen mark her face too, his small fingers tracing over her forehead and the skin under her eyes. 'We're in the same tribe.' He's earnest, watching for her response.

'Of course we are. We always will be.'

Stephen breaks the moment by whacking her in the arm with his sword, hard enough that it hurts. Clara bounds away from him.

'Try not to tread on things,' she calls over her shoulder, laughing, 'or there'll be no food to eat.'

But all the time, her feet press into the earth that Auntie and Warren have toiled on for hours. Clara wasn't here to see them through the spring and early summer, digging the ground, laying the seeds, watering them, protecting them, watching the vegetables grow. They didn't see Auntie pick all that she could carry, for cooking and drying and pickling, leaving the earth perfect for when the time should come again.

Clara pulls Stephen to a stop when she sees Auntie appear from the corner of the house. In her hands she holds a plate, heavy with a cake now getting ruined by the rain. The children drop the courgette leaves, the broken green slipping through their fingers. As they make their way towards her, careful now to avoid the plants, the remorse that Clara feels is genuine.

In front of Auntie, she finds it hard to speak.

'I made a cake for you,' Auntie says, as water falls onto the sugar petals. She blinks away the rain and they follow her inside.

* * *

The steam curdles up through the bathroom, touching the walls, trapped by the windows. Stephen stands on tiptoes to draw a face in the mirror – a rough circle, three dots for the eyes and nose, and a straight line for the mouth. Clara watches Auntie in the reflection, sees how she bites her lips before the clouds of moisture erase her.

'This is you, Auntie,' Stephen says, changing the mouth he's drawn into a big smile.

'Me?'

And Clara recognises in Auntie the glow of motherhood, the one she's felt from her own mother so often, the warmth that never quite reached Stephen.

'Yes,' Stephen says.

It's the first time it's occurred to Clara to wonder why Auntie and Uncle Warren never had children of their own, when she can sense such a longing lurking there.

'Shall I wash your hair?' Auntie asks him. She's set the shampoo on the edge of the bath. 'I chose the one that smells of ferns,' she hurries on. 'I thought you'd like it the best.'

'I'll do it,' Clara says, mud from the garden still smeared across her face. 'You don't need to stay in here.' Auntie doesn't move. 'We'll let you know when we've finished.'

'Oh,' Auntie says. 'Thank you.' Although she shakes her head slightly as she speaks. They watch as she steps out of the room and closes the door. Clara hears her hesitate for a moment on the other side and then there's the sound of Auntie's hand flat against the wood that divides them. 'You're not his mother,' she whispers.

There are her footsteps soft along the corridor, becoming quieter before they descend the stairs.

* * *

Clara has changed into a clean, dry dress from home. She rolls up her muddy clothes and pushes them into a drawer.

'I'm going to wear one of my suits again,' Stephen says, the towel over his shoulders as he sits on the bed. 'Because we ruined the vegetable patch.'

'We didn't ruin it,' Clara says, although she thinks they might have done.

'We ripped up her courgettes.'

'They would've been ripped up in any case.' The ragged ends of remorse still reach into her, but she doesn't know what to do with them.

'We can help her cook,' Stephen wonders aloud, as he pulls another new suit from its hanger and puts the brown waistcoat over his shirt.

'She doesn't want us to.' Somewhere, Clara notices in herself the murmurings of sadness for Auntie, but her own grief is so tightly knotted, so difficult to unpick, that it's easier to only feel indifference.

'Do you think Uncle Warren will tell us off because of the garden?' Stephen asks, as Clara helps him with his buttons.

'Maybe.'

She doesn't want to look at his suit any longer, confused how Stephen can feel so comfortable in it, how he so willingly wants to wear it when the dresses that Auntie made for her fill her with dread.

Clara picks up her sketchbook and takes the pencil from where she keeps it tucked inside. She flicks through the pages, glimpsing into her life back home – the plum tree in their garden, the fish pond at the park where they sometimes walk with their father after lunch on Sundays. She stops on a drawing of her mother, one where she drew her face surrounded with a halo of flowers. The eyes have been rubbed out.

'Stephen. Have you touched my sketchbook?'

'No.' He pulls straight the front of his jacket.

Clara looks at the smudges where her mother's eyes should be.

Did I do it? The fire has scorched patches in her memory, enough to doubt herself. *Were they not good enough and I wanted to change them?* She turns the rest of the pages, anxious of what she might find, but none of them have been touched. On the final page she finds the pressed stem of fairy lace, the white already tinged with brown.

'Are you going to wear your new dress?' Stephen's voice finds her in her fug of uncertainty. 'Clara?' Hauling her back to be in the room with him again.

'The dress? Not yet.' She puts down her sketchbook, thinking she should hide it under the blanket on the bed, but now not wanting it close to the sheets she sleeps in.

Stephen stares at her, his arms straight by his sides.

'Do you think,' he asks, 'that Edwyn wondered where the earth had gone?'

'What are you talking about?'

Clara has a sudden urge to break something. If she could, she'd scream loud enough to scare the birds she can't even see. Instead, she grabs Stephen's hand, knowing that she's too rough, but at least it silences him as they run out of the room and down the stairs, the sound of their feet echoing through the silence of the house, to where Auntie is waiting for them in the hallway. As soon as she looks up, Clara sees the disappointment stark in her eyes.

'I made you dresses.'

'I'll wear them soon,' Clara says, aggravated now by Auntie's insistence that she should wear clothes other than her own, trying to ignore the sewn leather boy sitting frowning at her from underneath the hall window.

None of them move, until Auntie nods for them to go into the dining room. Clara steps ahead of Stephen, pushing open the door. In the centre of the table is a small, brown casserole dish. Clara is tempted to lift the lid to see what's inside, but she doesn't. Instead, they sit in their places and wait. Clara glances to the ticking clock, notices that the photographs of Auntie and Uncle Warren are pushed close together now.

When Auntie comes in, she carries three plates with hot, buttery potatoes, the soft white encased in dark brown skins. Clara is unsure what she ladles from the pot onto their plates.

'Beef stew,' Auntie says proudly. 'Warren's favourite.'

Clara moves her face away from the steam, but at least the smell doesn't turn her stomach as the fish did.

'Is he coming to eat with us?'

'He'll be here later.' Auntie tucks a napkin into the front of Stephen's suit. 'That's better,' she says, patting it gently before she sits down.

'He works a lot,' Stephen says.

'Indeed, he does,' Auntie agrees. But Clara wonders if he's staying away on purpose and as she looks up at his photograph on the mantelpiece, just for a moment, she wants to catch his eye to tell him that they'll be good for him.

'This food looks nice,' she says, trying to mend the cracks that have crept between them.

'Thank you.' Auntie beams. 'You may start.'

The cutlery still feels so different to what Clara is used to at home. She wants to put it down, even eat with her hands, but she knows she can't. And she's hungry, swallowing the first mouthful so quickly that it almost burns her. It must do the same to Stephen, as he spits his potato back onto his plate.

'Ouch,' he says, oblivious to the line his manners have crossed. The knife and fork in Auntie's hands stop their scraping on her plate, a lump of stew falling back into its juice.

Stephen grabs his glass of water and it's when he's swilling it cool into his mouth that he notices the silence, the statues looking at him.

'Stephen,' Clara says. Normally, spitting his food out would make her laugh, but there's a thread tightening the inside of her throat that warns her not to. 'That's disgusting.'

'It was hot.' His eyes still water slightly from his burnt tongue.

'Blow on it, then,' Clara tells him. He scoops up a clumsy mouthful, juice dripping from the fork and blows so hard that brown specks splatter the arm of his small suit jacket.

Auntie looks about her like a frightened animal as the children eat. The piece of potato on her fork is soaked yellow in butter and she hurries it into her mouth, swallowing without even a glint of the heat appearing on her face.

'Sorry,' Stephen says, wiping the food from his face with his sleeve.

There's only the sound of Auntie's chewing, the wetness of it, the muffled churning spilling around the room. It nibbles at Clara's skin, making everything seem wrong. The polished table, the pictures on the walls. She's not sure she likes any of it.

The intense silence reminds her of the time when Stephen refused to eat his dinner at home, their mother smashing a plate in rage and their father storming in. Stephen forced to stand against the wall with his back to them all, his food congealing among the broken china as the meal was finished in a painful absence of words.

Auntie straightens her knife and fork before she stands up.

'I'd made hazelnut cake and fresh custard.' She leans over to pick up Stephen's empty plate. 'But I can't reward behaviour like that.'

'He said he was sorry,' Clara says, desperate for her brother not to feel disappointment.

Auntie stops and looks at them. 'What would Warren say?'

A door in the hallway closes. Please, Clara thinks. Don't let him come in here, not now. She feels unsteady as she stares towards the dining-room door. But the handle doesn't move and no one comes in.

There's the soft scrape of china as Auntie puts Clara's plate on top of the pile. 'You are children – not animals.'

Clara thinks again of the graveyard and the pets sunk into the ground. And she wonders how so many of them died.

'You can go to your room now.' Auntie may as well be speaking to the viscid air, her eyes looking everywhere but at the children.

'Should we help clear away?' Clara asks.

'No. Just go.'

'Fine,' Clara says, before she gets up and marches around the table, holding Stephen's hand as he stands. He looks up at her and she knows what he's thinking. What if Uncle Warren is out there? Yet she knows too that they have no choice but to leave this room.

Together they go into the hallway, where there's no sign of anyone; there's only the lingering sound of Auntie's breathing behind them.

* * *

They've brushed their teeth and are lying in their beds, each of them sketching the vase of harebells. Stephen presses his pencil hard into his notebook. Clara is more thoughtful, using light strokes the way their mother taught her. She's so engrossed in her drawing, completely taken by a world where only stems and stamens exist, when Stephen rips out his page, hauling her back into the room.

'Rubbish,' he says, screwing up the paper.

'I bet it wasn't,' she says, irritated at being interrupted. 'Try it again.'

'I don't want to.'

They both stop still at the sound of the bedroom door opening. Auntie appears with a fresh apron tied around her waist, a mug of hot cocoa in each hand, as though earlier never happened.

'I thought you might like this,' she says, still standing at the threshold, almost needing to be invited in.

Stephen sits up straight and gives her a smile that should wash away all the damage of the day. Auntie goes to him and puts down the mugs on the table next to the toadstool lamp. She leans close to Clara.

'You're drawing.'

But Clara feels exposed, that Auntie has intruded on something too personal.

'It's nothing.'

'Can I see?' she asks, as Clara closes her sketchbook, sitting up to put it in her lap. Auntie's face shows no emotion. 'Another time, then.' From her pocket she gets the brown bottle. 'Here's your malt treacle.' Clara watches Stephen swallow the thick drop of liquid, before she takes her own.

Auntie keeps the smeared spoon in one hand and with the other she touches the top of the toadstool lamp, the colours still bright after all these years.

'It was our brother's.' She seems lost to them, lingering in the shadows of her life.

Stephen shuffles awkwardly, until his back is against the wall. It makes Auntie notice him again. She has to put the sticky teaspoon in her pocket before she pulls the pillow from the bed, plumping it up and placing it behind him, putting her hands under his arms to help him to sit properly.

'That's right,' she says. Clara watches Stephen's face light up and she wants to cut in, but her thoughts are taking too long to make sense, caught in the thought of Edwyn's eyes looking at his lamp. 'Shall I read you a story?' Auntie continues, her confidence gathering. 'I've waited a long time.'

'Yes please,' Stephen says.

'No,' Clara interrupts. Even before the accident, their mother had never read to Stephen – that job has always fallen to Clara and now she's pierced with a need to keep her role defined. 'I've already read to him.'

'Oh.' Auntie's tiny word is uttered on an intake of breath. She hovers by the edge of Stephen's bed, but stays standing apart from them, like residue.

'Good night,' Clara says.

She knows that Stephen wants to speak. He'll want to somehow defend this woman who brought them a hot drink. And he'd like another story – he can never have too many. But Auntie starts to walk away. She closes the door without even looking back.

'That wasn't kind,' Stephen whispers. He reaches for the mug nearest him, but it's too hot, so he leaves it there.

'She didn't give us pudding,' Clara reminds him, although she knows that her reasons are far more complicated than that.

'She wants us to behave like good children,' Stephen says. 'We promised daddy we would.'

Clara slips her sketchbook underneath the bed, before she pulls herself up to a sitting position, moving the pillow so that it sits between her and the cold wall, knowing to be careful so that the doll underneath won't fall. 'She made the pudding for us and she wouldn't let us eat it. That's weird.'

'Do you think she threw it away?'

Clara leans towards the mug and blows gently on the coloured milk. The skin on it ripples slowly, the liquid caught underneath.

'I think she's probably eating it now,' she says. 'Stuffing her face.'

'Can we go down later and see if there's any left?'

'You wouldn't dare.'

'I would. If you come with me.' And Stephen picks up the handle of his mug, the heat from the drink pressing into his knuckles. It feels almost too heavy to hold, but he won't let go. He waits to drink it.

When their mugs are empty, the remains of the chocolate drink staining the inside, Clara keeps hold of hers, swings her legs off the bed and goes to stand by the door.

'Come on, then,' she says. 'She made the pudding for us, so we should eat it.'

'But she might not be in bed yet,' Stephen tells her.

'If she sees us, we'll say we're bringing back the mugs.' Clara beckons him to her. 'Don't be a wimp. You're the one who wanted to go down.'

'But what about Uncle Warren?'

'I bet he's scared of us.' This thought suddenly makes absolute sense for Clara. 'He'll hide if he sees us coming.'

Out on the landing, she feels vulnerable in her nightdress and Stephen looks so little, with his pyjamas inching up his ankles, his hand clutched around the handle of his mug. She looks down the corridor towards the outline of the window. One of the dolls on the sill must have been their mother's and Clara is tempted to lay claim to it, but right now it's hidden in the darkness and she's too afraid to step there.

The stairs feel clammy, their bare feet tacky on the floorboards. At the bottom, all of the doors leading from the hallway are shut and there's still no sound anywhere in the house. Clara goes straight towards the kitchen, Stephen creeping beside her, holding onto her elbow as she pushes open the kitchen door. There doesn't seem to be anyone inside the room.

'Do we have to?' Stephen asks, his lips barely moving.

'You don't,' Clara tells him, knowing that he'll neither stay out here, nor go back up the stairs on his own. She feels engulfed by this small act of rebellion, her heart pulsing under her ribs, her mouth suddenly dry as they hold hands to step into the kitchen.

Clara senses Auntie in the room's memory, expects her voice to admonish them, but nothing is said as they put down their mugs on the sideboard. The fridge door feels foreign to Clara, sturdier than the one at home, and inside it she finds six tomatoes on a shelf, next to a carefully wrapped block of butter. On the back of the door sits a row of eggs, their bald heads waiting.

'We could draw faces on them,' Stephen whispers.

On the bottom shelf, a grey lump of meat in a bowl of salted water. Clara pokes it with her finger, pressing into the cold, waxy flesh. She picks up a bottle of milk. The foil lid has already been pressed to open it, so all she has to do is lift the edge of the creased silver and bring the bottle to her lips. The milk is surprisingly sweet. She can almost taste the colour of it on her tongue.

Stephen shakes his head when she passes it to him. 'She'll know we've been in here.'

'Suit yourself,' Clara says, fitting it back into the fridge, closing the door and wiping the curve of white from above her mouth.

She holds his hand as they creep over to what she thinks is a cupboard, but behind the door is a small room filled floor-to-ceiling with wooden shelves stacked with packets of food.

'A larder,' Stephen says, eyes wide. Clara feels along the edge of the wall until she finds a switch. She closes the door on them before turning on the light. In front are rows and rows of jars. Clara runs her fingers along them, fruit floating in one, pickled vegetables jammed tight into another.

'Look,' Stephen says. On a shelf to the side there's something sitting on a plate. The paper wrapping rustles as Clara lifts it, a faint scent of hazelnut creeping out. She shreds a chunk of the pudding bread with her hands and passes it to him and he shoves the sweet sponge crumbling into his mouth. His cheeks bulge out and he coughs as a speck of it catches in his throat.

'Shh,' she whispers, before she too takes a mouthful from the bread, nodding, chewing slowly.

There's a bowl next to the cake, filled to the top with custard. Stephen presses his finger through the yellow skin, before popping it cold into his mouth. Clara can tell he doesn't like it. It looks thick, like mucous, and must spoil the taste of the hazelnuts.

'You'll have to swallow it,' she whispers. But he opens the larder door and rushes back into the kitchen, where he stands on tiptoes to spit into the sink.

Clara wraps the pudding loaf, tucking the paper under it. 'Let's get some food for our adventure tomorrow.'

'What adventure?' Stephen asks.

'To the buildings,' Clara says. 'I've seen them from our bedroom window. We're going there.'

Already she's unscrewing the lid of a larger, rounded jar and taking a biscuit from the top. She passes one to Stephen, but he hesitates. 'Quickly,' she says, irritation stepping towards her as she nudges it into his hands. She takes one for herself before she screws the lid tight again.

The air hums hungrily as they each choose a jar, rearranging the others so a gap won't be seen. Stephen holds onto his jar of pickled pears as if it's treasure.

Clara's nerves are alive to the house exhaling around them as they leave the kitchen, pulling the door almost shut. It's when they're tiptoeing across the hallway that they hear voices coming from the sitting room. Clara stops still. She wants to hold Stephen's hand but he's clutching the stolen food, his eyes struck by fear. Uncle Warren must have come home.

'Is it worth it, for you?' The man's voice has a hard edge and it puts that feeling in the pit of Clara's stomach – as though an egg is nestled there, splitting in two as tiny insects hatch.

'Yes,' they hear Auntie reply.

'There was mud by the door.'

'They went in the garden.' Her voice strains towards them.

'I don't want them there.'

'Children like to play.'

'They're not ours, Helen.' Clara feels her heart pummelling into the silence. 'They never will be.'

'They are. For now.'

'It was a mistake.'

Clara starts to pull Stephen's elbow and he willingly goes with her.

'I'll make it work,' they hear Auntie say, as they run up the stairs.

In the bedroom, Clara hurries Stephen into his bed. He looks even younger, curled up with his Walrus, his eyes looking to Clara for answers she doesn't know to give.

'Tomorrow will be fun,' she tells him, as she tucks their stolen jars into her satchel.

'Was this mummy's room?' Stephen asks.

'Maybe.'

'I think they shared it together.'

Clara finds it too difficult to imagine Auntie shrunk back to a little girl, her small hands clutching at the blanket, whispering to their mother in the dark.

'With Edwyn too,' Stephen says solemnly.

'We need to sleep now.' Clara turns off the light and darts so quickly back into bed, the rug touching her toes before she slides herself under the sheet.

'I like it here,' Stephen says.

'I do too,' Clara replies. Although she's not sure how much of that is a lie.

She thinks of their father alone at home and wonders whether he's happier with it this way; here she can admit the coldness between her parents. Even before the accident there was such a hole in the fabric of their family, sometimes it felt like only a frayed thread was keeping them all together. When he was at home, their father would lock himself in his study, reappearing sometimes at meals. And there were her mother's wayward moods that were so hard to pin down, like fragile moths' wings.

Clara feels bitten by the dread of insomnia, her thoughts burrowing into her blood. She pinches the skin on her arms to try to feel physical pain instead. Now that her nails are a little bit longer she feels their sharpness. She can taste the shape that they make, acid on her tongue, dull in her bones.

There's a long, low whispering, a humming that slips under her blanket and fills inside her. She rocks her head on the pillow, but the noise doesn't want to go.

* * *

*A*untie finds herself unable to concentrate on the tapestry lying flat across her lap, so she lays the material on the table next to her and gets up. Warren's eyes don't look at her, not for a flicker of a moment. She's tempted to wave her hand in front of him, but she doubts he'd even notice then. Since their children have come, he's coiled himself even further away from her. 'It will get better,' she whispers. 'It just needs time.'

She feels a freedom as she leaves him behind by the tinkering flames. In the empty hallway she steps around the rug and pushes open the door with the wooden horse inside, where it sits with chunks of its mane slung pitifully over its back.

She averts her eyes as she passes it, instead going to the doll's house, the one she, Jane and Edwyn had as children. It gives her that same rush of feelings as it did then, when she could barely see over the tabletops. The bricks on the front are so perfect that they could have been painted yesterday. There's not one chip, one crack in the windows or door. Auntie lifts the latch on the side and the whole front opens. The old, creased smell is comforting to her and she drinks it in.

The kitchen is as she left it, the table, the clean sides, the tiny tea towel tucked neatly from its hook on the oven. Her hands are clumsy as she opens a cupboard and takes out a pan smaller than her fingernail. She holds it under the tap, still amazed how she can twist it on. It's not a big step for her imagination to see water coming from it, turning off the tap before the pan spills over.

She puts the pan onto the hob, pressing a button on the oven's front. There's a level of dismay when the ring doesn't light up, but she doesn't want to waste time by searching for a battery now. From a drawer she pulls a baking tray made from layers of tin foil and has to hold it so carefully that her older fingers don't dent the edges. She's quick to make the bread with flour poured from a pot, mixed with milk from the cardboard bottle in the fridge. While it's baking, she drops imaginary vegetables into the pan, their earthy smell greeting her as they turn into soup.

When the food is ready, she serves it onto the tiniest plates and bowls. The tray used to have a painting of a cat, but over the years the colours have scraped away gently, leaving just a hint of the animal and a solitary eye.

She takes it in her fingers up the stairs, careful not to spill the soup from the bowls and at the top she opens their bedroom door. But the children are not there.

'I've made this for you,' she whispers. There's not much space for the tray as she squeezes it onto the table. She lifts the curtains, looks under the beds. It's only when she opens the wardrobe door that she sees the girl pushed towards the back, her legs twisted. 'What are you doing in there?' Auntie chides, pulling her out and brushing back the hair from the doll's face. The eyes, nose, mouth have been scribbled out in an angry green pen. 'What's happened here, my pretty thing?' Her head leans slightly as she licks the cuffs of her cardigan, scrubbing it across the doll's face. It's enough to lift away some of the dark lines, but it leaves her features smeared, her skin sickly.

Auntie looks a while longer for the little boy, pulling back the blankets on the bed, checking again behind the curtains.

'Where are you hiding?' she asks.

All the time the girl sits, staring ahead. Auntie picks her up gently, holding the doll close, feeling her heartbeat mimicking her own. When the girl turns to look at her, Auntie knows that she came from her flesh. She closes her eyes and her daughter stands up and throws her arms around her neck. It is the lightness of these vulnerable limbs that illuminate the weight of Auntie's responsibility. A weight she has longed for, that she bears willingly. And she knows for sure that she won't ever let anyone take it from her again.

5

Clara wakes when it's barely light. She tries to sift through the remnants of her unsettled dreams, but finds only dead-ends, blank spots in her mind. She lies still for a while, listening to the comforting sound of her brother sleeping, but it isn't long before she drifts to her mother, to the tubes helping her to live. Thoughts press in, hard and clammy. She wants to strip them off as though they were clothes, but she knows that they're sewn into her skin now.

Clara reaches under her bed, careful not to wake the floorboards as she sweeps her hand across to find her sketchbook. She doesn't want to see the picture again, the one with her mother's rubbed-out eyes, but she can't bear the thought of her left blind like that. Ignoring the ache in her chest, she turns to the right page and starts to mend her. Clara feels herself sinking into the time she drew it, when they'd sat together in the garden. She'd found it difficult to get the angle of her mother's head right and had made her stay still for what felt like an eternity.

When she's finished, Clara hugs the sketchbook to her chest, imagining her mother here, the sweet smell of perfume so strong that when she opens her eyes she's surprised that she's alone on the bed. The absence makes her soul ache.

'I'll see you soon,' she whispers. 'I'll see you soon.' Over and over, believing that the repeated incantation will reach her mother and just at this moment she'll open her perfect eyes.

Clara turns to the final page, wanting to show her mother the fairy lace that she has pressed there. It's gone. She turns to the previous page and the page before that, but the flower isn't there. She picks up the whole book, holds it by its spine to shake it, but nothing falls out.

'Stephen,' she says, as he shuffles in his sleep. She leans over to shake his shoulder and he opens his eyes. 'Where've you put my flower?'

He sits up, the night still caught in his hair, unable to look anywhere other than the sketchbook that Clara holds in front of him. He blinks and rubs his eyes.

'I haven't got it.'

'Who has then?'

He shrugs. 'It fell out.'

'But it's not on the floor.'

'How should I know?' His voice is irritable now and Clara hasn't the energy to bring him down from a tantrum if he starts.

'I'm going out,' she says, closing the sketchbook.

'Where?'

'On an adventure.' She gets out of the bed, and slips her sketch-book into the satchel that hangs from the wardrobe door.

'Where's Auntie?'

'Probably asleep.'

Clara starts to get dressed, unable to articulate how she feels as Stephen reaches into the wardrobe for one of the suits. The inexplicable sense that the empty jacket somehow has a strength beyond its stitching and hanging sleeves.

'You could wear your normal clothes,' she says, 'as we're going to play in the garden.'

He ignores her, only stepping closer so that she can do his buttons for him. When they're ready, Clara picks up her satchel with the two jars of pickled food inside.

'What if Uncle Warren sees us?' Stephen asks. 'He doesn't like us.'

The room tightens around Clara. 'How can he dislike someone he's never even met?'

Outside the bedroom, Clara hopes that the air will feel fresh and wash her lungs clean, but instead it's cluttered with the taste of damp. The children stand on the landing listening to the house, before their hands are on the banister, their feet on the stairs.

By the front door, their shoes sit neatly together once more. They've been cleaned of every trace of mud and Stephen's laces have been tied in a bow. Clara is sure she can feel eyes watching her as they put them on and she waits for a voice to stop them, but it doesn't come. So they slip unnoticed out of the front door.

On the step is a gnarled, half-eaten body of a mouse.

'Look what the cat left,' Stephen says.

'Don't touch it,' Clara tells him, but already he's bending down, his face close to the tiny, stiff legs.

'It ate most of it.' Stephen picks up a small stub of a stick from the gravel. He pokes the remains of the animal and it turns under his direction, flopping onto its side. 'It looks like someone's stepped on it, it's so squashed.' He drills the stick gently into the tiny teeth and flicks the sinewy tail.

'I'm going,' Clara tells him. 'You can stay looking at that thing all day if you like.' But she only has to take a few steps before Stephen joins her.

The morning touches cold hands on their faces as they run next to the vegetable patch, where there's no evidence now of the damage they caused. This close, Clara can see that it's a string of empty nutshells hanging from the birdhouse. She pictures Auntie sitting threading them, alone in her kitchen.

They rush along the top of the walled garden, Clara reaching out to feel the bricks with the tips of her fingers, her skin tinting orange with their dust. She wipes it on her cardigan just before the wall ends and they stand in front of a wooden fence. On the other side are the buildings – broken, scarred, but still standing.

Clara glances back at the house, the side of it facing them, before she buries any hesitation and climbs over the fence. She holds out her hand to help Stephen, but he shakes his head, his anger at being asked manifesting in rough movements that end with him landing heavily beside her.

They walk forward together, stepping on concrete that's stubborn against the weeds and they approach the first giant barn, with its gaping mouth. Stephen runs inside, his arms outstretched as a plane, tipping himself one way and then the next.

'Hello!' he shouts. He's waiting for an echo, but the sound just gets snatched and swallowed by the stillness.

Clara looks up to the iron ceiling high above, at the wooden beams below it. The space is huge, empty, yet she feels her mother's childhood forcing itself in, sharp enough to hear the echoes of laughter, of whispers, of tears.

'Clara.' Stephen is pulling at her sleeve.

'Let's look somewhere else,' she says. Stephen runs past her now, his chin tipped up and laughing. She envies how free his mind is.

They hurry through more long grass until they stumble into an empty circle, where nothing grows.

'What's this?' Stephen asks.

'I don't know.'

Lined up on the ground are little sticks that have been stripped of their skin and look almost polished. Stephen picks up one and brings it close to his eyes.

'I thought they were bones.' He drops it, disappointed, into the pile of stones at the centre.

'Children have been playing here,' Clara says.

'It's a game.' Stephen nods, kneeling to push his hands through the sticks.

'Not one I want to play.'

'Where are they now? The children?' Stephen looks up at Clara, squinting in the early sunlight.

'Who knows? Maybe they were here ages ago.' And Clara runs on through the grass again, away from the odd circle, hoping that Stephen will follow.

The next building is far smaller than the first, with a door that Clara has to yank and shove, ripping weeds from underneath it before she can scrape it open. Dead air crawls out as Stephen scurries to stand behind her.

'Hello?' Clara calls, unsure now that they really are alone.

It's darker inside, but enough daylight slides through to show them a room divided up into stalls where cattle must have been kept. There's still straw scuffed on the floor and locks on each of the shoulder-high doors behind which the animals would have lived.

'I think we should go in,' Clara says, but she's not sure why.

'What do you think was in here?' Stephen asks, more confident now. He finds an unbolted pen and goes in.

'Cows, I suppose.'

'Do you think Auntie played in here with mummy when she was younger?'

'Possibly.'

'And their brother too?'

The trace of the child grasps at Clara, but she pushes him away.

'Maybe,' she says, shaking open a stall door. Inside, the floor has been swept clean.

'Look,' Stephen says, rushing back to her. He's holding the

curled body of a spider, its legs dried and bent in on themselves. He tries to stretch one of the legs straight, but it snaps in his fingers. 'Oh. I've broken it.'

He holds it up to Clara as if she'll want to see.

'It doesn't matter,' she reassures him. 'It's too dead to feel it.'

'Do dead things not feel anything at all?'

'Of course they don't.'

'Why?'

'Because they're dead.'

Stephen pulls off another of the spider's legs and puts it into his palm.

'It's very small,' he says. And slowly he shreds the legs, until all that's left is a berry-sized body, with eyes that don't see.

'What hung on the hooks do you suppose?' Clara points to the row of curled-up metal, clad with rust.

But Stephen isn't listening; he's laying the shredded spider on the ground, the legs almost spelling out a peculiar, new word.

'I bet there are lots more dead things in here,' he says, going into another pen.

'She'll be frosted if you get filthy,' Clara tells him, watching as he crawls about on his hands and knees, the blue suit getting covered with dust. Hoping that it'll be enough to stop him wearing the suits again.

'Look at this.' He picks up a lifeless moth by its wing. 'It's furry.'

Clara doesn't like its sand colour, its stillness.

Stephen holds it close, looking into blank eyes.

'It can't see me,' he says.

'Of course it can't.'

The wings rip in his fingers when he pulls them. They're just scraps now and he looks disappointed. The wisps of antennae slide out easily and he walks back and lays the pieces next to the dead spider.

'Has its soul gone already?' he asks.

'Yes,' Clara replies. Although she's never thought about whether insects have them; whether they even have hearts.

'Does someone come and get the soul?' Stephen asks.

'I don't know.'

'Has anyone ever seen it?'

'Seen what?'

'The soul being collected.'

'I doubt it.'

'Do some souls get forgotten?'

'I don't know.' Clara drags straw in a circle with her foot. 'Maybe that's what ghosts are.'

Stephen stares at her intently.

'Mummy's soul hasn't been taken yet.'

'No,' Clara says. 'And it won't be.'

'If it does, can the soul collector give it back?'

'It won't need to. Mummy's going to be better soon.' But that familiar spot of anger, of guilt, spits within Clara. 'I'm going to see the last barn,' she says. She doesn't need to reach out for Stephen's hand – he instantly goes to hold hers, the powder of the moth's wings still light on his fingertips.

It's another barn with no door, but Clara can see that there was one once, the hinges now left useless and waiting. It's the smallest of the three, with a rough floor and murky air. There are four big containers lined up together, with hatches at the bottom. Stephen steps towards the nearest one and puts his small hand against its metal wall.

'This is where he died,' he says.

'Who?'

'Edwyn.'

'Don't be a germ, Stephen,' Clara says.

'I'm not. It was here.' His arms raise and he starts to circle them slowly. 'He played with the grain.'

It's so real, as though he's not pretending anymore. Clara watches with fascinated horror as the imaginary grain swamps his hands, his shoulders. She's sure she can taste it, the brittle grit of it in her teeth.

'It was here,' Stephen says again, his hands now starting to claw madly at the air around him.

'Stop it.' Her brother's face is twisted in some grotesque pain and Clara tries to hold his arms down, but he pulls them free. His breathing is distorted, bubbling and choking and she thinks he might drown here in the open air. 'Stephen,' she shouts, as she slaps him hard across his face.

He stands stunned, his mouth left open and flailing. Clara thinks he'll cry, but instead he just stares at her, shaking.

'I hate you!' he suddenly shouts. 'I wish you weren't here. I want to stay here without you.'

'Stevie,' she says, an apology just out of reach.

But he moves under her arm and out of the barn, down the side of the building, thrashing through old grass to escape. Clara has to run, away from the flames of shame wanting to scorch her. She follows her brother's path, his stab of angry blue suit and swiping arms, her satchel banging against her hip. She won't call out, knowing that she's quicker than him and when she catches up she holds tight to the back of his jacket to drag him to a halt.

'We haven't eaten our food,' she reminds him, but when Stephen turns to look at her she sees his cheek blazing red, knows she has to do this properly. 'I'm sorry I hurt you,' her voice sincere. 'Look, these are for you.' And she undoes the buckles on her satchel and takes out the jar of beetroot.

'I don't like them,' he says, pointing to the purple bulbs swimming in brine.

'You've got pears.' She holds his jar high so that the light shines into it. She knew it'd make him smile and it does. The thought of the sweet fruit calms him and he sits, just where he is, and waits for her to unscrew the lids. When she passes him his jar, he brings it close to his face to smell the juice.

Clara digs her fingers into the pool of vinegar, gripping a slithery piece of beetroot and pulling it free. She likes the sting it makes in her mouth, the soft release of earth as she bites into it, before she reaches for another.

Stephen eats all of his pears too quickly.

'You'll feel sick,' Clara warns him, knowing the syrupy fruit will be too much for his empty stomach.

'I'm keeping my jar,' he says, as Clara throws hers, still swimming with two small beetroot heads, far into the undergrowth.

'You'll have to put it back in my bag to hide it, then,' she tells him.

'I'm going to use it for my experiment.'

'What experiment?' She's thirsty now and wishes they'd brought a drink.

'To find a soul.'

She stops and looks at him.

'You don't need to do that, Bean.'

'But I want to,' he says. He pulls up some grass and rubs it around the inside of the glass. There are gummy remnants of juice on the stalks, and when he's satisfied he scrunches them in his fist and drops them to the ground.

'If you follow me, you have to be quiet,' he says.

'Where are you going?'

'I'm going to get something to keep in my jar. And I'm going to watch it when it dies so I can see the collector come and get its soul.'

'You can't just let something die.'

'I have to. I might be the first person ever to see the soul collector.'

He's walked to the edge of a clog of bushes woven with nettles. He kicks at them to make a clumsy path.

'Come on, Stephen,' Clara says. 'Let's go back. You're going to get stung.'

'I won't. I'm protected.'

'By who?'

'I just am.'

He pushes aside the broken nettles with his sleeves and peers in closer.

'She'll wonder where we are,' Clara says.

'Shh.'

His fingers rummage in the earth, picking back weeds, lifting stones, before he darts forward and clamps something in his hand.

'Quick.' He's holding a beetle, squeezing tightly on its back to stop it running away. 'I can't take the lid off on my own.'

So Clara does it for him. She doesn't know why – she doesn't want to be part of his killing experiment. And he drops the wriggling insect inside, its legs wheeling the air wildly, until it manages to stand against the glass bottom of the jar.

Clara thinks it's beautiful. It's almost the size of her thumbnail, its back a shiny blue-green, like liquid.

'How is it that colour?' Stephen asks.

'Nature's a clever thing,' Clara says. Yet even she never knew they could exist like this.

They stare closely at the segments of its legs, its black button eyes.

'You can have it as your pet,' she tells him.

'Until it dies.'

'It doesn't have to.'

'It does.'

'Not if we keep it well.'

'Have you forgotten?' He squints up at her, his eyes nearly closed. 'It's got to die.' He screws the lid on even tighter as the beetle tries to crawl up the wall of glass, frantic to escape. 'Maybe its soul will be even more beautiful.'

'Stephen.'

'I wonder where the collector takes them?'

'I've had enough of this,' Clara says. 'I'm going back.'

But Stephen holds the jar out towards her. 'Will you hide it in your bag?'

She doesn't want to feel the weight of it in her hand, to have those desperate thread-like legs so close to her. But she takes it from him because it's what her brother wants, and, without looking at the trapped insect again, she puts it in her satchel.

Together they head back through the grass and over the fence, Stephen skulking next to Clara down the edge of the wall. At the corner they hear only silence and so they feel safe to walk back the length of the vegetable patch.

Clara looks up to see Auntie watching them from the kitchen window, her face so perfectly framed that it might be a painting, hanging there on the side of the house. When they get to the front door, Auntie is already there, her spotless apron tied around her waist, a cloth in her hands.

'You went out again,' she says.

'There's a lot to explore.'

Stephen looks on the floor for the dead mouse, but it's gone.

'We found the farm,' he tells her, as they go inside.

'I thought you had.' Auntie's mouth barely opens as she speaks, her reluctant words thin as smoke. 'I'd made you shiny toast.'

'How's it shiny?' Stephen asks.

'I fry it in oil. On both sides.' And now her face picks up slightly. 'It was my favourite when I was your age.'

'How lovely,' Clara says, the thought of oil on her teeth making the taste of bile rise to her tongue.

'We can eat it together,' Auntie says.

Stephen runs ahead into the dining room and Clara follows, knowing that in her bag there's a secret Auntie knows nothing about, as the beetle's legs scratch uselessly inside the jar.

* * *

The breakfast is painfully empty of anything but the sound of eating. It's only at the end, when every plate is clean, that Stephen speaks.

'Could we go and see your chickens?' he asks.

Auntie's fingers fidget in her lap. 'We could collect the eggs,' she says.

'I've never seen a real one.'

'A chicken, or an egg?' Auntie's crease of a laugh changes her. 'Why don't you two pop upstairs to wash your hands and when you come down I'll be ready.'

Stephen runs from the room before Clara can blink. She's more careful, her satchel hanging from her shoulder, her hand pressed against the shape of the jar.

* * *

Auntie is coming out of the kitchen as they come down the stairs. She holds a small basket, the curved handle painted with fading colours.

'This is what I use,' she says, beaming up at them. 'You won't fill it, but it's enough to share.'

'Thank you,' Stephen says, running the last few steps to hug her. They all look stunned. His desperation in needing a mother is painful, yet when Auntie folds her arms around him, jealous tears threaten Clara. She stares at them, wanting this resentment to crumble. She needs to be happy that this woman is standing here.

'This will be fun,' Clara says, her cheeriness too forced. 'Let's get your shoes on, Stephen.'

Clara passes them to him, but he doesn't untie the laces enough to slip his foot in easily and she has to kneel down, feeling Auntie waiting. She won't rush, enjoying the comfort of helping Stephen into something that's his from home, something their mother chose. She almost wants to kiss the shoes, wondering if the soft leather might remind her of their mother's cheek. But she can't stay crouched like this forever. When they stand up, Auntie gives Stephen the basket and opens the door.

The sun touches them as soon as they step outside. The sky is clear, any rain forgotten. Stephen skips ahead, something Clara doesn't remember him doing before, and she has to hurry behind him until they turn around the corner of the house and wait for Auntie to catch up.

'It's through there,' Auntie says, pointing at a small arch in a hedge. Clara feels the leaves as they duck through it, the smell of smooth green on her fingers. Now they're on a brick path, surrounded on either side by long grass. Clara likes it brushing against her palm and she squeezes her fingers shut against the stalk of one, gently pulling until the grains come away in her hand. She holds them, like tiny little beads, before she blows them to be taken by the wind.

At the end of the path there's a small shed, surrounded by a tall mesh fence. Stephen stops and stares. Then Clara sees what he sees – feathers are scattered in the enclosure. A chicken lies on its back, its eyes wide, one leg pedalling slowly in the air.

There's a strangled intake of Auntie's breath.

'You went in here,' she says.

'No.' Clara shakes her head.

'You didn't close the door properly.'

'We've never been here,' Clara tells her truthfully, the sky warm on her neck.

Stephen stares at the feathers in the mud-pecked ground. The only thing that moves is the scrawny stick of that chicken's foot, three claws curled tight at its end.

'Where are the other chickens?' he asks, although he must know already.

Auntie lifts the latch of the gate in the fence and pushes her way through. She swings wide the door to the hut, so that they can all see the emptiness gaping out.

'You left the door open and the fox got them.'

'Maybe Uncle Warren did,' Clara says, but Auntie ignores her as she paces around the inside of the fence. It isn't long before she finds a ripped hole through which the fox has taken its bloodied brood.

'Will they come back?' Stephen asks.

'It's killed them all,' Auntie states flatly. And they wait, with the emptiness and that knowledge, before she goes back to the one chicken that's left, where it stares upwards, blinking when it sees her. Clara is aware of the fear in its eyes.

Auntie picks it up and Stephen goes to her, wanting to help make it better. He's about to reach out when Auntie grasps the chicken's head, balled up in her palm, and twists it with a rough click. The leg stops turning its circles, the whole body collapsed down, released of its air.

Stephen screams. Clara clutches him to her, but still he sees Auntie holding the dead animal by its feet, its wings swinging uselessly from its body, the eyes still open, beak slightly parted in shock.

'You need to collect any eggs that are left,' Auntie tells them, before she goes back out of the gate and down the path, the lifeless chicken knocking against her leg as she walks.

The children stare after her. 'I think she had to do that,' Stephen says. 'Because it was hurt.'

Clara isn't sure what to believe. Auntie's hands had seemed too powerful against the soft neck. She hadn't even winced as she'd snuffed out its life.

'We need to get the eggs,' she says.

'I don't want to.'

'We have to.' Clara pulls away from him. 'She already thinks we left the door open.'

'But we didn't.'

'I know. But she's going to be angry, so we need to do something to make it better.'

She takes the basket from him, sensing briefly the hint of a child, their mother hiding behind the fence. Clara holds Stephen's hand in hers, as much for her own comfort as anything, and pulls him towards the shed. Inside, in the darkened room, she can smell death.

'We won't be long,' she says, barely opening her mouth.

There are straw and feathers all over the floor and Clara doesn't know where to start to look. She steps further inside, kneeling down to feel her hand across the surface.

'There's some,' Stephen says. 'There.' He's pointing towards the back of the shed, where three eggs curve their soft white shells in the dim light. Clara doesn't want to touch them. She's frightened that the fox's teeth aren't far away. But she has to walk into the gritty-smelling air, to gather them quickly, placing them in the basket in the crook of her arm.

'Is that enough?' Stephen asks.

'It'll have to be.' And they run from the shed, past the gate and back down the path where Auntie had been just moments before.

* * *

Back in the house, they forget to take off their shoes as they step through the silence into the kitchen. Clara doesn't expect to see the dead chicken lying on the side. It stalls her and she doesn't go further than the doorway, instead she just stares at Auntie standing there.

'Are you going to bury it?' Stephen asks.

'You've got some eggs.' Auntie comes towards them and takes the basket. 'Only three?'

'Yes.'

'They'll be the last ones. Dead chickens can't lay eggs.'

'We didn't leave the door open,' Clara says. 'We've never even been there.'

'I'll bring your lunch to your bedroom later,' Auntie says.

'To the bedroom?' Stephen asks.

'You're not to go in the garden again,' Auntie tells them. She sounds like a toy, wound up with a key.

'Ever?' Clara laughs at the absurdity of it.

'Go now.' She turns to take the almost empty basket into the larder, and Clara remembers how not long ago Auntie had handed them the same basket, hope woven in with the wicker, her skin glowing so much with happiness that her cheeks blushed red. Yet now the children stamp their way up the stairs and slam the bedroom door behind them.

* * *

It is a new sound for Auntie, this protesting rage of the children and it both terrifies and compels her. She wants to stop them – should stop them – and bring down a safe veil of quiet again, but there's a moment in her that wants to join them too. To be a child again, where consequences were too distant to care about. To have her brother running beside her, have him holding her every word and copying her footsteps.

Auntie needs to settle her mind with the comfort of cooking. The clean slice of cold butter, the careful sprinkle of flour. Edwyn's soft voice so close as she adds a dash of freezing water to the dough mix and begins to bring it all together. It's always magical to her, the flakey grains in the bowl turning into a malleable solid she can roll and stretch, shaping it with cutters, pressing each disc into tiny pie cases.

It's only when she must use an egg for the filling that Auntie's composure stalls. The albumen is stringy as it hangs from the separated shell; she scrapes and uses every last bit of it. Her terror is diluted, but it's still there. That the chickens have gone. That soon Warren will know.

She hopes that he'll be pleased with her solution. It's clear that the children must stay inside for a while. They are excited to be in

Ballechin, but they must have boundaries. What good is a child if it doesn't know right from wrong?

Auntie gets a knife from the drawer. From a bowl in the fridge she takes one tomato. She's sure that the children will like it on top of the pie, softened in the oven, blackened just slightly on the edge. She cuts a slice and then another, careful to make them identical in size. And when she's finished, Auntie licks tomato pips from her fingers, one-by-one.

6

It's much later, in the thick fog of boredom, that Stephen sits on the bed and holds his jar above his head, turning it slowly as he looks inside it.

'How long will it take?' he asks. 'For the beetle to die?'

'I think you should let it go. It's been in there long enough.'

'That won't help my experiment.'

'So you're really just going to keep the lid closed on it?'

'Yes. And then I'll find the soul catcher.'

'It's too pretty to die,' Clara says. If it wasn't trapped she would draw it; she'd like the challenge of capturing its liquid colour on the page.

'Even pretty things die.' Stephen leans forward to put the jar next to the toadstool lamp, where the light filters into it and makes the beetle's back shine. Clara feels her mind slip inside the jar, where the lid keeps her trapped with the insect's segmented legs clicking against the glass. Her mother's fingers are here too, clawing to get free. It's difficult to see through the stench of smoke, but she's sure it's her mother's arm, the cream material of her dress engulfed by flames.

'Clara.' Stephen is poking her elbow hard. 'You're doing your staring thing.'

She's in Ballechin. The two beds are here, the rugs, the beetle in sharp focus.

She can still taste smoke. 'It's wrong to keep it like this,' she says.

'It doesn't react at all. Look.' Stephen knocks roughly against the jar. 'If it was a cat or something, it would at least move.' He picks up the jar and shakes it, enough to make the beetle scuttle into the glass.

'It's cruel,' she tells him. 'He'll be really confused, wondering where the earth has gone.'

'Like Edwyn?'

'I doubt Edwyn looked anything like a beetle,' Clara says, trying to steer them from a creeping darkness.

Stephen stops still. 'Will mummy wonder where the earth has gone?'

'She's not going to die.' Clara is adamant.

Stephen shrugs. Clara sees her words fall like leaves around him and she wants to gather them back up so she can say it again and again until they both believe it.

Stephen brings the jar close. 'It doesn't look confused. It doesn't look anything.' He scrunches up his face, but his eyes stay open. 'What if it doesn't even have a soul?'

'Of course it does. Everything has a soul.'

Clara needs to be somewhere else and knows that only the scratch of pencil on paper can take her there. She goes to where her satchel hangs on the wardrobe and takes out her sketchbook, the familiarity of it in her fingers already helping her. She settles back on the bed, knowing she'd like to finish the picture of the harebells; the tiny petals are beginning to crisp and she wants to show their change with just a few deft strokes of sharpened lead. There's the sound of the pages turning, the soft definition of them against her thumb.

She stops, dumbfounded. The words *hate bells* have been scrawled across her unfinished drawing of the flowers, the letters so angry that in places they've torn through the page.

'Stephen,' she says, but he's engrossed by the trapped beetle. Clara has to lean over and poke him hard. 'You spoiled my picture.'

He's annoyed to be distracted, barely glancing at her sketchbook.

'I didn't do that.'

'Who else did, then?' Clara knows she has to control her anger, that she can't risk her brother starting.

'It wasn't me.'

Clara softens as she recalls his attempts at drawing the harebells, how useless it made him feel when he couldn't get it right.

'My drawing was only better because I'm older than you, Bean,' she says.

'I don't care.'

Clara feels trapped by his bewilderment. It makes her unsure where to place her thoughts. The walls watching in silence don't help. She wants to rip up the picture, but doesn't want to touch the page again.

When there's a faint knock on the door and Auntie walks in, doubt about everything lands heavily on Clara.

'Did you touch my sketchbook?' she asks.

Auntie stands in front of her, carrying two plates filled with little parcels wrapped in greaseproof paper and clasping a blanket and small flask under her arm.

'What a funny thing to say.' She puts down the food on top of the chest of drawers. 'Of course I didn't. It's yours. But what I did do is make you a picnic.' She turns to face them again, smoothing her apron.

'For indoors?'

Auntie's eyes flick involuntarily to the window, at the sun tipping through. 'It will be exciting,' she says.

'If we go outside, I promise we'll only sit on the grass,' Stephen says and Clara sees him slip his jar underneath his bed. Inside the jar is the beetle, motionless, but alive.

'No. If I give in to you now, a flood of disobedience will start,' Auntie says. 'You'll be fine up here.' She lays her hand on one of the parcels. 'I've made you cheese and onion pie.' She looks at them, waiting for their smiles, but they don't give her any. Clara wants to tell her that she hates onions, but she's too unsure of this person who's replaced the one in her imagination.

'There'll be just enough space for the blanket,' Auntie says,

LISA HEATHFIELD

holding it out for Stephen to take. His own disappointment keeps his arms by his sides, so she has to put it folded on the bed. 'I'll come and get the plates when you're finished.'

'We'll bring them down,' Clara tells her.

Auntie hesitates in the doorway. For a moment Clara dreads that Auntie might want to stay and join them, sit with them on the floor, pulling her skirt to cover her knees. But it doesn't happen.

'I hope you like it,' she says and when they don't answer, she leaves them.

As soon as she's gone, Clara gets her satchel and pushes her sketchbook inside. There are so few places to hide it in this room and she chooses the back of the wardrobe, hoping that the dresses might disguise it.

She knows she has to touch the picnic and goes to peel back the paper of the first parcel. The smell of two hard-boiled eggs drifts into the room, the stench of an infected lesion.

'Yuck,' Stephen says. Clara goes straight to the window and tries to open it, forgetting that it's locked.

'Wrap them up again,' she tells Stephen. 'I'm not staying in here. We'll go outside.'

'What if she sees us?'

'She won't.' She folds the picnic into the blanket and grips the corners to hold it all together. 'We'll go quietly.'

Stephen nods, unsure. Clara understands his hesitation. She's beginning to think there's instability lurking in Auntie, yet it hides just beyond her comprehension.

At the top of the stairs, they peer down. From the kitchen, Clara can hear the sound of Auntie.

'Run flat out,' she says.

They skim so swiftly down the stairs, staying to the carpet in the middle, anxious of wooden creaks. Stephen has to open the front door as Clara's hands are full. He struggles with the handle, jittery with anticipation. When he manages, it feels too loud and Clara is sure that Auntie will hear.

'Don't close it completely,' she whispers, so he pulls it almost shut behind them.

'Which way?' he asks, and Clara recognises the thrill of adventure in his bones. She knows they can't go on the front lawn as they'll be too exposed to Ballechin and all its eyes. And she never wants to go near the chicken shed again. The only place where they'll be hidden is through that old door in the heavy brick wall.

'Follow me,' she says as she darts around the corner of the house, the blanket of food awkward in her hands.

At the small window in the kitchen they stop. Clara puts a finger to her lips and motions for Stephen to crouch down low. He's on the edge of laughing, the excitement reaching out from him in all directions, but he won't want to be found yet. He wants his picnic in the garden.

Together they almost slide along the ground and Auntie doesn't see a thing.

Before Clara can breathe again, they run the short distance to the walled part of the garden, Stephen close to her heels. 'Open it,' she urges and he holds the heavy metal handle and twists them into the world behind the bricks, the reek of chrysanthemums ready to greet them.

With the door closed, Stephen lets out a snort of a giggle.

'Shh,' she scolds him. 'She could still hear us.' The silence is instant. It sits like fog.

This place is exactly as they left it. The graveyard is rimmed by overgrown grass and in the middle is their clearing of ripped, neat stubble, with five crosses sticking up crudely from the ground. Stephen is already ambling towards them, but Clara is regretting it. She doesn't want to eat here, she doesn't want to taste death on her tongue.

'Put down the picnic then,' Stephen says, from where he stands in the middle of the crosses.

Clara wants to say that she's changed her mind and they should go somewhere else, but her brother has that expression of impatience, the one that sometimes precedes him stamping his feet in the wail of a tantrum and she can't risk Auntie following the trail of their noise and finding them.

Heat strikes her arms as she tumbles everything from the blanket, before she spreads it so he can scramble on.

'She's made a lot of food. They're like little presents,' he says, as he unwraps what Auntie has given them, clumsily knocking pastry, denting it with his fingers. 'She's very kind.'

The cheese and onion pie has been cut into neat triangles, the edges of it flaring up into crumpled ruffles.

'I'm not so sure anymore,' Clara says.

'Because she's angry about the chickens?'

'Maybe.'

'I still think she's nice.'

The second parcel holds two small potato pies with discs of tomatoes planted on the top.

The eggs stay wrapped.

'I'm not going to eat those,' Stephen says.

'They stink.' But it's not only that. Looking at them, Clara sees the chicken with its throttled neck, the movement of its leg, the disappearance of the others dragged away by the fox.

'I think we should bury them,' Stephen says solemnly.

'The eggs?'

He nods and she knows from the look on his face that she mustn't laugh.

'Here?' she asks.

He nods again. 'They can share this cross.' Stephen points to the one closest to them. He picks up the two forks and starts to dig near the small, carved stone.

'I'm not sure we should,' Clara says.

Stephen pauses to look up at her, his face showing only unwavering certainty. 'We must.'

Clara feels strangely detached as she takes a fork from him; together they make a hole in the earth.

Not far down, Clara spots the corner of a piece of cloth. She pulls at it and it slides up through the mud, fragile in her fingers.

'You've found a map,' Stephen says.

There's darkness at the rag's centre, leaking out in thick tendrils, making a pattern Clara can't decipher. Stephen twists the rag around and over, stares closely for any tiny clue of treasure. He can't find any, so he drops it onto the blanket and instead points to the bundle of eggs.

'Can you put those into the grave?' he asks her.

She doesn't want to touch them, so she opens the greaseproof paper and rolls their soft flesh from it and drops them into the hole. They stare up blankly, so she brushes over the earth.

'That's better,' she says, although she's not convinced that it is, not completely.

'Yes,' Stephen whispers.

'I might save my food till later,' she says, putting her pie slices on top of each other and wrapping them tight again. The paper keeps opening and she wishes she could find some twine to knot around it. It would make her feel that they're really deserted, really alone, that this small patch of garden is an island from which they can escape.

'It won't feel like a proper picnic if you don't eat with me.' But this time Stephen's pleading eyes won't work. She keeps the parcel in her hand and there's nothing that will make her eat food in here.

She watches Stephen, his greedy munching through the layers of his pies. He picks out the onion from among the cheese, each bit pulling like a piece of string. He giggles, wriggling a bit under

Clara's nose and she laughs as she grabs it and throws it to get eaten by the long grass.

'I wanted that,' he says, a scowl whipping suddenly across his face.

'You don't like onion,' she reminds him.

'I do,' he says, picking again for another bitter thread, which he pulls free and stuffs into his mouth. 'See.'

They don't hear as Auntie walks across the lawn, just the other side of the wall. They don't know how close she is, her hand on the round handle, pressing open the wooden door. They don't even notice, at first, how she stands and stares.

'What are you doing?' Her voice staggers through the earth towards them.

Clara looks up and stops still. 'We're eating our picnic.'

'We made it nice,' Stephen says, sweeping his hand over the beaten-down grass.

It's as if Auntie is being pushed forward to where they sit among the graves, where she sees, in the middle of the blanket, the stained scrap of cloth. It seems to fill her mouth and choke her as she flounders.

'You've dug it up,' she says.

'The map?' Stephen asks.

When Auntie screams, Clara expects the sky to crack and fall. She's running with Stephen, the injured call of Auntie echoing on their backs, the picnic scattered. They flee across the tangled ground to the door, which Clara pushes, pausing for a second, brief enough to let Stephen grip the edge of her dress so they can stumble together over the mowed grass, towards the rose-walk.

They run through the tunnel of flowers and Clara sees the swing in the distance, but she chooses the other way, the quicker route to a hiding spot in the hedge, bending low, scraping their palms and knees on the ground, squeezing close to the roots, pushing themselves into its bristly insides.

The children stop, curled in nature's womb. Clara tastes the strength of her heartbeat pressing into her throat, her tongue. Stephen is circle-eyed in the gloom. The small branches bend their way over his body, making it difficult to settle, to find a position comfortable enough to hold.

'Shh,' Clara tells him. She has enough space to part the dense leaves with her fingers, watch the cracks of daylight on the other side, to see as Auntie stumbles from the walled garden. Clara knows that they've somehow torn happiness from her, and in the moment before Auntie turns, Clara sees bewildered loss drawn painfully on her face. There's the defeated huddle of Auntie's shoulders as she lurches up the steepest part of the lawn, the picnic blanket held close, past the bird table with the trailing nutshells, the vegetable patch, until the corner pulls her to disappear.

'Where is she?' Stephen whispers.

'She's gone.'

'Gone?'

'Only inside.'

Stephen nods solemnly. 'Shall we go to her?'

'Not yet.'

And so they wait, the rusty smell of the earth holding close to the soles of their shoes, the damp creeping close to their ankles. As Clara's heartbeat slows, her knees begin to ache from crouching so low, but still she doesn't move, only watching the house to see which window Auntie might appear in.

'Will she forgive us?' Stephen asks.

'There's nothing to forgive.'

'But she didn't want us there.'

'Then we won't go in there again,' Clara says, glad of an excuse not to see the crosses.

'Do you think she still wants us to stay with her?'

Clara looks over at her brother, hunched like a gnome, a spindly branch resting on his forehead. She manages to reach through the twist of leaves to push it from his skin.

'Of course she does. She loves us.' Although she is less sure now.

'We'll be extra good for her,' Stephen says.

'You can be.' Clara starts to crawl backwards, feeling the way with her feet until she's free. She stands, brushing away the loose fingers of branches, unpicking the hedge's bitten nails from her hair. She has to blink away a piece of grit fallen in her eye, the scratch of it as she opens and closes her lid, the water in her lashes until it gets washed away. It's not so easy to untangle her emotions, to find the roots of one, the ends of another. There are so many weaving, conflicted feelings and she's too tired now to do anything other than leave them seething where they are.

* * *

The children are alone in the bedroom when they hear the shouting start.

'Uncle Warren is in the house,' Clara whispers, the worms of fear spilling open in her stomach as their uncle's voice rolls in waves up the stairs.

'She told him what we did.'

'We didn't do anything wrong, Stevie.'

She curls Stephen into her side, picks up a book and starts to read, sitting in such a way that her arm covers one of his ears as he glances towards the door. She keeps reading, wrapping Stephen in a different, paper world, a safer, more predictable one, far from Uncle Warren and his violent rage.

Time ticks by, the clock on the wall counting out the seconds, mingling with the rumblings of their hunger. There's no sound from downstairs anymore. The night begins to creep over the hills, coming closer to Ballechin, close enough to feel the brick walls and step inside. Clara feels a hate for this place gathering speed, an unsettling blame for Auntie, too intricately woven to their mother trapped in the fire. She turns on the light, needing to forget as she watches Stephen play with his wooden truck. He fills the back of it with shredded balls of paper, tipping it so that they fall onto the floor, a dry heap of snow. She's glad that his attention has moved away from the soul catcher, and thinks that maybe soon she can take the jar back to the garden and set the beetle free.

It's only now that she notices a tiny mound of salt on top of the chest of drawers, drifting in a small trail towards the edge.

'Stephen.' She nudges him with her foot, but he shifts away.

There's a knock at the door. They both look towards it as it opens. It's Auntie standing there. Her head is bent down low, but she can't disguise the thickening bruise spread purple on her face.

'What happened to your cheek?' Stephen asks. He stands up to go to her, but she steps back. 'Does it hurt?'

'I need help with this,' she says. Behind her a small table stands on the landing. Clara doesn't have room in herself to argue, not with the guilt and reluctant pity fighting for space inside her, so she stands up and together they push and drag it into the room. 'I think by the window would be nice,' Auntie says and they squeeze it past the beds and move it right up against the sill. It fits perfectly, as though it was always meant to be there. 'I'll get the chairs.' And she goes from them.

'Why's she putting that in here?' Stephen asks.

Auntie comes back in, struggling with a chair in each arm. Clara helps her and together they put them by the table.

'Were these mummy's?' Clara asks, needing to feel their mother near her.

Auntie only taps the back of the one nearest her. 'Warren and I think it's better that you should eat up here.' She's unable to look at them, keeping her eyes instead on the edge of the bed. 'Tea is nearly ready. I'll bring it up.'

The children don't complain. In fact, Clara in particular feels relief. 'Shall I help carry the food?' she asks.

But Auntie seems cut from her mooring and Clara watches, detached, as the woman runs from them.

'Why are you happy?' Stephen asks. 'I don't want to eat up here. I want to eat with her.'

'But up here,' she replies, 'you can spit out as much hot food as you want.' She watches him, expecting him to laugh, but he doesn't.

They're waiting at the table when Auntie comes back. Clara has managed to squeeze the chair between the bed and the table so that she's looking out of the window. Stephen is next to her, having only the wardrobe as his view. Clara keeps her back to the door, but she can hear Auntie walking across the room, seeing her only when she's putting down the plates of food. Fatty steam rises and Clara nearly gags.

'If you eat all of it, you can have pudding,' Auntie says, her hand shaking slightly as she puts down Stephen's plate.

'Thank you,' he says.

Part of her is broken, Clara thinks, before Auntie leaves the room and they hear the sound of her footsteps fading.

'Why has she got a bruise on her face?' Stephen whispers.

'She must have fallen against something.'

It's not the honest answer Clara should give, but she doesn't want to fill Stephen's head with the possibilities in her own.

'This looks revolting,' she says, turning her face away from the smell. And she's so hungry. She'd still had the pies in greaseproof paper clutched in her hands as they fled up the stairs, but she hadn't wanted to eat them. She'd given them to Stephen, who'd been happy enough to finish every last crumb.

'It's nice,' Stephen tells her, already starting to eat.

Clara picks at her potatoes, chewing them and swallowing without breathing so that none of the taste of the stew gets through. When she's finished those, she knows that she has to start on the meat, so she jabs at the chunks of white with her fork. Suddenly, she realises what it is – unrecognisable now from the feathered animal banging against Auntie's leg as she'd walked away. Clara thinks she'll vomit as she remembers the wide eyes expecting help, that stick-like leg circling in the air.

'I'm going to the toilet,' she says, walking as slowly as she can from the room and then running to the bathroom and locking herself in. She leans her back against the door, but the air in here is still too tight, so she goes over and pushes the window. It opens easily and she leans out, taking big gulps of the dark.

'Dad,' she whispers, willing him to hear her, to come and find them. She hadn't wanted to cry, but now she can't stop. The thought of him, so far away. Clara grips the window ledge and it feels like her whole body is weeping. And when her legs are shaking too much to hold her, she curls into the floor of this strange house.

'Clara?' It's Stephen knocking. She doesn't know how long she's been lying here, but her body hurts as she stands up.

'I'm coming,' she says, turning on the basin's tap and splashing her face. She leaves the water running and holds her hands under it as it gets hotter, counting to ten until her skin looks soaked in red. It calms her enough to open the door and Stephen is standing here, his arms hanging down, the toes of his small feet pressing into his grey socks. 'I'm fine,' she tells him before he can ask, and he follows her back to the bedroom.

Stephen's plate is empty. Clara thinks he's even licked it clean. They sit back down and she pushes her plate of congealed food away.

'Don't you want it?' Stephen asks, surprised. 'It's nicer than the stew we had before.'

'I'm not hungry.'

'We won't get pudding if you don't finish it.'

There are faint footsteps on the stairs.

Clara jumps up, grabs the small bin by the chest of drawers and scrapes in her food. She scoops up the tiny screwed-up bits of paper that Stephen spilt from his truck and piles them on top. She's only just sitting down when the door opens.

Auntie smiles at the empty plates.

'Did you like it?' she asks.

'It was delicious,' Clara says.

'Oh good.' Clara is sure that if Auntie hadn't been holding the pudding bowls, she would have reached over to stroke Clara's hair. 'I've made baked apples with cream.'

Clara hurries to pick up her spoon. The apple is sweetened with syrup, and melts almost as soon as it passes her lips. Auntie stands, watching them from the doorway, one hand barely touching the wood. Clara wants to tell Stephen to stop eating so weirdly –

he's only taking food from the end of the spoon, swallowing in exaggerated gulps.

'You're really here,' Auntie whispers.

'Yes,' Stephen replies.

Unkindness almost spills from Clara. She longs to say how she wishes she wasn't here, in fact more than anything she'd like not to have her fingers on this spoon, her blood ticking in this room. Maybe she doesn't even need to say it to crush Auntie. Maybe her silence, her accusing stare is enough.

'Warren is waiting.' Auntie's voice has been ground down, crumbled to dust, as she turns from them. 'He likes his pudding too.'

The children don't speak to each other as they scoop up the soft fruit swimming in cream. When they've finished, Clara runs her finger around the inside of the bowl, licking off the last trickles of white.

'Do you think there's more?' Stephen asks.

'I doubt it.'

'Shall we take these to the kitchen?' Stephen asks.

'I don't know.' Something has changed. The walls of the house have stepped closer, the rules somehow shifted. The bruise on Auntie's cheek and the thought of going downstairs frightens Clara, so she stacks the china bowls one on top of the other. She notices that the salt on the chest of drawers has been swept away, as they wait.

* * *

Auntie makes Clara swallow her sulphur pill and both children lick sweet malt treacle from the spoon.

'Can we go downstairs and play?' Stephen asks.

'No. Not tonight,' Auntie replies. 'It's time for bed.'

'Already?'

Clara knows that Stephen had been hoping to play with the train track again – it's partly the reason why he ate every bit of food – yet Auntie's resolve is stone, and Clara needs to find a way to chip away at it.

'The dolls on the landing,' she says. 'Which one is mummy's?'

Auntie stares at her and Clara wants to tip her up to make her blink.

'One of them must be,' Clara continues. 'One for mummy, one for you, one for Edwyn.'

All the air leaves the room.

Clara hadn't expected to feel shame, but she does. A gross sense that she's forcing an injured mouse towards the teeth of a waiting cat.

'They're precious,' Auntie finally says. 'They're not yours.'

Clara and Stephen follow her back to their bedroom and Clara doesn't even glance at the dolls. The children change in silence, Auntie waiting in the corner. Clara wants the day to end so that sleep will creep to her quickly, to blot away all that's real.

'Good night,' Auntie says once they're in bed. She stares at Clara as she turns off the light. 'May the bugs not bite.'

Clara looks at the silhouette of Auntie in the doorway. Has

she found out about the beetle hidden under Stephen's bed? Can she somehow sense the hopeless winding of its legs? Clara turns away, pulling the blanket over her shoulder up close to her chin and pretends that the soul catcher hasn't found a way into her thoughts, isn't nestling inwards, sticking to her skin.

* * *

*A*untie sits alone at the empty dining-room table, staring into a garden now painted with deep black. She hums a lullaby to herself, one that only she can hear as she picks at the skin around her thumbnail, nibbling it free with her teeth.

They hadn't known, the children, not to go behind the wall. She needs to remember that. She needs to find and hold some perspective, or she'll lose herself in a maze of hostility. They couldn't have realised – could they? – that as they pulled the material from its burial place, their hands touched the beginnings of her fourth child, wiped away with her blood all those years ago, as her heart splintered again.

She aches with the effort of thinking about what is and what should have been. Aches with the strain of filling up five earthen holes with empty futures and trying to forget. Dreams missed and souls lost, the hope of motherhood disintegrating at the edge of her vision, despair so complete that it skulks in and smothers her.

7

The next afternoon, the children sneak out to the garden again. If Auntie could see through the walls of her kitchen and past the hedge, she'd find the girl standing on the swing, pulling on the ropes to make herself ride higher.

'What is it?' Clara asks her brother, noticing his sudden stillness as he sits cross-legged on the grass. Maybe he's found more of the rose petals that were scattered here before.

'Nothing.' But he's poking around in the spindly roots, dragging a sharpened stick among them.

She watches as he holds his breath, his lips stuck tight together until his chest heaves and he's gasping.

'Why are you doing that?' she asks.

In reply, his eyes follow her as she swings.

'Well, I'm going to climb the mountain,' she says, scrabbling for normality.

'It'll be too big.' Stephen lifts the stick and picks at the dirt on its tip.

'I think it's only a hill. We could just climb a bit of it.'

'If you want.'

'I do want,' she says, sensing that he's with her again. She jumps down, landing without falling. 'Come on, then.' Reaching out for the comfort of Stephen's hand in hers.

'Do we have to go in the forest?' he asks.

'Only for a bit. And it's just a few trees.' But Clara hasn't forgotten the squirrel's brutal death. 'Then we'll be out the other side.'

They step in and Clara tells herself that she's not afraid; she's safe here, with only the towering pine trees rocking high above her head, cracked patches of blue sky beyond. The dry, primeval smell of the land, the brittle step of fallen ferns. She won't touch the solid lines of the trunks, instead weaving a path to keep her skin, her clothes, from them.

'I don't like it in here,' Stephen whispers.

'There's nothing to be scared of. We came in here before. Remember?'

'That was different.'

'Well we can't turn back now.'

And she doesn't want to. She needs to put distance between them and Auntie and the brewing anger of Uncle Warren. Have time away to try to untangle the knot of confusing emotions beginning to fester inside her.

They follow the silence, until the light in the distance grows, Clara pulling her brother through the trees until they're out of the forest. In front of them a hill rises steeply, the grass scattered and unruly. Clara laughs as she lets go of Stephen's hand and starts to run.

'Race you,' she shouts.

The uneven ground wants to twist her ankles as she scrabbles upwards, the light breeze forcing itself stronger as her hands grasp at stalks. She knows that Stephen can't keep up and she knows too that she'll never be able to hide the grubbiness on her clothes from Auntie. The hill makes her calves ache as she climbs, but she needs this – the sharp air in her lungs, to feel completely alive.

'I hate you.' It's Stephen's shout that makes her finally stop. He's there, on hands and knees, crawling up the hill, fury in his knuckles and cheeks.

'I didn't really win,' Clara says as he gets closer.

'It wasn't fair,' he yells. 'You're bigger than me.' Flailing his arms as though he's drowning.

'Stop doing that and don't be a spoilsport. It's just a game.'

'I'm not a spoilsport,' he says, a stone in his fist.

'Put that down.'

It's no bigger than a magpie's egg, but he throws it hard, just missing his sister's eye as she ducks out of the way.

'This isn't even a mountain,' he says, climbing closer.

'It sort of is. And we're nearly at the top.'

'I bet I get there before you.' Stephen rushes past clumsily, not even glancing at her.

'I bet you will,' Clara says.

There's comfort for her in his tantrum, a blanket of familiarity that she wants to keep close as she walks, challenging herself to stand straight without using her hands, the wind gathering to push against her back and arms.

'I'm here!' Stephen shouts and Clara looks up to see him balanced at the top, spinning in his small victory.

'We're free,' Clara whispers, joining him, her arms flung wide, her laughter caught on the clouds.

Below them, the tops of the trees. Beyond the trees, the lawn waits for the children to return, the knotted hedge small enough to balance on Clara's thumb. And then the house, a pocket-toy now, a smudge of grey roof, the windows simply holes with nothing beyond, the furniture and curtains impossible to see.

'We could keep going,' Clara says, the tumbling air taking the edges of her words.

'I want to be home for supper,' Stephen says.

It's not our home, Clara wants to reply, her clothes rattling loose against her skin as she leans into the wind. This is just a house where we're caught, where we don't belong. Our home is a beating heart, far from here.

'My ears hurt,' Stephen says, his hands clamped either side of his head. Clara feels the pain too, a blunt knife turning. She closes her eyes, feels the force of nature on her cheeks, accepts its hands in her hair, giving herself willingly to it. She thinks of her mother in the hospital bed, lets the wind unwrap the bandages, pull them back until her mother's body is free and healed and whole.

'We'll see you soon,' she whispers.

She opens her eyes, needing to hold her brother tight. But he's gone.

'Stephen?' Clara turns a whole circle, yet there's only the grass, the stones, the empty hill. 'Stephen?' She's worried that he won't hear her in this wind and she starts to run, unsure, a useless search behind the bigger tufts of grass, the larger rocks barely big enough to hide behind.

'Stephen?' She yells it, so loud that his name scratches her throat as it leaves her mouth.

The wind battles her and with the discomfort of it in her ears she thinks he must have tried to escape it and has gone back to the stillness of the trees. She runs quickly, all the time looking, expecting to see a flash of his green jacket, the tell-tale sign of his trousers hiding flat among the grass. It's steep, but Clara hurtles down it until she's at the edge of the pines.

Inside them, the wind stops completely, as if it was never here.

'Where are you?' Clara calls, reluctant to venture into the shadows on her own.

She stands still, listening for signs of her brother, but there's only birdsong and the creaking trees. She steps forward, wishing silence on her feet as twigs crisp and sink under her shoes. Dead needles catch in her socks, work their way through.

'You can stop this now,' she shouts. 'It's not funny anymore.' The sound of her voice knocks into her chest.

Anger seeps into Clara's fear. They should be playing together, could even now be on top of the next hill, gathered by that fierce wind. She starts to stomp, hoping Stephen will hear that she no longer cares.

'I'm bored now,' she calls, coming out from the trees by the empty swing. She was sure he would be here, sitting on the hanging plank of wood. Clara looks towards the hedge, at the arch and rose-walk, the slice of the house showing through. Stephen isn't on the lawn; there's no sound of him giggling.

Clara is too scared to go back to Auntie and tell her that she can't find him, realising that it could push the woman over some precarious edge that Clara can't see. She knows she must head into the trees again, into the sharp smell of the pines.

'We won't be able to play here anymore if you don't come out.'

She's searching behind fallen stumps, pushing back clumps of fern. Picking up a stick that's taller than her, she thrashes through leaves never big enough to hide him. And all the time there's a creeping knowledge that he's gone.

'Stephen,' she whispers, peeling back layers of this forest, stepping through and under and over, pushing into its web of secrets until it will give back her brother.

She sees his shoe first, the end of it poking out from behind a tree, the other neatly by its side. And as she gets closer, there are Stephen's knees pulled up to his chest, his little hands clasping his legs. He's smiling up at her.

'You've been here all along,' she says, fury squashing any notion of relief. 'Why did you do it? You knew I was worried.'

Stephen's answer is only a shrug.

'Mummy would thrash you for that,' Clara says.

'Well mummy's not here.' Stephen stands up, so small against the looming pine, brushing his trousers clean. 'I'm going to see the rocks.'

'What rocks?'

'The ones by the hedge.'

He walks away, as if he hasn't just dragged his sister to a new level of fear. And Clara finds herself forgiving him because he's all she has, following him until finally they're out of the trees, past the swing and across the lawn, to where the giant slabs of crooked boulders look anomalous and uninviting. Stephen doesn't run ahead as Clara expects, instead slowing enough for her to be next to him.

'How did they even get here?' he asks.

'They were probably here before the house.' Maybe they even watched the house grow.

The children walk alongside the curve of the rocks, needing to lean in slightly where the apple tree stands too close. Clara lays her palm flat against the hard, grey stone, liking the touch of it, warm in the sun and a darker cold where the skin bends in a crevice.

'Can you feel it?' she asks, more to herself than to Stephen.

'Feel what?'

'The heartbeat in it.'

Tendrils of knotted plants hang down and when Stephen goes to touch the shredded hair, his hand disappears right through. He parts the plant and peers beyond it.

'It's a cave,' he says, looking at his sister in wonder.

'Oh.' Because she knows what comes next.

'We can explore.'

'We don't have to.'

'We do.' And he's stepping his small feet onto the rocks, holding back the fringe of green so he can slip his body through. Clara is alarmed at how quickly it closes behind him and knows that any choice she had is gone.

Inside, it takes moments for her eyes to adjust to the dampened light. She pushes aside the tendrils behind her as far as she can so that she can see the small cave, with its uneven ground.

'This is the best,' Stephen announces. He cups his hands around his mouth. 'Is anybody here?'

'If you're loud, she'll hear us,' Clara tells him, the taste of mildew on her lips.

'She won't.' He runs his fingers along a natural shelf between the boulders. 'This can be our secret place. We can bring things here.'

But it's so cold and Clara thinks she doesn't ever want to come back.

'There are other places to play,' she says. Stephen ignores her, drawn instead to five silent figures standing almost hidden in the darkness.

'What are those?' he whispers.

They're made from lumps of clay. One is no more than a stump of an idea, the vague shape of a child; others have pressed-in eyes, the curve of a nose, the point of fingers.

'Don't touch them,' Clara tells him.

Stephen picks up the one nearest to him, holding it in both his hands before he snaps it in two. It's such a tiny cracking sound.

'We don't want these in here,' he says, throwing down the broken figure and pushing away the rest with his feet.

Clara wants to leave the dank cave, but Stephen's stepping further in behind a man-made wall of rock, where he stops.

'What is it?' Clara asks.

There's just enough light for them to see the neat pile of clothes – trousers on top of a large green coat, a pair of heavy boots. And next to them an old metal spade, its handle resting against the stone.

'Uncle Warren's,' Clara says. She knows she should run, they both should, but her feet are wedded to the ground.

'Why does he have his gardening clothes here?' Stephen whispers.

'Maybe so he can keep away from us,' Clara says.

'It's not our cave, is it?' Stephen reaches for her hand as he looks up at her.

'No. We should go.' She pulls her brother away from the stuck air, with its unfamiliar clothes and unnerving clay figures, back to where the sky is still and clean. Clara wants to stand just for a moment, but more than that she wants to get away.

Auntie is waiting for them on the patio, just standing there, pinching the apron in her hand.

'Where did you go?' she asks, trying for authority.

'Just out,' Clara replies, seeing as the eyes judge the dirt on her clothes.

'I wanted you to stay inside.'

'We didn't like being cooped up.' Clara and Stephen carry on walking down the side of the house, where clammy baking smells creep from the kitchen window.

'I knew you'd gone,' Auntie says, hurrying to catch up with them. 'Yet I let you.'

'Thank you, I suppose,' Clara says, smirking at Stephen.

By the front door, crunched so close to the step that Clara almost doesn't see them, is a broken pair of spectacles. She picks them up, holding them by one of the twisted metal arms, touching the frame where the lens has splintered.

'These are daddy's,' she says simply.

'No,' Auntie says, taking them from Clara. 'They're Warren's. You found them for him.' She laughs briefly. 'How funny that your father should have some just like his.'

'Has daddy been here?' Clara asks, refusing to move forward, wanting to hold the glasses again.

Auntie pats her on her shoulder, dares to brush back a lock of Clara's hair.

'Been here and not seen you?' She laughs again. 'I think you've had too much sun for one day.'

'How can they have the same glasses?' Clara asks, immobile now after Auntie's touch.

'Most men do. Have you not noticed?'

'No,' Clara says, but she's unsure now, losing her grasp on certainty as she looks at the spectacles in her aunt's hand.

'Come on, then,' Auntie says, opening the front door. 'You'll like what I've made for you.'

Her hand on Clara's back is firm enough to move the girl inside.

* * *

Auntie lies awake in her bed. It's the darkest part of the night, the clouds outside are thick and drifting. Dreams don't settle on her, however much she wants them to. Instead, she finds herself stuck in the mysterious mist of motherhood – something she can't make sense of.

She moves her legs to the side of the bed, sits up and pulls down her nightie as close to her ankles as she can. The floor under her feet feels unfamiliar at this time of night and she's unsure of it, but still she walks from the room, finding her way down the corridor in the dark. She touches the wall, knowing when she reaches the door that the children sleep behind. Slowly she turns the handle, before she steps inside.

Here, now, they are simply shapes, little hills rising from each bed. She pauses and listens, their breathing a lullaby. Her nerves begin to ebb away as she matches their breath with her own. She imagines them growing in her stomach, soothing them, giving them life.

She finds her way across the room to where earlier she'd seen

Clara throw her clothes onto the chair. She picks up every piece of them, before she pulls a drawer quietly from its case to find all the old clothes and she gathers them too, leaving only their underwear.

Auntie stands and wants to stay, to meet her children in their dreams, but she knows that she can't. Instead, she tiptoes away. She doesn't close the door completely, pulling it gently as far as she dares before going back to her room.

For now, she must leave their clothes under her bed. She folds each garment neatly, flattening the creases with her hand, not liking the feel of their other life against her skin.

Tomorrow, she will burn them.

8

The morning light sneaking through the window wakes Clara and she stretches under the sleep-heavy sheets. Today will be different. Today will be better. She looks over to where Stephen is sitting cross-legged on the floor, the jar with the beetle on his lap.

'How will it get in?' he asks.

'How will what get in?'

'When the beetle dies, how will the soul collector get in here to take its soul?'

'I doubt it works like that.' Her cheek is soft on the pillow as she blinks away the final fragments of her dreams.

Stephen stands up and goes to the window, opening the curtains before he pulls himself up to stand on the windowsill.

'Careful,' Clara tells him. 'You could fall out.'

He pushes hard against it.

'It still doesn't budge,' he tells her, jumping back down to the floor.

'You could open the door.' She doesn't know why she says it. She shouldn't really encourage these thoughts of his.

'That's a good idea,' he says. 'Will you watch the beetle for me?'

'It's not going to die in the few seconds it takes you to cross the room and back.'

'It could. It only takes that,' he claps his hands once, 'to die.'

He runs backwards to the door and finds it open. He pulls it further, just a bit, before he sits down again, his eyes steady on the shiny insect in the jar.

'Is mummy going to die?' he asks.

'Of course not. She's in a hospital and that's where they make everyone better.'

'Not everyone. James Pilter's daddy went into hospital and died.'

'Well our mother won't,' she says.

'If she does, I'd like to stay here.'

Clara feels her whole being shrink. 'That'll never happen.'

She needs not to think now, so she picks up her book and starts to read, her mind locking onto the pages to try to block out all her piercing doubts.

It isn't long before she hears the scrape of the jar lid being opened.

'Are you letting it go?' she asks.

'No. It's taking too long. I'm going to do it myself.'

'Do what?' She puts down her book.

'I'm going to make it die.'

'You can't.'

'I have to,' Stephen says, as he squeezes his hand into the jar. 'Or the experiment won't work.' His fingers flail around slightly before they pincer the beetle and drag it out. He holds it by its shell, its legs spinning uselessly.

'You mustn't do it,' Clara says.

'It won't hurt, if I'm quick.'

He stands up, clutching the beetle in the noose of his hand, and reaches over to the mantelpiece for the china statue of the boy.

'She'll kill you if you break that,' Clara says.

'I won't break it.'

Stephen lays the beetle on the table, keeping one finger pressed on it so that it can't escape.

'It wants to go back outside,' Clara tells Stephen, needing him to see.

'It's going to a better place,' he says, as he slams the blind china boy hard onto the beetle's back. Stephen peers closely, his gaze steady as he slams it again and again, splintering the insect into shards of dark and light.

Clara feels sick.

She should have stopped him.

There's silence, filled with too much Clara doesn't understand, before Stephen jumps up, wide-eyed.

'I saw it,' he says. 'I saw the soul collector.'

There was nothing there. There was just the crushed and dying beetle.

A headache begins to spin at the corner of Clara's eyes.

'Did you see it?' Stephen holds the figure of the boy in his hand and leans in. 'It was him.' His face looks calm, the answer to the puzzle given. 'You came,' he whispers. 'I knew you would.'

Clara is cold. It feels as if the beetle has risen and scuttled down her throat. Yet Stephen is filled with energy as he studies the cracked remains of the insect's back, the air buzzing around him.

He grins at the china boy. 'He was here all along, in the same room as us. If we die, he'll collect our souls, so we won't get forgotten.'

'We're not going to die, Stephen.'

'Of course we are,' he says.

'You need to clear that up so she doesn't see it.'

Clara thinks she should help him, but she doesn't want to touch the beetle's shattered remnants. She looks away as he scrapes it up and drops it back into the jar. It's only when she hears the twisting of the lid that she gets up.

'I'm getting dressed. We should go out.' But her clothes aren't where she left them. She looks under the bed, although she knows that they can't have tumbled there. In the wardrobe and drawers are just the new suits and dresses.

'Where are our clothes?' she asks Stephen. 'Have you hidden them?'

'No.' He leaves the jar on the windowsill and goes to sit on his bed.

'She's taken them,' Clara says.

'Why would she do that?'

'I'm going to ask her.'

She's cold in her nightdress, scuttling down the stairs. At the bottom, Auntie stands with a heavy tray of food, as though she's been there all night.

'Good morning,' she says. 'I've got your breakfast.'

'I don't want breakfast. I want my clothes.'

'You have clothes.' Auntie keeps her smile. 'You'll get cold, standing here. I've made you breakfast. I can bring you cocoa too, to warm you up.'

'I don't want the clothes you made. I want my proper ones.' Clara stares hard at her.

'Has my sister not taught you any manners?' Auntie's voice is so quiet, that Clara barely hears her, but she recognises the insult directed towards her mother, senses the swell of sibling rivalry that it brings with it.

'It's not good manners to steal someone's clothes,' she seethes, trying to hold strong to her confidence even as she feels it slipping from her.

'She taught you nothing good.'

'I've been taught to speak the truth,' Clara shouts. 'And the truth is I don't like it here and I'm going to speak to daddy and I'll tell him when he comes to see us that I want him to take me home.' She stamps her way towards the small table where the telephone sits and lifts its handle. There's silence at the other end. Clara shakes the phone slightly. Puts it down and lifts it up again, but there's nothing.

'The line came down in a storm,' Auntie says. 'I'm afraid that there's no way you can speak to him.'

Clara won't look at her. Instead, she presses the handle back into its cradle, picks it up again. It's the silence at the end of the line that terrifies her the most.

'You told daddy you'd telephone him. I heard you. You said

that you would.' She's angry at herself now, at her voice cracking to expose her distress. 'How will you speak to him? How can we find out about mummy?'

She sees a glimpse of her mother standing next to her aunt. How different they are. Her mother tall, elegant, hands brushing back loose tendrils of hair. Hair that turns to smoke.

'Clara?' Auntie remains calm in the centre of this unexpected tempest, unaware that the child in front of her feels the heat of flames. 'Clara? It's all right. Warren uses the telephone at his work.'

Auntie's mouth coming into focus. The hallway's smell of polish. The circle rug with its threads of colour.

'It's not all right,' Clara screams, running back up the stairs, pulling at her nightdress so she doesn't trip. She storms across the landing and slams the bedroom door.

Stephen sits staring at her. He hasn't moved from where he was, not even an inch. 'Will she still bring us breakfast?' he asks.

'Of course she will,' Clara snaps. 'She won't exactly want us to starve, will she?' She gets into her bed, trying to hide the fact that she's shaking.

'I don't want you to phone daddy. I like it here,' Stephen says. 'I don't want to leave.'

'I can't at the moment, in any case. But I will. As soon as the telephone is fixed.'

Clara hates the feel of the bed's blanket, but still she holds it close, rubbing the wool repeatedly over her nails. The broiling mess within her doesn't settle as she thinks of her mother and her aunt sitting side-by-side, hands clasped in their laps, jealousy oozing like thick tar between them. The ghost of their brother unable to find his space there. The dreadful, gaping hole he left that perhaps their mother was never able to fill, not even with Stephen.

* * *

It's a long time before there's a soft knock on the door. Clara doesn't want to open it, but Stephen's hunger makes him. Auntie is standing, the same tray in her hand, the same pieces of bread spread thick with butter and raspberry jam.

'What a beautiful day,' she says brightly. She puts down the tray on the table by the window and turns to look at Clara. 'I made the jam myself, from raspberries we grew in the garden. I have some of the preserved fruit in the larder – maybe we could make some together soon?' Clara feels Auntie's shattered expectations scattered by her feet.

'I'd like that,' Stephen says. And it's there – his basic need for a mother.

'Oh good,' Auntie replies.

'You can go now,' Clara tells her.

Auntie looks defeated as she leaves, barely closing the door behind her.

'That was unkind,' Stephen says.

'Put a lid on it,' Clara says, passing him a plate. 'We can eat in bed now and spill crumbs onto the sheets.'

'I don't care,' he says, taking a large bite of bread, not bothering to swallow it before he speaks again. 'The jam looks likes her bruise.'

Clara forces herself to eat. Pretends that it was her mother who spread the butter across the bread. When food catches in her teeth she wriggles it free with her tongue, chanting her mother's name. More than anything, Clara wants to get her sketchbook and get lost in the pencil drawings, but she's scared of what she'll find there. The pages no longer feel such a safe place to be.

When the plates are empty, they drink their glasses of orange juice.

'We'd best put on some clothes, if we want to go out,' Clara says, opening the wardrobe door. She shifts the hangers along the rail, so she can pull out each dress in turn. 'They're all hideous.'

'You'll look nice,' Stephen encourages her.

She yanks down one of the dresses. The material is covered with faint yellow flowers, with lace around the neck.

'It's like a sack. And the sleeves are horrible.' But she puts it on, changing from her nightdress in an instant. 'Do me up,' she tells Stephen, standing with her back to him so that he can pull the zip. He takes the responsibility very seriously, balancing on the bed.

'I think you look a knock-out.'

'You're joking, aren't you?'

'No.'

There's a green ribbon tacked lightly around the waist that Clara knows she's meant to tie at the back. Instead, she knots it into an absurd bow across her belly.

Stephen screws up his nose. 'Not that bit, though.'

'It's the finishing touch.' She laughs.

Auntie enters their room without knocking this time. She looks stunned by Clara's transformation.

'Do you like it?' she whispers. Clara realises the hours it must have taken to sew, with its ribbon and the buttons to the cuffs and she doesn't have the heart to tell the truth.

'I'll have to put a coat over it when Stephen and I explore the hills,' she says, hoping that any concern of the dress being ruined will be enough for Auntie to give back her own.

'The bow is meant to tie at the back,' she says, stepping forward as if to help.

'I like it like this,' Clara says.

'But it's not right.' Clara senses it even stronger than before, an unsteady rhythm to her aunt that's threatening to unravel. Before she can protest, Auntie is tugging the end of the ribbon so that it trickles loose. She ties it behind Clara as it's meant to be, pulling the edges to make it perfect.

'Better?' Clara asks, spinning around.

'Much,' Auntie says, with something resembling happiness soft on her skin.

When Auntie has gone, she looks outside at the garden to where greying clouds push their way over the tops of the hills. Clara wishes she could be roaming there now, with her mother when she was full of sparks rather than thunder. They'd travel all the way home, their heads together, creating a story of the hidden creatures they meet on the way.

Stephen is already in the blue suit when Clara turns to him. He sits cross-legged on the floor, an old tiger puppet dangling from the strings in his hand and as he treads the tiger across his ankles, Clara knows she has more than enough love to make up for what their mother never gave him.

Stephen sees her watching and nearly topples as he stands, the puppet buckling at the knees as he carries him over to his sister.

'What's in the garden today?' the tiger asks her.

She looks through the glass again and this time there's a man there, by the rose-walk.

'Uncle Warren.'

They both stare down at him, at the brown coat heavy on his back, the thick winter boots, the hat pulled low on his head. He's bending down, his spade in the ground.

'Can we go and say hello?' Stephen asks.

'I don't think that'd be a good idea.'

'Because he doesn't want us here?'

Clara picks a chip of white paint from the window frame, dropping it from her nail onto the floor. It sits, a scrap of an eye, watching her.

'I bet he wants you,' she says. 'It's just weird girls he doesn't like.' And she pulls her hair up into absurd bunches, a wild smile on her lips.

'Stop it.' Stephen giggles. 'You look horrible.'

'Come on,' she says, jumping up. 'If Uncle Warren's in the

garden, that means he's definitely not in the house. So we can go and play.' She's trying to pretend that the bruise on Auntie's cheek doesn't linger in her. 'How about the train track?' She knows it's enough for Stephen to leave the tiger puppet slumped on the rug and he puts his small hand in hers.

But outside the bedroom, Clara turns the other way.

'Where are we going?' Stephen whispers.

'I just want to see.' And she's sneaking to the furthest door. She turns the handle, but it doesn't open. 'It's locked. What about that one.' She points to the one back nearer to the bathroom.

'I'm not going to touch it.'

'You're a wet rag,' Clara scolds.

'You said we were going to play with the train,' Stephen reminds her.

Clara nods and even though their Uncle Warren won't be able to hear them, the children are as quiet as they can be as they tiptoe down the stairs, across the patterned rug, to the doorway under the stairs.

'Ready?' she asks and Stephen nods.

Clara turns the handle and darkness greets them. She remembers that the light switch is halfway down and now wishes that she'd never suggested this. She keeps holding Stephen's hand and they go down the steps together as the door swings shut behind them. She keeps her fingers on the cold wall.

'Where is it?' she mumbles.

'It must be there.'

Clara sweeps her arm against the flat surface, ignoring the need to run back up to the daylight.

'I don't like it.' Stephen's voice is made smaller by the dark.

'I've found it,' she says, relief and light flooding around them.

'Can we go now?'

'Not yet. I want to hear the birds singing again.'

'I don't know how to work that bit.'

'We'll find out.'

Clara pulls him with her, every step taking them towards the basement's damp skin. They stop at the bottom, and the rotten smell worms its way into Clara, settling on the roof of her mouth. She tastes it as she speaks.

'How do we start it?'

The train looks lonely. The emptiness around it is filled with secrets and Clara wants the clatter of movement to drown them out.

'Somewhere over there.' Stephen's reluctance has fallen from him and he's eager now to hear the engine, to see it move.

The children both poke their fingers around the station building, pulling back plastic shrubs, moving people.

'It's here!' Stephen shouts, forgetting to be quiet. As soon as he presses the button, the wheels on the train spin into life, speeding down the track. Stephen jumps up and down and runs to follow it.

'Look, Clara. Look at the tunnel.' The train disappears completely, before it appears on the other side.

'How do you think we get the birds to start?' she asks.

'Maybe you have to wait until it happens.'

Clara isn't sure. She's busy separating the trees to find more buttons, pulling them right down to their roots, when her elbow knocks the train as it passes.

'Clara!' Stephen shouts. But he's not close enough to catch the spinning carriage, can only watch as it crashes to the floor, a corner of it cracking off like a chipped tooth.

The children stand and stare at the stationary wheels.

'You've broken it,' Stephen accuses.

'I didn't mean to.' Her temper feels reeled short. Suddenly she's not bothered with hearing the delicate singing. 'It's a stupid train in any case.' And she's gripped by a blistering need to hurl it against the wall.

Stephen looks towards the stairs. 'What if Auntie comes down and sees what you've done?'

'She'll understand it was an accident.'

Stephen bends to pick up the train, passing it gently to his sister. She has to push closed a carriage door that's hanging loose.

'No one will ever know.' Clara puts it back just where they found it, ignoring how it now leans to the side, the small hole where part of the roof should be.

'She'll kill you,' Stephen says, disappearing on his hands and knees under the table.

Clara prods the train, trying to straighten it, but it doesn't work.

'What are you doing?' she asks.

'I'm looking.'

'At what?' But she doesn't want to see what has sent her brother so still.

'At this.'

Clara crouches down. On the floor, directly in the centre, is a small pile of stones, surrounded by thin polished sticks, as delicate as bones.

'It's the game,' Stephen whispers.

'It's not,' she says, determined to convince herself that he's wrong, that these are just things that have been swept here and forgotten.

'Where are the other children?' Stephen asks.

'There aren't any.' But her words instantly fill Clara with dread. She has to leave this basement; they can't stay in here now. 'I'm bored. I'm going outside.' Already she's heading to the stairs.

'But she said we couldn't.'

'Well I say we can. Besides, she'll want us to get some fresh air so we don't get rickets.'

'Rickets?'

'When your body goes funny because you don't go outside enough,' Clara says. 'You don't want that, do you?' She's hurrying away from the game and the children, giving him little option to stay.

'I suppose not.'

'Me neither. Come on.'

In the hallway, Clara can see into the kitchen and Auntie isn't there.

'Will my suit get ruined outside?' Stephen asks, the train already forgotten as he strokes the jacket pocket.

'Why should you even care?' Clara asks. 'You didn't before.'

'I do now,' Stephen says.

'It'll be fine,' Clara tells him.

'I'm going to bring my jar.'

'Why? You've already done the experiment.'

'I might have to kill something else,' he says and he scuttles away from her, up the stairs to their room.

Clara is lost as to what to say. She wants Stephen filled with life, not death. She tries to remember the immovable core of who he is, her little brother who paints pictures on their father's used newspapers back at their real home, who plays hopscotch with his mouth open as he concentrates on not slipping into the cracks. She misses that, the surety of him and she's determined to find it again as he runs back down to her, the jar in his small hand.

She helps him balance as he slips on his shoes, before together they're out of the front door, Stephen waddling awkwardly behind his sister, one hand clamped firmly over his lips to staunch his giggles. Clara stops by the birdhouse. The thread of nutshells has fallen down and is crushed and scattered in sharp-looking lumps among the birdseed.

At the top of the lawn, Clara remembers Uncle Warren. He'd been here when they'd seen him digging in his garden. She signals at Stephen to stop, but he ignores her, oblivious to the terror spreading from his sister's heart to her palms. Their uncle could be anywhere. She thinks of his eyes glaring at her from the frame on the mantelpiece, the tenor of his voice thundering around the house.

He doesn't want us here.

She runs past the flower bed with the fairy lace, holding her breath through the rose-walk, until she's through the arch in the hedge, to where Stephen stands, shiny-faced and red-lipped. There's no one else around.

'We did it,' he says.

Clara brushes the sun from her face, sees now the boulders that hide the entrance to the cave, thinks only of the fear she'd felt when she'd seen the neat pile of Uncle Warren's clothes.

'Let's keep going,' she says, as Stephen skips beside her.

She stops only when they get to a clump of brambles at the forest edge, tangled thick with blackberries.

'Can we have one?' Stephen asks, looking up at Clara.

'Of course we can. They're ours.' She picks a ripe one and it comes away easily in her fingers. The sweet taste sits on her tongue before she swallows it. Stephen copies her, squeezing too hard and spilling tiny beads of the berries onto his skin where he licks them off.

'It's a bit sour.' He wrinkles his nose.

'Get a better one. Here.'

And so they stand and then crouch as they pick, the gentle hum of the outdoors around them. Twice, thorns scratch the back of Clara's hand, but only enough to draw the faintest line of red. She barely feels it, her mind filled entirely with the deadened motion of picking and eating and not thinking.

She realises after a while that Stephen has stopped. He's sitting cross-legged on the ground, a small hole dug in the earth in front of him. He's tugging at a worm, pulling it until it pops free and dangles from his fingertips.

'I'm going to see if it's true,' he says, berry juice still bruising his lips.

'If what's true?'

'What Sam said.' Thoughts of the boy from his school swirl up, but Stephen forges on through the memories of pinched arms and legs. 'That if you cut a worm in half it doesn't die, but makes two worms.'

'There's nothing here to cut it with.'

'I'll keep it, then.' He picks up his open jar and tips it upside down, the broken beetle scattering to the ground. Stephen forces the worm in, having to push its reluctant body deep enough so he can close the lid. 'I'll get a knife from the kitchen.'

Clara stares at the twisting line of faint pink and wishes he'd just let it go.

'Let's explore before she finds us,' she says.

'But what about Uncle Warren?'

Uncle Warren. His name shifts the ground under Clara's feet.

'We live here now. We should be allowed where we want.'

Stephen scrambles up and they follow the path until the blackberry bushes dwindle to nothing. Someone has been here recently, the grass short enough to catch only ankles, the way clear.

'Do you think then there'll be two souls?' Stephen asks. 'When the worm is cut in half?'

'I don't know,' Clara says. 'Let's go down here.' And she grabs his arm, darting away among spindly, squat trees where there's enough daylight still poking in. Clara touches the moss on their bark as they pass, the ground becoming softer, slowing them down.

'Remember how the soul collector forgot to take Edwyn?' Stephen asks, fragmented sun bright on his cheek.

'What do you mean?'

'You know,' Stephen continues. 'That Edwyn's soul is still here.' He picks up a withered stick and knocks it against the jar, but it snaps in two. With the stub of it in his hand he hits each tree they pass, the dead sound of it hanging where he touches. Clara watches him, tries to reconcile this boy with the brother she thought she knew. She needs to erase his words before they imprint on her mind.

'Let's not stop until we find another house,' she says. 'We could find some friends.'

'Maybe.' Inside Stephen's jar, the worm slowly uncoils, pressing its ringed body against the glass.

Clara wants to keep trekking until they get lost in the nooks and crannies of the hills where she's sure they'd survive. She picks a long stalk, yanking it from its roots. The end is strong enough to press into her arm without breaking as she spells her name in looped handwriting, the letters appearing slowly, rising in faint welts on her skin. She sucks the end of the inkless piece of grass, imagining she can taste honey in its bones. Thinks now of their mother's arms like white sticks in the hospital bed. Sees her finally waking to find herself trapped in a jar, with Clara on the outside looking in.

'Look!' Stephen shouts, running towards a strip of water glancing at them through the leaves.

'I'll come back for you,' Clara whispers to her mother, as the loch gets closer.

The water in front of them now, a brilliant rippling slab of black stretching to a distant shore. It greets them by sliding over mud and fine stones, crumbling apologetically at their feet.

'She didn't say there was a lake,' Stephen says.

'It's not a lake, it's a loch,' Clara corrects him. Daddy had told them, on their way up. It was one of the few things he'd said on the long drive, when they'd passed a vast stretch of water like this.

Stephen runs forward and kneels at the damp edge. He stirs his stick through it, laughing as he loops splashes into the air.

'Be careful,' Clara calls out, yet there's a part of her that wants to wade into the thick of the water.

'I love living here,' Stephen shouts.

Clara stands and watches the trees' reflections, sturdy in the liquid. She wonders what it would feel like to reach over and touch them, jump into branches that don't exist, into leaves that would give way under her and ripple and crack. Maybe she could find a way to swim home.

'It's freezing!' Stephen shouts, putting his hand palm down, as clouds strike at the sun. 'It makes my fingers look funny.' Behind him, his jar lies tipped over in the wet ground. 'Can we swim?' He looks up at Clara.

'No. It's far too cold.'

Across from them, too far to reach, the mountains rise sharply from the loch, their curved tops tilting against the mottled sky. The sun appears again, and Clara holds her face towards it. *Maybe we could build a camp and live out here instead*, she thinks.

She trails after Stephen as he ventures along a part of the shoreline where the water doesn't quite touch, leaving just an expanse that looks like clammy sand. Her shoes are getting damp, but she doesn't care. She likes the thought of stomping them into the house, leaving them scattered and muddy on the floor.

'What's that?' Stephen asks, pointing to a shape sticking from the ground further out.

'An old branch or something,' Clara says. But Stephen is running, drawn by the wooden ribs with planks holding it together, the remains of red paint clinging to its side.

'It's my boat,' he shouts over his shoulder. He's moving in a peculiar way now, with a gait that Clara doesn't recognise. 'Auntie painted it for me, next to my name in the dining room. Remember?'

As he nears it, the beach of treacly mud begins to collapse under his feet.

'Come back,' Clara calls, but he ignores her, pulled forward by some need to see.

Stephen suddenly sinks up to his knees.

'Don't go any further,' she shouts to him, seeing as he tries to turn towards her.

'My legs are stuck,' he calls, already with fear in his voice. Clara watches it all as if through a shroud of smoke, how his hands press down to pull himself out, but he only sinks lower.

'Clara!' He's scrabbling with his hands, but the mud wants to keep him.

'I'll come and get you,' she shouts, running to him. But she's heavier than her brother and too quickly her feet are sucked down. Her ankles are clamped and as she tries to get free the freezing mud fixes its weight over her shoes.

Stephen is crying. He should stay still, but panic is shaking him as he tries to heave his body out. Clara is so close, but she can't reach him. The mud wants to swallow her too. She spreads her fingers wide into it, desperate to find something, anything solid to push against, but each movement makes the loch's sweat creep up her body. She feels the grip of it now covering her knees. It holds the hem of her dress in its fist and slowly, languidly, pulls her down.

'Stephen,' she says.

There's a strange stillness. The water, the trees, even the clouds stop moving. And a silence too. She can see Stephen struggling, his mouth open, but she can no longer hear him. There's just the underlying thud of blood near her ears, beating into her skin.

A roar cracks through it all. A man is suddenly here behind them, dragging branches, making paths across the mud.

'Stay still,' he shouts, his voice bellowing to the dome of the sky. He moves steadily, fury shining from his skin as he lays down thick branches to balance on, until he's almost at Stephen. The loch reaches his shoes as he slides his belt from the loops in his trousers and throws the buckle-end at him. 'Take hold of it,' he says.

Stephen pushes up his elbow, freeing a hand enough for him to grab tight to the metal-clad leather. There is a battle for him now, between the man and the loch, each holding tight to the little boy. Stephen's body is seized by the mud's thick ink, but still he's dragged forward by the heaving effort of the man. The stench of stagnant water as it smears its claim on his cheeks, his eyelids. Until suddenly he's free.

'Step along there,' the man tells him.

Stephen is too shocked to speak. He stumbles, crawls, along the sinking branches.

Clara feels the man's eyes on her. She focuses on lifting her arm through the tar-like substance, waging a conflict she refuses to lose. Her hand reaches a branch and she heaves herself up, kicking at the mud to make it let go. Now she's able to struggle along the make-shift floor, her chest tight as she reaches her brother.

'It's all right,' she says, as he sinks his head into her and starts to cry.

'It's not.' The man stands next to them, his voice flecked dark. 'Have you any idea how dangerous this place is?'

Clara looks up at the man. 'Uncle Warren?'

'I'm no one's uncle,' he says, contempt twitching his jaw. 'Now you get away from here.'

The children scramble to their feet and try to hurry away, slime cold on them, smeared across their clothes and touching their skin. Stephen is still shaking, the mud sticking to his fingers, his neck, tight in his hair.

The trees seem different, moss sunk deep into them, as the children flee through them and break free from the forest, retracing the way, following the path alongside the blackberry bushes, until they're rushing across the lawn. Auntie comes to them before they even reach the house, her arms outstretched.

* * *

'It's too hot,' Stephen says.

'We have to get you clean,' Auntie tells him, pushing on his shoulder so he'll sit still in the steaming bath. Clara knows that the sinking mud has wriggled a path deep into him. He's altered now. She sees it in his eyes, in the way he moves.

'I can wash him,' Clara says, standing just back from Auntie.

'No,' she replies. And Clara feels something shift in the air. 'Lie back,' Auntie orders Stephen. She holds the tilt of his head, his hair splaying out in the water as she rubs away any specks of the loch that might be stuck there. She helps him to sit up, water circling his stomach and running in dripping lines from his neck.

He looks like a fish, Clara thinks, and she wonders if somehow he might swim away.

Auntie is brisk with the soap, wiping the foamy lather over his skin. It feels like a violation to Clara, but Stephen closes his eyes and lets her sweep the flannel over his face, nuzzling it into his ears.

'That's better,' Auntie says and Clara sees the smile. 'Isn't it?' she asks and Stephen nods.

'You're nicer than mummy,' Stephen says. 'She's rough when she washes me.'

The shock of his disloyalty scalds Clara's tongue, stopping her speaking. She glares at him, biting hard into her bottom lip until she tastes blood.

It's when Stephen steps out of the bathtub and Auntie wraps him in a towel that he starts to whimper.

'You're safe now,' she says, rocking him tight.

'I didn't want to go there,' he says.

'I know,' she tells him. 'It wasn't your fault.'

Auntie looks at Clara blankly, as if she can't really see her. Or doesn't want to.

'We were just going for a walk,' Clara says.

Stephen clings to Auntie. 'I want to stay with you,' he says.

'You will.'

Auntie rubs the towel through his hair and Clara watches as she helps him into his pyjamas, first one foot and then the other.

She's furious as she follows them from the bathroom, her pull of responsibility for Stephen still stronger than her desire to run.

She'd promised their mother, whispering to her in that hospital that she'd look after him, and although this promise now seems blurred she's determined to keep it.

Sitting in her bed, Clara can feel the vague shape of the little boy doll pressing his bones through the pillow towards her. She doesn't know whether it comforts or frightens her, as Auntie stands watching them, playing with a key in her hand.

'This will be for your own good,' she says. 'Your own safety.'

'What will?' Clara asks. Although already, she knows.

'I can't risk losing you,' Auntie says.

'Well you certainly can't lock us in.'

'It's the only way.'

'But there'll be no air. We can't even open the window.'

'I don't want you falling out,' Auntie says.

Clara stares at her, hoping the look will penetrate enough for Auntie to feel it in the centre of her bones.

'You can't do this to us.' Her voice rising for them all to notice. 'We're your family.' She uses the word to shock Auntie, to shine some sort of light of reason.

'We can't trust you, Clara. We can't trust you to keep your brother safe.' Auntie strokes her hand over Stephen's hair. 'We don't want her taking you anywhere again.'

Clara closes her eyes when Auntie leans in to kiss him and only opens them again when she hears her footsteps going towards the door.

'What if we need the toilet?'

'I can take you.'

'But what if you're not here? We can't use the bin.'

'I'll bring up a chamber pot.'

'A potty?' Clara asks. She turns to Stephen again, expecting to see him giggling at the absurdity of it. 'She wants us to use a pot as a toilet.' But danger still drifts too close to her brother.

'I understand,' he says and Auntie smiles at him.

'I'll see you soon.' There's the rustle of her clothes as she brushes against the door, before she closes it and locks them in.

It's the sound of the key that whistles panic into Clara.

'What if there's a fire?'

Stephen looks at her. 'There won't be.'

She smells her mother's hair melting, the heat burning away the present. Ballechin, with its savage loch of awful water, the tiny graves, all twist away from her until she's in her own garden back home.

'Why did she ever go in that shed, Stevie?'

Whispers start around Clara's ankles, find their way up through her skin. They want her to see her mother's fire-red fingers on the handle, the flames swallowing her dress as she pulls at the door.

The slap to her cheek is furious. Stephen stands in front of her, his arm hung in the air.

'Stop it,' he says. 'You're scaring me.'

The shock of it wrenches her back to the bedroom. Her brother's hand, the vicious sting of it on her skin. She wipes away tears as she blinks at him, confused by the violence. She's failed him, of that she's sure. She's protected neither his heart nor his soul and now they're here, trapped inside.

* * *

The hours whittle away. Clara has tried to draw, but nothing takes shape in the way she wants it to. Instead, she pulls all of the dresses from the wardrobe, turns them inside out, rearranges them. She rolls and unrolls the sleeves, examines the fine stitching on the hems, busying her hands to stop herself listening for Uncle Warren, to block out the punishment he'll want to mete out to her.

Stephen doesn't seem to notice the ticking of the day. He pulls the beds slightly away from the wall and lets his mind be taken by the truck that he pushes in circles under chairs, over the table and up the window. Clara, watching him, is struck by a memory of being in the kitchen with their mother, Stephen spinning the truck around their feet, the spilt flour, the sudden slap to the back of his legs.

Sometimes he whispers to himself as he plays now, words that Clara struggles to understand.

* * *

The clouds are coming closer, as she thought they would. She holds up her thumb to the glass, closes one eye and smudges them over the hills. They hang there where she leaves them, just waiting, as boredom grinds its teeth into her, clamping its jaw and shaking her senseless.

'I'm sick of this room,' she says, banging her head gently on the sill.

'It's your fault we're in here.'

Clara looks over to Stephen and sees the faint beginnings of accusations on his face, before he turns away from her, his shoulders hunched over the little wooden soldier he holds on his lap, twisting its arm back to see how far it'll go before it snaps.

When Auntie eventually comes back to them she seems surprised to see Clara in another of the dresses, hesitating before she scuttles across the room and puts a chamber pot next to the bin.

'I'm not going to wee in that,' Clara tells her.

'Well, it's here if you need it.' Clara is sure that Auntie's smile is one of satisfaction, that she's pleased with this solution, that all problems are being covered.

'I'm sorry that we went to the lake,' Stephen says.

'I am too,' Auntie replies, as she goes to undo the curtain ties so that the white material falls, pulling them tight to meet in the middle.

'We've been very bored,' Clara says, determined not to let her fear in. She doesn't move from her position on the bed.

'I'll bring some more toys.' Auntie's hands reach for the comforting twist of her apron.

'We'd prefer to come downstairs,' Clara tells her. 'Stephen would like to play with the train track again.' Stephen doesn't exhale as he waits for an answer, but defiance settles in Auntie's eyes.

'We don't think that would be right. Not yet,' she says, without looking at them. 'I rushed you. I'm sorry.'

'What do you mean, rushed us?' Clara asks.

'It was a big adjustment for you coming here. For us all. It would have been better to start you in this room, while you got used to everything.'

'You didn't do anything wrong,' Clara says calmly, aware of Auntie's increasing unpredictability, trying a different way. 'It must be difficult for you too, us being here, as you've never had children around.'

Clara sees Auntie pause and look at her.

'I'll go and get your supper now.' Auntie's shoulders slope as she nears the door.

'Thank you,' Stephen says, but she doesn't see how he beams just for her.

'Well that went well,' Clara whispers. She's hoping Stephen will laugh, but he doesn't.

When Auntie comes back, she puts the plates of food on the table.

'I hope it's tasty,' she says. 'I spent a long time cooking it. Garlic is always tricky to cut as it's so small.' Clara looks down at the chicken leg on her plate. The skin has been dislodged by the garlic slipped inside. It's a sweetened, fatty smell that lingers in the bedroom now, tempting her to be sick.

Auntie winces as Stephen picks up a pea and squeezes it between his fingers before he pops it into his mouth. 'Are you still very angry?'

'A little bit,' Auntie says, as she takes one of the napkins, snaps it into the air and lays it across Stephen's knees. 'You need this.'

'It feels like being in a restaurant,' he says.

'I'll fetch the plates when you've finished,' Auntie says, her hand gentle on his shoulder.

'We can bring them down,' Clara says.

'No. It's best that I get them.' Auntie edges back across the room.

'Best for you, or best for us?' Clara challenges. Auntie answers by closing the door behind her.

Stephen looks down at his food.

'Will you cut it for me?' he asks.

'You can eat it in your fingers.' Clara doesn't want to touch it, even with the ends of a knife and fork.

'It's like me when I'm cold,' he says, poking the white skin flecked with goosebumps. His sister waits for him to notice the shape of the leg, remember it clutched in Auntie's hand. 'I don't want it,' he says, dropping it back onto his plate.

'You have to eat it,' she tells him.

'You do it, then.'

'I'm eating my potatoes first,' she says, piercing one with a fork. 'See. They're delicious.'

Stephen copies her, putting one into his mouth and then another. Clara picks out the chunks of carrot, swallowing them before she pokes at translucent squares that she hopes are onion and not skin. They scoop up their peas, until there's nothing left on their plates apart from the chicken legs. Clara touches hers with the fork. Her stomach slips and rolls at the thought of it, but she has to do this to make her brother eat. She knows this. She retches as the chicken touches her lips. It makes Stephen giggle nervously. This time, she opens her mouth and sinks her teeth into the bruise-tasting flesh.

'I can't do it,' she says, dropping it onto her plate. 'I'm sorry.' She drinks from her glass, swilling the water into every crevice of her mouth. She doesn't want to swallow, but there's nowhere to spit it out, so she has to. 'You must eat yours, though. I just don't feel like mine today.'

'I won't,' he says, pushing himself further back from the table.

'There won't be pudding,' she says.

Stephen gets up with his plate in his hand and goes to the bin. Carefully he picks out the top layer of scrunched-up paper and slides the chicken leg inside. He leaves the paper on the floor, knowing that she'll follow him. Clara goes and throws her food in too, scattering the paper back on top. But it quickly gathers up the wetness and she watches the juice spread through the knotted pieces of dry white. They change colour and flatten and she knows they'll give the deception away. Stephen instantly understands. He takes two pieces of paper from the side and rips them into pieces.

'There,' he says, dropping them into the bin. 'She'll never know.' He sits back neatly in his chair, his suit buttons done up, his collar straight. 'She'll let us out to play now.'

It feels like a long time before Auntie comes back, bearing apple and elderberry pie with vanilla cream.

'We finished your food. It was delicious,' Clara says. 'We're much better now. We could come downstairs with you and sit and read books together.'

She feels Auntie listening, can almost touch the woman's emotions as they start to creak and turn, lips forming around words that don't appear, her eyes darting like a cornered bird.

She stops still when she sees a seeping stain on the floor by the bin. Looks at the children's empty plates, before staring hard at Clara.

'Where are the bones?' she asks. 'Or did you eat those as well?'

The children watch as their aunt goes to the bin, kneels and tips it slightly. Broth drips from it. Auntie touches the juice with the tip of her finger and smells it. She puts the bin flat again and picks up the top pieces of paper. Underneath, soggy bits stick to two wet chicken legs.

'Why?' Auntie asks. It sounds pitiful, pulled from her mouth.

Clara struggles to reply, looking down at her crouching there. 'I didn't like it,' she answers. 'I'm sorry.'

She watches in horror as Auntie starts to cry, wretched sounds crushing her forehead to her knees, her head forced down with the weight of something Clara can't see. Stephen looks to his sister, unsure and scared. The giggles that come from him aren't mean – they've got their roots in uncertainty and Clara knows he's mortified as they tumble from him.

'Stop it, Stephen,' Clara says sharply. But she feels her own laughter bubbling mercilessly too. She looks out of the window, chews her lips, digs her nails into palms, but none of it's enough. She can barely stand, so sudden and hideous is the noise that comes from her.

Auntie crawls through the sound of them, each shard of laughter killing another part of her. She pulls herself up to the table and gets hit again as she piles the bowls and pudding plates onto the tray. She staggers from the room, the final pellets peppering her back, before she locks the children in.

She won't hear, as she hurries down the stairs, how Stephen's laughter turns so quickly to tears. She doesn't see Clara go to him and rock him as shame sweeps around them. Auntie will never know that they weren't laughing at her, not really – that it came from nowhere, meant nothing, yet scars them all in different ways.

* * *

Auntie drops the tray into the kitchen sink. One of the bowls shatters against the ceramic side, breaks into a kaleidoscope pattern that she can't fix. She crumples to the floor with her back against the cupboard, as though her own soul has gone, leaving only a carcass that in time will rot.

How can her children not need her, when she needs them like air?

This loss erodes her bones, takes her essence and scatters it into the oncoming storm. She drifts, listless.

Touching the back of her fingers to her cheek, Auntie finds tears, and as she licks the salt she feels the weight of five small hands resting on her shoulders.

It is all the evidence she needs, to show her that somehow she's survived.

9

When Clara wakes in the morning, the bin has been emptied and cleaned. The floor underneath it has been scrubbed and dried, so that none of the food remains. They both notice it, but they don't say anything. Stephen won't want to remember yesterday; Clara doesn't want to think that Auntie crept in when they were sleeping again.

It's porridge that Auntie brings up, two steaming bowls of it laced with wild honey.

'You need to sit at the table,' she says and they both obey. 'Stephen, this chair is for you.' She points to the place where he's sat before and he goes to it. She pushes in the chair behind him. Clara has already got out of bed and is in her place by the time Auntie turns to her with the onset of a smile. She tucks a napkin into the front of Stephen's pyjama top and Clara grabs the other napkin, tucking it into her nightdress, straightening it across her front.

'Good,' Auntie says, before she picks up a spoon and digs it through the hardening top of the porridge, to the gluey texture below. She blows on it, the steam spreading away from her lips. 'Careful, it's still a bit hot.' She holds it up to Clara's mouth.

'I can feed myself, thank you.' Clara reaches out for the spoon, but Auntie holds it tight.

'I'll have to feed you until I can trust you to eat properly,' she tells her, but Clara turns her face away. 'You have to eat, or you won't survive.' Between them, the porridge sits cooling on the spoon. 'I won't feed Stephen until I've fed you. He'll be very hungry and his food will go cold.'

'Clara,' Stephen says. And it's enough. She turns to look at her brother, his body too small in that chair, the napkin tucked in and waiting. However much she resents it, even resents him in these brief-long seconds, she opens her mouth and lets Auntie feed her. The gloopy whiteness makes her gag as she holds the porridge on her tongue. If she swallows it, she's sure she'll vomit, but she has to force it down, closing her eyes and squeezing her teeth together.

'Good girl,' Auntie says, spooning in another mouthful.

Clara opens her eyes, but not once does she look at Auntie, not even at the hand on the spoon, staring instead at the tops of the trees huddled in front of the mountains, wondering what it'd be like to jump on the top of them, from one spike to the next. She takes her body, her mind there until she can no longer taste the curled worm of porridge in her throat.

She can tell by the sound of the spoon in the bowl that she's finished.

'Your turn,' she hears Auntie tell Stephen. He eats more noisily and Clara wants to tell him to close his mouth when he chews, as their mother would have done.

'It's delicious,' he says, and Auntie slides the spoon into his mouth again. And again, until Clara hears the sound of the bowls being piled up.

'You need a drink,' Auntie says, holding a glass of water clumsily to Clara's lips before she has a chance to complain. The liquid rushes in too fast and after three rough gulps she pushes away Auntie's hand. Water falls onto the napkin and Auntie is quick to pull it from Clara's nightdress and dab it at her face, all the while Clara sitting motionless.

When Auntie has tipped drink into Stephen, she picks up the tray.

'You should get dressed now,' she says, before once again she goes out of the room and leaves them with difficult silence.

'That was weird,' Stephen finally says. 'I'm not a baby.' He slumps back, disgruntled, folding his arms across his chest.

'She shouldn't have done that,' Clara encourages him, licking away the grainy taste in her teeth.

'I don't like her anymore.'

Clara feels his burgeoning blaze of discontent just within her reach. 'I'd never treat you like that.'

Stephen only raises his eyes to look up at her. 'Do you promise?'

'Of course. You can trust me. And we won't let her do that again.'

'But what if she doesn't give us pudding?'

'Then we won't have pudding.' Clara doesn't mind the simplicity of it, but she knows that for Stephen the thought of no cake will pockmark the day ahead with coal-like holes.

'She said we should get dressed,' he says.

'You can.' Clara purposefully gets back into bed and pulls the blanket to her chin. 'If you really want to.' She reaches for her book and opens it, tries to concentrate on reading, but the memory of that spoon in her mouth puts a finger of distraction between her and the page.

She finds herself half-watching Stephen as he diligently undoes the buttons of his pyjamas, how he tries to fold them neatly and put them in a pile at the bottom of his bed. She suspects that his small smouldering of rebellion has already been snuffed out and the smoke of disappointment sticks in her throat. He struggles to get the suit from the hanger, but he manages and concentrates as he puts it on. When he does the buttons wrong, leaving the front of the jacket at an awkward tilt, Clara puts down her book, gets out of the bed and goes to him. It's easy to put right.

'There,' she says. 'You look lovely.'

'Do I?' He wants so much for her to be telling the truth, as if looking nice will give him the ticket to leave the room and go to play downstairs.

'Of course you do.' She forces a smile.

It's the vulnerability of sitting too close to Stephen that makes Clara change from her nightdress. The responsibility she feels makes her open the wardrobe door and reach into the dresses, grabbing the first one she touches, yanking it from its hanger. It's different to the one she wore yesterday, a faint orange, gathered in at the waist. Auntie has embroidered flowers in lines down the skirt and she must have worked hard to get the sleeves to puff like bubbles over the shoulders.

Clara thinks it's hideous, yet she takes off her nightclothes and steps into the dress.

'You'll have to do the zip for me again,' she says, and Stephen does, pulling it right to the top just as Auntie appears. She's holding a large, flat wooden toy. It looks like a maze with tiny walls zigzagging all over it. There are holes too, dotted around.

'Warren made it a few years ago,' she says, her voice childlike as she sits on the bed, the toy on her lap.

'Where is he?' Stephen asks. 'Does he still not want to see us?'

Auntie bends her head to the side, just slightly.

'He's gone,' she says.

Clara experiences a sudden jolt of relief, the lifting of a darkness she hadn't even been able to vocalise.

'Gone where?' Stephen asks.

'He's gone for work. He'll be back soon.' Auntie is blind to a bleakness seeping into Clara once again. 'See,' she carries on, 'you get the ball from this tiny bucket here and then you have to tip it so that the ball rolls but doesn't fall down the holes.' Stephen kneels on the bed next to her. He watches as Auntie moves the board and the ball hurries along the side of a wall. She doesn't lift it up in time and the ball falls through one of the hollow circles, landing in the folds of her skirt. She laughs, before picking it up and putting it back to the start.

'I'll go slower this time.' She glances up at Stephen and moves the board, rolling the ball around the corner so that it avoids the hole it fell in before.

'Yes!' Stephen shouts, leaning closer, putting his hand on Auntie's shoulder. She stops. Clara senses a significance in the small gesture, as a bewildering bliss now layers over Auntie's features.

'Is the ball stuck?' Stephen asks.

'No.' Auntie holds the game tight. She tips it and the ball rolls again. Once more, it hugs close to a wall and once more it falls through a hole, this time dropping all the way to the floor and rolling away.

'I'll get it,' Stephen says, jumping away from her, already on his hands and knees, squirming his way to fit flat under the bed. Clara feels Auntie look towards her, but she stays where she's sitting in the chair, her eyes on her book, trying to keep deep in another world.

'Can I have a go?' Stephen's voice has a bizarre tilt in it.

'Of course,' Auntie says, and as he sits back on the bed she passes him the toy, balancing it carefully on his lap. 'Have you got it?'

'Mm,' Stephen says, already lost to the maze in his hands.

Clara glances up enough to see Auntie watch in fascination as he concentrates, his eyes staying almost still, his tongue poking, just a bit, from his lips. When the ball drops into the first hole, she sees the strike of surprise flash quickly across his face.

'I'll get it,' Auntie says, mirroring his words. The small ball rests against the chest of drawers and it's easy for her to pick up and place back in his palm.

Together they play the game. The ball knocks and glides against the wood, falls and is gathered. They're with each other and Clara is on the outside. Stephen is laughing and it's not with his sister.

'Do you want to do something else, Stevie?' she asks. She feels him being pulled away from her and has a sudden desperation to claim him back.

'No,' he says. 'I'm enjoying playing this.'

Auntie pauses. Clara can almost see how she gathers his voice to her.

'Yes, we're playing together,' Auntie says, and Clara nearly snatches the game from them and stamps on it.

It's a long time before Auntie pushes on her knees to stand.

'The chores won't do themselves.' She stops and looks at Stephen. 'I do miss you when I'm downstairs. Both of you.' She smiles at Clara too, knowing that she's listening.

'Then can we come with you?' Stephen asks.

Auntie pauses, matches her breath with his.

'Not this time,' she says. 'Soon, though.'

She stares with such love at him that Clara wonders if she even notices the beginning of a scowl drawn across his forehead.

* * *

Later, when boredom is burrowing into Clara, she goes to the wardrobe, takes out one of the dresses and starts to dance with it.

'I'm Lillian,' the dress says, and she turns it so that it bows in front of Stephen. 'What's your name?' the dress asks, thumping him on the shoulder.

'Stephen,' he says.

'Well that's not very imaginative, is it?' The dress sways towards him again, slapping a sleeve at his face. 'I said, what's your name?'

'I told you.'

'You have to think of another one.' Clara is unmoving now, the dress hanging from her fist like a gutted fish. 'We can pretend that we're different people. That we're not here.'

'But I want to be here.'

It's unfathomable to Clara. But somehow Auntie has hold of Stephen and is dragging him away. She makes the dress grab at his ankle and Stephen laughs as he knocks over a chair in his attempt to escape.

'You're mine.' The shape of Lillian has him and starts to tickle him. 'All mine.'

They're hysterical together now. It's a sound that the house has been waiting for, aching for, and it wants to keep the feeling trapped within its walls. It's only the door unlocking that instantly silences the children, their laughter torn from them as Auntie comes in.

'You don't have to stop playing,' she says, although Clara knows she's stung by the sight of them standing on the beds and has clearly noticed the fallen chair.

Stephen suddenly runs to hug Auntie, his arms clumsy as he tries not to knock the tray of food.

'How are you?' she asks.

'Hungry,' Clara replies. 'And bored.' She takes Stephen's toy truck from the table and puts it on the floor. 'You can leave the food here.' She's relieved when Auntie does as she's asked and puts down the tray, taking the two plates from it to leave in their places before she turns back to her. 'Stephen needs more paper,' Clara says. 'He's almost run out.' She can sense a soft point in Auntie, one she just needs to find and press her thumb inside.

'Paper?'

'Yes. To draw on.' Clara speaks slowly, as though to a child. 'And some colouring pencils would be good.'

'Of course. I'll bring some up. Would you like that, Stephen?' He nods so enthusiastically that a little piece of Clara's heart splinters.

'We made some slides,' he says, pointing to the drawers that they've taken out and slanted against his bed.

'I can see,' Auntie says, but there's not the shiver of annoyance Clara thought would come.

'They're for my trucks.' His voice is sing-song as he picks up one and holds it out towards her. 'That's the best one because its wheels go quickly.'

Auntie doesn't take it from him. 'You'll have to play later. It's time to eat now.'

If Stephen is disappointed, Clara can't see it. He simply puts the truck on the floor before they sit at the table.

'Do you have a brush?' Auntie asks.

'A brush?'

'A hairbrush,' Auntie says. 'I could brush your hair while you eat.'

'Brush my hair?' Clara can't help but look disgusted.

'Yes.'

'No thanks,' she says, twisting her hair over her shoulder to move it away.

'You can brush mine.' Stephen sees only the two puddings on the edge of the tray. Clara can smell the sweetness of cooked blackberries.

'You don't have to, Stephen,' she says.

'I don't mind,' he says. 'That's Clara's comb.' He points to the small table between the two beds. It's there, lying flat next to the toadstool lamp. Auntie picks it up and starts to pull at a piece of Clara's hair caught in the neat rows, but hesitates and leaves it coiled there in the dark teeth.

The children sit and watch her. Clara feels awkward, being let into a part of Auntie's mind that she doesn't want to see, so she picks up a knife and fork to break the spell.

'Do you want me to cut your food, Stephen?' she asks, already slicing the end from her baked potato. The steam escapes, freed from the skin.

'I can do it,' Stephen says.

'You'll have to hold your fork like you normally do, then,' Clara tells him.

'I am,' he replies. But he's not. He's got the handle in his fist, as though he's only just learning as he slices his ham. He's busy pushing the tiny balls of peppercorn out of the way when Auntie brings the comb through his hair. He ducks away from her in shock.

'Did it hurt?' she says, mortified.

'No. It's fine,' he says, sitting slowly straight again.

She perches close to him on the edge of the bed and gently puts the comb through his hair again. When there's a knot, she teases it out, checking his face constantly. If he winces she stops, before dabbing at the knot with the tip of the comb's tooth, until it works loose. Clara concentrates on forcing herself to eat, the blistering food stinging through her alarm. Auntie keeps brushing even when Stephen's hair is smooth, waiting until the children have finished every last scrap of their food, before she pulls Stephen's strands caught in the comb and puts them in the pocket of her apron.

'I can feed you your pudding,' she tells him. He hesitates and Clara knows he's worried that he won't be allowed any if he refuses.

'He can feed himself,' she says for him.

'No. I'll do it,' Auntie says.

The custard, even under its skin, is already going cold as Stephen sucks it obediently from the spoon. Clara knows she has to eat, working her tongue around the jellied lumps to try to swallow. It's easier to concentrate on the blackberry crumble, the fruit melting into its juices, the topping still dry and sugary and soft in her mouth.

'Good boy,' Auntie says, as she pulls the final empty spoon from Stephen. He doesn't say anything. 'I'll take these downstairs. And when Warren and I have eaten, I'll take you to the bathroom to wash.'

'We can do that ourselves,' Clara reminds her.

'You're not quite ready. Not yet,' Auntie says. She stands up and gathers the plates and bowls onto the tray. 'I won't be too long.'

* * *

Clara is reading to Stephen when Auntie comes to put a mug of hot cocoa on the table next to Clara and another closer to Stephen.

'Bedtime now,' she says.

'I'm going to finish reading this book first.' Clara doesn't look up from the page.

'But it's late.'

'It won't take long.'

'I could read it instead.'

Clara suspects how much Auntie longs for this, yet still she feels a curious balm of satisfaction. But this feeling of power begins to slip from her as Auntie sits on the bed and listens to her reading. She's aware of Auntie watching, can feel her face being studied. It makes her lips feel clumsy and she drops words and letters into the wrong place as she hurries to the end of the story.

'Hop into your own bed,' Auntie says as soon as it's finished.

Clara wants to hold Stephen's wrist, *stay close to me*, but he does as he's told, jumping into his bed, sitting with his back against the wall. Auntie straightens the blanket over his knees, giving his legs a playful tap before she hands him his cocoa. Clara is desperate for her to leave them and so she takes big gulps of her warm drink, watching as Auntie goes over to the window, where the moths outside mingle with her reflection before she pulls the curtains closed.

'There were enough blackberries left to put some in the fridge,' Auntie says.

'Can we have crumble again tomorrow?' Stephen asks.

'There's not quite enough for that.' She smiles. 'But maybe biscuits.'

Stephen takes a mouthful of the sweet drink. 'I'd like that,' he says and Clara watches how his happiness touches Auntie.

When their mugs are empty, Auntie carries them with her and stands by the light switch. She looks to Clara like a painting, the doorway framing the fresh brushstrokes that bring her to life. The moment is broken when Auntie lifts her hand to turn the room into darkness.

'Goodnight,' she says.

'Goodnight,' says Stephen.

But Clara doesn't reply.

* * *

*W*arren doesn't ask about the children. Through the evening meal they sit in their usual silence, dotted only with mumbled appreciation of the food. After, in the sitting room, he reads in his chair, barely noticing his wife sewing. And later, as they get into bed, he talks briefly about the changing season and the colder weather, before he turns his back on her. She looks away from him, to where the stitched boy in his blue suit now sits in the corner, his leather hands in his lap. He may be blind, but Auntie knows how much he sees. His mouth is pinched shut, but she knows how much he wants to speak.

She waits for the familiar sound of her husband's snoring, the low whistle from inside him. She wonders if he even thinks of the children and can't conceive that he wouldn't. They are there in her mind every waking moment. Their hands, their faces, their voices. They are part of her now, as she pushes back the covers on her side and steps from their bed. She takes the torch from under her pillow, puts on her dressing-gown and her slippers and goes silently from the room.

The darkness of the landing greets her. As a child, she would have been scared, but now she knows that there's nothing there. They are the same walls, the same bare floor, the same pictures looking out. She only clicks on the torch when she turns the children's door handle, the sound of it amplified by the night. She covers the beam slightly with her hand, muffling the light as she slips into their room.

Stephen and Clara are as she left them, but now they're in a drug-induced sleep, their mugs of hot chocolate satisfyingly empty.

The comb too is where Auntie wants it to be, on top of the chest of drawers. She doesn't sit on Clara's bed because she's unsure how deep the powder has sent the girl, thinking it better to kneel next to it, the torch on the floor tucked almost under her dressing-gown to give barely enough light to guide her. Clara's eyes are closed. First, Auntie gently presses her shoulder. Clara doesn't wake, the sleeping pill nestled heavy within her, so Auntie holds some of the ends of her daughter's hair and pulls the comb through. It snags on knots almost immediately and she has to hold her hand steady to work at them.

The hair is softer to touch than Auntie had anticipated. It looks so wild that she thought it would be rough against her palms. And the more she brushes it, the smoother it becomes. When she's finished a whole section, she puts the comb on the floor and divides this part of Clara's hair into three. She weaves it slowly into a plait, the action of it healing the depths of her. When the plait curls into a thin point at the end, she unravels it and starts again.

Clara smells different to her brother, she thinks. Somehow tangled, more complicated. Auntie knows she will need more patience with her and resolves not to take her daughter's coldness to heart.

'Ice doesn't melt in minutes,' she mutters to herself, as she undoes the plait once more.

It's difficult to reach all of the hair, with some tucked underneath, but Auntie does the best she can. She keeps going until the comb runs freely and she's satisfied. Tomorrow there'll be time to style it properly. She'll ask Clara how she'd like it and they'll do it together.

Auntie pulls the hair from the comb before she places it back on top of the chest of drawers. She waits for the ache in her knees to subside as she watches her sleeping children.

'Such pretty things,' she whispers, before she clicks off the torch, preferring to go back in the dark.

10

Clara notices it as soon as she wakes up. Someone has touched her hair, someone has brushed it while she slept.

'Stephen,' she says loudly, even though he's awake. 'Did you get up in the night?'

'No,' he replies.

'She came in and brushed my hair.' She looks at him, reality hanging too close to her.

'What do you mean?'

'She came in here and combed my hair when I was asleep.'

'That's nice of her,' Stephen says.

'It's not. I don't want her coming in here at night.'

'Did you wake up?'

'No.' The thought of it slips uneasily into Clara. She sits still for a moment, unwillingly absorbing it. She tries to remember, to think that somehow she felt it, but the black hole of the night sits stubbornly on her thoughts and all she knows is sleeping, and waking.

Her head is throbbing as she goes to the wardrobe, opens it and reaches to the back where her satchel is hidden. She sits for a moment with it on her knees, needing the familiarity of the buckle, running the tips of her fingers along the bumps of stitching.

She takes out her sketchbook, smells it first and it's as she left it, with faint traces of how she's sure the inside of a stick would taste. She turns to a drawing of Nancy, freckles exaggerated across her nose. No one has tampered with it, and as she touches her friend's face she hopes by some miracle that her palm will press through the page and find her there.

When she hears the rattling of plates on the tray as Auntie walks up the stairs, Clara shoves the sketchbook and satchel back into the wardrobe. There's a pause long enough for Clara to get back into bed, before the key is turned and she's here.

'Good morning,' Auntie says, ignoring Clara's glare. 'I've brought your breakfast. I saved the last two eggs for you.' She puts down the tray and stands back, her hands wringing the flowers from her apron again. 'You need to sit and eat.' Clara doesn't move. 'I was thinking of making you orange juice,' she blunders on. 'Would you like that?'

'You brushed my hair,' Clara says.

'Yes,' Auntie replies.

'You had no right.'

'It needed it. I wanted you to look nice.' Auntie seems proud that she's standing her ground, even in the beam of Clara's furrowed eyes.

'It was nice already.' Clara won't look away. She feels a power in her, needing to make Auntie see.

'You'll look better when I brush the other side,' Auntie says, her head slightly tilted as she examines the asymmetrical confusion of Clara's hair. 'I'll do it when you're eating breakfast.'

'I won't let you touch it again,' Clara tells her, grasping for victory.

'I'll have to brush it when you're asleep, then.'

'Let her do it,' Stephen whispers. 'You look pretty.'

'Your food is getting cold,' Auntie says.

Clara feels defeat creeping in. She shoves back the blanket, steps out of bed and goes to sit on the chair. Stephen scurries after her, allowing Clara to slam his eggcup down in front of him, his plate of bread.

'Look,' Auntie says, her voice forced happy. 'You can dip the bread in like this.' She reaches over Stephen and picks up a butter-soaked slice. She has to push it quite hard into the top of the egg, the white bulging up before the bread pops through and a stream of orange leaks out. 'See?' She holds the dripping food to Stephen's mouth, and he eats it obediently. 'Is it nice?' Somehow, so much is held in his answer.

'Yes,' Clara hears him say.

She's already scooping her egg quickly with a spoon. It's runny against the roof of her mouth and her throat clutches it before she forces herself to relax so she can swallow.

Auntie picks up the comb from on top of the chest of drawers and gets to work on the unbrushed side of Clara's hair. There's solely the sound of the scrape of the comb's teeth and her children chewing. When it's done, Auntie gathers the hair into three parts, which she diligently plaits, looping it over and under her fingers.

'I've finished my breakfast,' Clara says abruptly, banging down the empty glass and pushing away the plate.

'Do you have any ribbons?' Auntie asks.

'No.'

'You must have a hairband?'

Clara could lie and pretend she hasn't, but she thinks then Auntie will choose something herself and she couldn't stand to have something of hers stuck in her hair.

'It's in my washbag. I'll get it.'

Before Auntie can think or protest, Clara runs from the room, along the corridor and into the bathroom. She doesn't even want to touch her hair, fearful of any memory of those fingers. She almost holds her head upside down and shakes her hair free, but she knows if she does that, she'll have to go through it all over again. Instead, she finds two bands in her washbag and twists them over the straggly ends of the plaits.

'You need to come out now,' Auntie says, tapping her knuckles on the door.

Clara looks wildly around the bathroom. There's no secret door, no magic archway, no safe way to escape.

'I'm going to brush my teeth,' she says, needing to grasp onto the weak tails of power she feels slipping away.

She squeezes the toothpaste along the length of the bristles, closing her eyes to taste it sharp against her gums. She visualises her mother standing with her, just by her side, and when she opens her eyes again, as she rinses and spits the water into the basin, it's impossible for her to understand that she's truly alone. She looks around the empty room and it feels swollen with loss, pressing so hard against her that it's too painful to cry.

In her washbag, the hollow eyes of her nail scissors watch her blankly. She picks them up and pushes them into the pocket of her dress. She uses the toilet quickly before turning on the tap, letting it run too hot and forcing her hands into the water, the steam enough to blur her scorching skin.

Mummy. Did it hurt, or was it quick?

There's a momentary release from everything, only the searing pain remaining. Her fingers ache to the bones as she unlocks the door. She strides past Auntie, turning her invisible as she goes back to Stephen waiting in the room.

'We've finished breakfast,' she says, getting into bed and picking up Stephen's book with scalded fingers. 'Get in with me,' she tells him, lifting the corner of the blanket. 'I'll read to you.'

Stephen looks up at Auntie. 'You could read to me later,' he says. 'I'd like that.'

Over my dead body, Clara thinks, as she turns the page.

* * *

The day is immeasurably long, pockmarked only by a lunch of cheese and bread and the sound of Uncle Warren arriving home.

When Auntie comes in with paper and colouring pencils, she hovers at the table and Clara is aware that she's expecting them to thank her.

'You need to empty the chamber pot,' Clara tells her. 'You shouldn't have forgotten.'

'Of course,' Auntie chides herself.

Clara sees how she struggles to pick up the pot and imagines Auntie's stomach squeezing, bile rising against the base of her tongue.

'It's not very clean,' Clara says, revelling in the woman's discomfort. A part of her hopes the urine will lap up over the edge and spill down Auntie's hands.

There's a moment of unlocked freedom as Auntie hurries to the bathroom. Clara hears how the toilet lid is lifted, the sound of liquid falling heavy into the bowl. She hopes Auntie is retching as she puts the pot onto the floor, the tap turned to wash her hands.

* * *

When Clara wakes in the morning, there's a ribbon tied in her hair. She sits, sleep still pressing heavily upon her as she touches the gentle material. She yanks at it, but it's stubborn at first and she has to pull hard to get it free.

She doesn't tell Stephen that Auntie has been in their room again. Instead, she finds the scissors and starts to cut at her curls. Stephen wakes to find her hacking her hair into spikes.

'Clara!' he shouts, but her eyes are so wild that he doesn't come too close. 'What are you doing?' He starts to cry, but she doesn't stop.

She holds the clumps of her hair until her fist is too full and she has to let them fall onto her nightdress. She cuts and cuts until it's nearly all gone. Frightened, suddenly, that Auntie will find the scissors, she makes a small gash in the hem of the curtain and slips them inside.

'I don't like it,' Stephen says, his tears worsening. Clara puts her hair on top of the chest of drawers, before she goes to slide herself into the bed next to him.

'I'm still me,' she says. 'I just look different.'

'I want your hair back.'

'It'll grow.'

She strokes his own, waiting for his tears to slow and exhaust themselves.

'Why did you do it?' he asks, not looking up at her.

'It's easier this way,' she says. 'I won't have to wash it.'

'But I don't like it,' he tells her again, reaching his arm across her tummy as if needing to know that it's really her, that she's still here.

'I'm sorry,' she says, stroking his fingers one-by-one.

They stay like this, safe together, until Auntie walks in. The immediate sight of Clara nearly forces her from the room, but instead she falls forward, the tray dropping from her hands to hit heavily on top of the chest of drawers. She doesn't see the pile of hair waiting for her there.

'What happened?' she exhales.

'What's wrong?' Clara asks.

'Your hair.' Auntie is struggling to think.

'Oh, this?' Clara touches it, trying not to reveal shock on her own face at the stubble under her palms. 'It got cut.'

'How?'

'I don't know,' she says. 'It just did.'

'It can't have just got cut.'

'Maybe you did it?'

'Me?' She sees Auntie struggle to remember – surely she wouldn't have? She couldn't have? 'I didn't.'

'Well, no one else did,' Clara says.

Auntie lies her hand flat on the chest of drawers and it's only now that she feels the bundle of hair beneath her fingers. She grasps the shreds of it.

'Where are the scissors?' she demands.

Clara feels Stephen's hand grip hers tighter.

'There are no scissors,' she says, her gaze unwavering.

Auntie looks around. She starts to move, kneeling to look under the bed, pushing her hands as far as she can under each mattress.

'Where are they?'

'I don't know what you're talking about,' Clara says. Auntie opens the drawers and shakes out each item of clothing before she folds them and puts them back in. She feels along the base of the wardrobe and sweeps her hands down the dresses and miniature suits.

'There's no point looking,' Clara says. 'You'll never find them.' She stares hard at Auntie. 'You can't find something that's not here.'

* * *

Auntie stumbles at the top of the stairs and has to hold tight to the banister to stop herself from falling. If the children could venture from their room now, they would find her curled on the top step, her hand across her mouth to stop her tears.

She remembers when her fourth child died, so close to birth. How her dreams had been cruel and constant – the plaits and bows and ribbons – leaving her to wake empty-handed, her soul destroyed. She feels her womb bleeding again now, can feel loss seeping out of her, clots heavy and thick as she loses her grasp on her new daughter. She wants to howl, have the floorboards open up and swallow her, take her from this pain.

She lets herself feel it. She has to feel it – she has no choice.

And when she has settled, she touches her cheek for signs of tears.

'This won't get a dog a bone,' she whispers, as she pulls on the banister rail to help herself stand. She wants to be in her kitchen, sweeping the floor, needing the regular rhythm of the broom pulling towards her, the appearance of piles of dust for her to gather and tip away.

11

'I've brought something for you,' Auntie says. They're sitting at the table and Clara turns over the paper she's been drawing on, so only a blank piece of white looks up.

'What is it?' she asks.

'Close your eyes,' Auntie says.

'No,' Clara replies.

'You have to.'

'I don't have to do anything,' she tells her.

'Yes,' Auntie says. 'Yes, you do.'

'I'll close my eyes,' Stephen says.

'No,' Clara says. 'I will.'

'Good,' Auntie says and she sits on the edge of the bed. 'You'll like it,' she insists. 'But you have to keep your eyes closed.'

Clara hears the zip of a bag and a faint smell gives away the make-up. She can't move, held down by the gnarled hands of responsibility, by the withered bones of confusion and by grief and fear. She's shaking when Auntie touches the brush to her eyelid, repulsed by the soft pressure on a part of her that no one but herself has touched before. She feels naked, defenceless, even as she grips her hands into fists.

'You'll look so pretty,' Auntie says. And Clara hears her dab the brush back into the powder, before she sweeps it over Clara's other lid. With a pencil she shades over the girl's eyebrows in an arc, Clara grimacing at the pull on her skin. Auntie digs through the bag for something and there's a click that might be a compact being opened. Soft sounds before a bigger brush is rubbed hard in circles onto Clara's cheeks.

'Perfect,' Auntie says.

Clara tries to pretend that she's somewhere else. She takes her mind with her and floats through the window, catching onto a cloud and hanging by her fingertips as it drifts her across the mountains. She barely feels the pencil being dragged along the outline of her lips, the filling in with the petal-smelling lipstick, dabbed and then rubbed to make the colour strong.

'I think I've finished,' Auntie says and Clara lets go of the cloud and feels herself drop. She opens her eyes and is surprised to find that she's sitting here. 'Do you want to see in the mirror?'

'No.'

'But you should.'

Clara doesn't recognise this aunt sitting in front of her, can only grasp at fragments of the cracked mind she senses is growing there.

'You can go now,' she tells her, watching as Auntie's heart deflates. Clara throws the make-up back into the bag. She hates the touch of it, the traces of crumbling powder it leaves on her skin. She struggles with the zip, the material bulging, but eventually forces it closed. 'There. You can take that with you.' And she shoves the bag into Auntie's hand.

For a moment, Auntie sits stunned.

'This wasn't how it was meant to be,' she says quietly.

'No,' Clara says.

But Auntie somehow gathers herself, a steely determination creeping into her eyes.

'Don't rub it off. Or there'll be no tea for you, or Stephen.' She stands up, grabs Clara's shorn hair from the chest of drawers and leaves them.

The room is different now. Clara doesn't know whether it's trying to comfort her, or turn its back in shame. Stephen is opposite at the table, Clara starkly aware that she can't make sense of any of this for her brother.

'How do I look?' She goes cross-eyed for him, but he only screws up his face in reply. 'That bad?'

'Yes.'

'We could make me a mask.' She holds up a piece of paper to her face.

He doesn't laugh, so she peers around the edge. 'Better?'

'Who's that?' he asks, pointing to the paper. Clara had forgotten her drawing on the other side.

'It's mummy,' she says.

'In hospital.'

'Yes.' He wasn't meant to see.

'Can you draw her before? When she was better?' he asks.

'If you want me to.'

'I do.' He passes her a new piece of paper from the pile and she picks up her pencil again.

It's harder to concentrate now, with the smell of the make-up on her face. She feels it pressing into her skin, venturing too far into the thoughts of their mother. She wants to remember what she looked like, those months ago, but she's struggling to find the shape of her nose, the curve of her chin. She has to cross out her first attempt, scribbling over the stranger looking back at her. She tries again, wanting her mother to appear from her pencil and rise up from the page. But the more she tries, the further away she goes. She screws the paper up and slams it onto the floor.

Again, Clara draws the outline of her mother's face, but knows it is too narrow. She rubs it out and draws a new one, the faint lines of the other still watching her. She thinks she remembers her hairline and has brief certainties about the shape of her eyes, but she struggles with the lips and wants instead to hear her. In the silence of the room she waits for her mother's voice, but there's nothing.

Stephen watches as Clara rips the picture into shreds, smaller and smaller, angrier and angrier. He doesn't want his sister to be like this. She gets up and kicks her chair, but when it doesn't fall, she picks it up and swings it hard against the wall. There's a crack of a splinter as the leg gets dislodged.

'No, Clara,' Stephen says, jumping in front of her. She holds the chair back, enough time for him grab it, wrestle it from her. Without it, Clara crumples hard onto the wooden floor.

Stephen tries to comfort her, patting her shorn hair that he hates to touch.

'Shh,' he says. 'Don't cry.' He keeps stroking her hair. 'She'll get better, you'll see.'

* * *

Later in the day, Clara has pulled out a drawer and is busy scratching her name into the back of it, as Stephen sits colouring at the table.

'It must be confusing,' he says, biting the end of a pencil, soft splinters almost breaking away.

'What must?'

'For that fly. Because he thinks the garden is there and he can fly into it, but something stops him.' Clara hadn't noticed it before, but there it is, knocking against the window.

Stephen puts the bottom of his pencil to the glass and starts to turn it.

'What are you doing?'

'Trying to make a small hole.' But after only a few seconds he gives up, realising it's useless.

'Maybe we could try to catch it?' Clara suggests. 'And then set it free when the door is open.'

'We've nothing to catch it in,' Stephen says.

'We could make a cup.'

And that's why he gets a piece of paper and folds it into a bowl shape in his palm.

'I don't think that one'll work somehow,' Clara says.

'It will,' Stephen insists. But every time his clumsy cup gets close to it, the insect flies from his reach. Stephen follows it with his eyes, sitting stationary as it clings to the ceiling and when it jitters jagged down the wall, close enough to almost touch. He watches its spindly legs rub over its eyes.

'You'll never get it.'

'I will.'

'Tell you what, I'll carve a picture of it on the drawer, so if you don't catch it, you'll still sort of have it.'

'Would you?'

'I've nothing better to do.' Clara says it to make him laugh, but instead it swings reality so close to her face that it makes her flinch.

* * *

When Auntie comes in, she has a line of plum colour on her lips. She puts the tray on the table and doesn't speak as she steps close to Clara, takes a tissue from her sleeve, licks it and sweeps it around the split edges of blusher on Clara's cheeks.

'The casserole has three different types of beans in it,' she says. 'I had to soak them overnight in a bowl in the larder.'

'That's a lot of work,' Stephen says.

'It's not Warren's favourite, but I like it.' She taps Stephen's chair and he goes to it, allowing her to tuck a napkin into his collar. She blows on a spoonful of food, the stew rippling and settling before she guides it into his mouth. 'It made my wrist ache, whipping up the potato to make the mash silky enough.'

He swallows quickly. 'It's delicious.' And she shines with pride. 'Does Uncle Warren mind that we're up here?'

'No,' Auntie says. 'He doesn't.'

'Won't he want to see us?'

Clara notices it – the briefest second when the truth comes in and trips up Auntie – but she recovers herself.

'Not at the moment,' she says.

'Not even for a bit?'

'He thinks it was a mistake. You coming here.'

'We don't have to stay,' Clara says, her mouth full of food.

Auntie looks at her as if she's said the strangest thing. It's a thought unfathomable that she should lose these children too.

'You have me, though,' she says, daring to touch both of them on the arm. 'And I promise I'll never leave you.' She scoops up more of the potato and holds the fork steady as she kisses Stephen's forehead. 'You're safe here,' she tells him, leaving the faintest mark of lipstick on his skin.

* * *

Later, Clara watches the darkness creeping over the mountains. The garden dims until the hedge and the trees are shapes that slowly disappear.

Now she's left with only her reflection looking back, and in this mirror she sees the blocks of make-up on her face. There's nothing in her that she recognises. She rubs a fingertip over her cheek, smearing the red so the colour bleeds.

'She said not to rub it off,' Stephen reminds her.

'I'm not,' she reassures him. 'I'm just smudging it in.'

'Will she mind?'

'I don't care.'

Their faces stare back at them from the window.

'You have to try to be better.' He has shadows of that unusual voice again, some of the words wilting as they leave his lips.

'Go and turn off the light,' she tells him.

'Can I put on the toadstool lamp?'

'Let's have nothing first. You can see everything outside more clearly without the light. If you don't like it, I promise I'll turn it on.'

Stephen steps over to the switch by the door. 'Really?'

Clara nods and there's a click as Stephen turns them into thick darkness. She reaches her hand for his as he comes back to her and although he seems reluctant, she pulls him onto her lap.

'See?' she says.

Outside, the garden has come alive. The trees have been painted back, the line of the hedge drawn across the bottom of the garden.

The evening has brought with it pinpricks of stars, swallowed in patches by clouds.

'Are you frightened?' she asks.

'A little bit,' whispers Stephen.

They can't see the mountains, which are set too far back, but Clara knows that they're there. She wonders what it'd be like to run up them now, dark stones against her feet, the feel of the night on her neck, her hair. She presses her hand against the glass and finds a comfort in its cold, the way it starts at her fingertips, sinks into her wrist and drifts into her body.

'There are a lot of stars,' Stephen says.

They bring faint memories for Clara of their mother spreading black paper on the grass. Brushes dipped into paint and shaken so that colour spattered in clumps and wild dots. Stephen watching from the window, not allowed to join in, in case he ruined it.

'They look like tear-drops,' she says.

'Is God crying, because we've been bad?' Stephen turns to look up at her. Even in the darkness she can see the earnestness etched in his eyes.

'We haven't been bad,' she tells him. 'But someone has.'

Stephen looks back towards the sky.

'Are the tears hot?' he asks. 'Like little bits of fire?'

'Yes,' she says. 'They've scorched lots of holes in the sky.'

Stephen nods, knowing the truth of it, not needing to question.

The night seems so quiet. Clara hears only Stephen's steady breathing locked tight into hers. She can almost feel his mind moving among the stars, feeling them burn his fingers. She pretends that those glinting sparks of white are their mother's eyes, multiplied and watching them. It should comfort her, but it doesn't, only making the distance loom larger.

She yanks the curtain over the glass.

'I was looking,' Stephen protests.

'It's bedtime,' she says, moving him from her lap.

It's easy for her to find the lamp, to turn it on and wash the room in a glow that reaches threads across the ceiling, all the way to the corners. She lifts up the edge of Stephen's blanket, giving him no choice but to climb into the sheets waiting for him. She kisses his head and tucks him in as a mother would.

* * *

In the morning Clara wakes to find the stain of her monthly menstruation remorseless between her legs. She moves to crouch on the floor, careful not to get any of the blood on the sheet. Stephen doesn't see her kneeling, impotent to the curse that brings with it a complex mesh of shame. She knows she didn't think to bring sanitary napkins; she knows too that she'll never ask Auntie for any.

She crawls over to the curtain, aware now that Stephen is awake and watching as she finds her scissors. She prays the blood won't drop onto the floor as she opens the wardrobe and cuts a square from one of the dresses.

'What are you doing?' Stephen asks, glancing wide-eyed towards the closed bedroom door.

'None of your business.'

She folds the cut material over and over and tucks it inside some clean underwear, trying to ignore the dull echo of pain in her stomach. Clara can tell that her brother wants to ask more, but this is too intimate, so she closes off to him.

Stephen gets up and starts searching along the walls, the mantelpiece, the chest of drawers. When he opens the curtains, there's the buzz of the fly and he smiles at it as it wakes to tap against the glass.

'Do you think we should feed it?' he asks.

'Feed what?' she snaps.

'My fly.'

'I've no idea what they eat,' Clara says, her harsh tone snagging slightly on her conscience.

'I'll give it some of my breakfast.' He tries to touch its back, but it spins away from him. 'It won't need much.'

'Do what you like.'

They hear the steady footsteps coming up the stairs. Clara feels an impossible desire to hide, but she forces herself to stay standing just where she is. When Auntie unlocks the door, she has that same expression as when she first saw them, the same sense of awe.

'I made you fresh orange juice,' she says, beaming at them both before she puts down the tray. 'I know some would consider it wasteful as you have to throw away the pulp, but you need your vitamins if you're not outside in the sun.'

'You could let us out,' Clara says, emboldened by the secret of her bleeding as she reaches for a slice of the toast.

'You must sit down to eat,' she's told.

'I want to stand up.'

Clara sees panic blinding Auntie momentarily, before she takes away Stephen's food, grabbing not only his plate but also the toast in his hand.

Clara glowers at her, defeated.

'You win,' she says, sitting down, feeling the wet material unsteady between her legs.

Auntie doesn't give Stephen back the food. Instead, she holds the toast close to his mouth for him to bite. He's obedient, careful not to spill a crumb.

* * *

In the evening they have their bathtime with Auntie standing outside the door. Clara leans over the edge of the tub to wash Stephen's hair, trying to hold his head to stop the shampoo from soaking into his eyes. When she's finished, he plays with the flannel, balling it up and throwing it against the tiles. She takes this chance to sit on the toilet and take the sodden rags from her underwear.

'Clara, you're bleeding.' Her brother scrambles to his knees in the slippery water, but he doesn't come closer.

'It's the curse,' she whispers. It doesn't stop her from feeling dirty in his naïve glare, as she puts the rags, heavy with blood, on the bathroom floor. 'It's normal.'

'You've cut yourself.'

'Shh,' she whispers, glancing to the door.

'Are you hurt?'

'No.'

'Are you going to die?' He blinks away quick tears, his cheeks tinged red in the faint steam.

'No. The bleeding is a good thing.'

'Good?'

'Yes.' She looks directly at him, needing him not to be afraid. 'When girls get old enough they bleed a bit every month. It means that they can have babies.'

'The babies grow in the blood?'

'It's complicated,' she tells him. 'But if there's not a baby there, then the womb bleeds.'

'Like it's crying?'

'I suppose so. But they're not bad tears.'

He nods solemnly.

She takes the new cut of material from her pocket, folding it tightly before wiping herself clean with toilet paper and pulling up her underwear. She doesn't like how he watches her, but she doesn't want him to be frightened. He's silent as she goes to the window, coughs loudly and eases open the latch, pushing on the glass. There's a pulsing ache inside her as she bends down to pick

LISA HEATHFIELD

up the rag, holding it far from her, dangling it in the outside air before she lets it go.

The material, thick with her blood, falls heavily to the ground, landing crumpled like a dead bird.

'Come on,' she says brightly, loud enough for Auntie to hear. 'Time to get you out.'

* * *

The following day, Auntie is filled with an impenetrable sadness. She feeds her children their breakfast in almost silence and Clara seems even more reluctant to have her make-up reapplied. Every time she feels that they're floating closer to her grasp, they close off from her and drift away. Her yearning to be near them is a bleak, gaping hole.

Alone in her kitchen, she picks up her empty blackberry bag.

'Here's one for you.' She passes air to the imaginary Clara. 'And one for you,' she tells Stephen.

It's easier to know that they're beside her, to hear the sound of her son's shoes skipping around the edge of the house. She crosses the lawn, one child on either side, happy that she's remembered to button their coats against the sudden chill tumbling down from the hills.

'Autumn is coming,' she says. 'Soon I'll read you stories every night by the fire.'

The branches are drooping with fruit, forced to ripen early by a summer of rare heat. Auntie shows Stephen which ones to pick, to ignore those not quite black enough and be gentle with those that are. He asks if he can eat them.

'Just one.' She smiles, and pops one in her mouth too.

It isn't long before the bag is full. Auntie wishes she could slow it all down, go back to the top of the lawn and do it all again.

'We can make jam with it,' she says. 'Then we can pick some more again soon.'

'I'd like that,' Stephen says, and when he puts his little hand in hers her heart aches with love.

Clara seems distant again, so Auntie takes her hand too.

'I'll teach you how to boil the fruit,' she says and her daughter rewards her with a full smile.

The lawn is still slightly damp from the morning dew and Auntie thinks it's wise that she's worn her boots. And wise that she's come out early as she's aware of rain in the air.

When she's by the side of the house she notices a small bundle on the floor close to the wall and she hesitates. It's a baffling shape – flat, yet twisted. She steps closer, knowing instantly that it's a piece of cloth holding old blood from her womb. Cloth she buried all those years ago. She'd wiped it between her legs, the beginnings of her child smeared onto it, as her heart shattered.

Auntie loses her balance in this world, dropping the bag of blackberries as she falls to her knees. She's scared of the material – her hope of motherhood that she dug into the ground – but she touches it to her cheek, feeling the fragments of the child she begged to keep.

Is this a sign? Is the child that came from her womb not happy that it's been replaced? Why else would it be sitting here now, waiting for her to find it?

'I'm sorry,' she whispers, holding it close as she stumbles towards the graves hidden behind the wall. It's an older hand that pushes on the door, but her tears are new, pulled up from the earth and poured down from the sky. She needs to know what her babies are thinking, needs them to understand that she hasn't forgotten them.

The grief starves her mind of sense as she sees the cleared grass around the crosses, knowing only that her children have clawed their way back through the earth, have tidied this bit of garden so she would come to them again.

'I'm sorry,' she says, sitting down among the crosses, not caring about the wet ground seeping through her skirt. 'I'm sorry.'

They're not happy at being replaced – she sees that now. They'd fought so hard to grow into existence, but she'd let them all go and, with the arrival of two strangers, she'd forgotten them.

'I'm sorry,' she says again, digging a shallow hole with her hands. The earth snags under her nails, the dirt creeping through her, but she has to do this. She digs until it's deep enough, kisses the blood-patterned material and sinks it into its grave, before she brushes earth over to smother it, locking it away from the world, from a chance at life again.

The pain engulfs her now as it did the first time, the teeth of grief gnawing wildly through her skin, scraping cruelly along her bones. She thinks she can't bear it, but she knows she must. So she

stays, touching each of the little crosses in turn. She feels her babies'
fingers and even faint kisses on her cheek.

How can it have been better to block out this pain, where here she
feels so near to them? She wonders at the time when all she knew was
hope, when two of her children grew enough to turn in her womb, to
kick their little feet until she could feel them. She'd lie naked in the
bath and watch the miracle of them moving underneath her skin,
knowing that soon she would meet them.

Yet they all left her.

Auntie stands up, unsure where time has disappeared to, but
knowing that enough minutes – maybe hours – have passed to seize
up her legs and make them ache to stand.

12

Clara doesn't need to look at the clock to know that lunchtime has been and gone.

'Has something happened to her?' Stephen asks.

'She's still downstairs. She's fine.' Clara can hear the sound of Auntie in her kitchen, the muffled noises drifting up the stairs.

'She's forgotten our lunch,' Stephen points out.

'I know.' Clara is trying hard to take away the sharp bruising pain in her empty stomach.

'She must be very busy.'

Stephen has been drawing on a piece of paper, scuffed heads of birds with unfinished bodies, their wings separate and uneven. The squeaking scratch of his pencil rubs at a patch of anger inside Clara, over and over until she thinks she'll explode.

'Can you stop that?'

'Stop what?'

'Colouring. It's bugging me.'

He looks up at her, confused, the pencil paused above a half-drawn eye.

'But I'm bored.'

Clara nods and bites her gum inside her mouth, enough so that it almost pierces the skin.

'Fine,' she snaps.

'It's your fault we're in here,' Stephen says. There's a soft sound as he puts down his pencil on the paper. 'You should be nicer to her.'

'She should be nicer to us.'

'I don't like you anymore,' he says.

'But I'm your sister. I'm all you've got here. You don't need her.'

'I do. It's you I don't need.'

Clara wants to squeeze his words dry, wring them tight so that they drip away. She can still hear them, though, the echo of them on her tongue. She picks up her book again, longing to lose her hurt in the written page. But it doesn't work and now she welcomes her menstrual cramps, almost indistinguishable from her hunger, concentrating on her rumbling stomach and counting in seconds how long it lasts, measuring it against the next time.

She watches the rain prowl over the mountains, rushing urgently across the garden and hammering on the window. She wishes it were strong enough to smash the glass to let them out.

The chamber pot begins to fill. Stephen doesn't mean to watch Clara as she uses another slice of rag to clean herself when she's been. He's disgusted as she pushes the damp material to the back of the bottom drawer and he finds it difficult to concentrate on anything now, with that smell of urine sitting sour in the air.

* * *

*D*ownstairs in the kitchen, Auntie's mind is so soaked with her babies that all other thoughts are washed away. She forgets everything else as she scrubs the oven, her hands clad in rubber gloves. She imagines her five children standing in a row. They're all smiling, their hair combed, hands clasped in front of them against neatly ironed clothes. She doesn't turn around but is comforted in knowing that they're here as she scrubs spots of grease and animal fat from the oven walls.

After her evening meal, Auntie goes to the only place that will calm her. The room is very still, devoid of sound and laughter. She thinks at first she'll go to the doll's house, but instead she opens her sewing cupboard filled with all her bits and bobs and reaches for a bag hidden at the back. Inside are the ragdolls she remembers making when her heart hurt so much that it scorched her mind.

There are five of them, and she kisses them all in turn and lays them side-by-side on the table before going to the drawer for her box of crayons. She takes the brown one from the packet and inhales its smell. She can't tell whether they are happy or sad memories it evokes – it's more like a haze of feelings, impossible to trap in her hands.

She picks up her first child and does what she should have done years ago – the waxy colour drags at the material, but she presses hard enough to leave a mark, to draw eyes, a nose, a mouth. She colours in the next and the next, unashamed of her tears, believing in some magic that the touch of the salt water will bring her children to life.

But the dolls stay still, now staring up at her, accusations in their eyes.

'Forgive me,' she says, again and again, gathering them all to her, holding them in her arms.

Auntie stays like this until the moon has reached its peak, when she should have been in bed long ago. But she can't bear to put the dolls back in the bag, not now that they can see. Instead, she lines them up in the rocking chair, slowly pushing the back of it until she's sure that they're asleep.

13

When Auntie appears in the morning, she brings only plain bread and two glasses of water.

'You forgot us,' Stephen says, sitting up. 'You didn't bring us our food.'

The stench from the chamber pot pushes between them. Auntie struggles to move past it, putting the tray on the table by the window.

'You'll have to do that,' she tells Clara, pointing to where the pot sits on the floor.

Clara is glad to, needing to escape these four walls. She picks it up, holding it far from her as she takes it to the bathroom, tipping away the heavy urine, gagging on the steam it leaves behind. She hurries to lock the door. Even though she's frightened to leave Auntie alone with Stephen, she's desperate for time on her own. She closes her eyes as she uses the toilet, trying to find a link in her thoughts, to remember when she stepped from her life and was hurled along the path she's on now. Unwanted by Uncle Warren. Auntie's love melting as hot wax, changing into something she doesn't recognise. Stephen willingly slipping into its stream. Clara pummels her feet, wanting to bruise the floor, urging a transfer of pain from her own body that doesn't feel strong enough to hold what she's been given.

There's a transient wisp of relief that there's only a small amount of her period on the rags in her underwear. But her head is aching and hunger whistles through her arms and legs, and it's this that moves her back to the bedroom once more.

Auntie watches as they shovel in every crumb of their breakfast, yet she can't see into Clara's mind, at the maze of thoughts clicking and ticking there. She doesn't know that Clara deliberately lifts her bread to her mouth at the same time as Stephen, can't see the threads that the girl tries to plait into a tight bond to bind her to her brother.

'I don't want you to hate us,' Stephen says as the trays are stacked.

Auntie seems stunned. 'I don't hate you. I could never hate you.'

'But why can't we come out and play?'

'It's not safe yet,' she says. 'You have to be better.'

'Better than what?'

'Just better,' she says, before she hurries away.

'I think she means you,' Stephen tells Clara.

'Me?'

'Yes. You're rude to her and you don't care about her toys.'

Clara feels the carefully plaited threads start to fray, her grip on them begin to fail.

'It's her that doesn't care about us.' Clara knows she's pushing him towards tears, but she's too tired to mind.

'She does,' Stephen says. 'She loves me.'

Clara cuts another strip from the cream dress and Stephen stares when she starts to fold it. She replaces the stained material with the clean bit, before she pulls open the drawer and pushes the old rag to the back.

'That's dirty,' he says.

So she doesn't reply.

* * *

A storm is against the window when Auntie brings them soup for their lunch. She doesn't flinch when a crack of thunder breaks the sky so sharply that Stephen clings to Clara's side.

'It can't hurt you,' his sister reassures him. She hopes that Auntie will see that he's scared, but she looks straight through them before she leaves, shedding a footprint of neglect in her wake. Clara recognises it starkly for what it is, but her young mind finds it too bewildering to process, how the steps of love can lead to this.

Stephen looks lost, despair settled in his eyes.

'It's not that she doesn't love you,' Clara says. 'She's just a bit angry still, that's all.'

'With you?'

'Yes,' Clara says. 'I'm sure it's just me.' Clara wants that to settle it, but Stephen is glaring at her.

'You're being bad,' he says.

They sit down to eat and though the soup tastes of little, there are chunks of vegetables that add bursts of sweetness. Stephen keeps his head low, his movements small. Clara feels the unit of them disintegrating and she needs him to come back to her.

'I think storms are beautiful really,' she says, 'the sound they make.' She points with her spoon into the distance, where the mountain has been stripped of its green and turned purple-black. 'Look, that was a different colour before, yet the rain has painted it. It's changed everything.' But Stephen ignores her as he finishes his food, tipping up his bowl to drink the last drops.

'I'm still hungry,' he says.

'I know,' Clara says, trying not to feel defeated.

When Auntie comes back, Clara holds onto her bowl.

'Please can we have some more? Stephen is still hungry.'

Auntie doesn't look at her, she just stands there with her hand outstretched, waiting.

'I haven't made any more,' she says.

There's something unnervingly peculiar about her now, as though she's been hollowed out and filled back up with a confusing tangle of thoughts.

Stephen looks at Auntie's hand before he passes his bowl into the waiting fingers. 'I am hungry,' he dares to whisper. 'And I'm trying to be good.' This awkwardness swamping them would normally make him laugh, but he doesn't even smile. Clara shoves her bowl into Auntie's hand.

'We've done nothing bad enough to deserve this,' she says, trying hard not to shout. Auntie piles the glasses and plates onto the tray. 'And if you don't want us here, you can send us back home and daddy will find someone else to look after us.'

'No.' Auntie's reaction is instant. 'No,' she says more to herself. And as she takes away the stacked china and cutlery, Clara distinctly hears more: 'I can't fail, not again.'

* * *

It's dark in the evening when Stephen turns onto his side and touches the tiny door in the glowing toadstool. He keeps his hand there and starts to hum very quietly to himself.

'Stephen?'

'Shh,' he says angrily. 'I'm listening to Edwyn.'

'Edwyn?'

'Her brother who died.'

'But you can't hear him.'

'I can.' Stephen sits up and crosses his legs, leaning closer to the lamp. 'He says he's coming to see me.'

A feeling of unease slips into Clara's bed.

'Stop messing about,' she says.

'I'm not. Edwyn says he's coming soon.'

He speaks too quietly for Clara, having a conversation she can't hear as he nods and smiles.

Anger scratches hard enough at Clara's chest to make it hurt.

She finds the lead for the lamp and yanks it, pulling it from its socket. The room snaps into total darkness. 'Go to sleep,' she says.

She expects to hear the rustling of sheets as her brother shuffles back down into his bed, but there's nothing.

'Stephen?'

'Edwyn says the soul collector couldn't find him when he died.'

Clara covers her ears, pushes her palms against her head. She wants to scream, but she knows she mustn't. If she can just block it all out, then she'll be able to sleep and if she can sleep, then she won't be locked in here anymore. She'll be free.

But through the darkness she can still hear Stephen's words reaching towards her.

'Edwyn is coming,' he says. 'He'll be here soon.'

14

Clara wakes in the morning to find Stephen sitting at the end of his bed. He's dressed in his blue suit, the statue of the china boy in his hands.

'Good morning,' he says, grinning at her. 'I can open the curtains now you're awake.'

She'd forgotten the strange end to last night, but now it comes rushing towards her as Stephen stands up stiffly and pushes the curtains wide.

'Stop talking in that voice,' she says.

'This is my voice.'

'You're being stupid.' Clara tries to ignore the distant look on his face, the smile that isn't quite his. 'She'd better not forget our breakfast.'

'She won't,' he replies. And he puts down his soul collector, before he goes to the closed door. 'I can't wait to see her.'

Clara won't speak again. She doesn't want to hear that voice reply. And she doesn't want to be in this nightdress either, so she changes quickly in the chilly room, hoping Auntie will notice how she's thrown it onto the unmade bed.

There are heavy footsteps coming up the stairs.

'Do you think it's Uncle Warren?' Clara looks at Stephen, but he doesn't seem to have a shred of the fear she suddenly feels.

The door opens and it's Auntie who appears. Stephen lets her put the breakfast tray on the chest of drawers before he wraps his arms around her waist, folding his little body into hers.

'Good morning,' Auntie says, tears creeping into her voice as she dares to hug him.

'I came back,' Stephen says, looking up at her, his arms still caught in the poppies of her apron.

'Came back from where?'

Clara recognises the panic in Auntie.

'I've come back to see you.'

'What are you talking about, Stephen?'

'I'm not Stephen,' he replies. 'I'm Edwyn.'

Auntie pushes him away, as though he's burnt through her clothes.

'I am,' Stephen says proudly, still reaching for Auntie. 'I've come home.'

'Why are you saying this?'

'My soul didn't get collected. I waited, but now I'm here.'

Auntie doesn't reply, only frowning into the shocked silence curling around them.

Stephen's smile doesn't waver, as Clara strides across the room and grabs the tray.

'You forgot us again,' she says. 'We're starving.'

Auntie looks over at her, but her thoughts seem knotted, the truth snarled up in them. Clara slams the tray on the table, hard enough to spill precious water from one of the glasses.

'If you want us to die of starvation, you're going the right way about it.'

'Die?' Auntie says.

'Yes.' Clara rips a piece of toast in half and shoves it into her mouth. Auntie has spread the butter so thick she can feel its oiliness against her tongue. 'Come and get your toast, Stephen,' she says, the food filling her mouth.

Her brother doesn't move.

'Stephen?' She holds out a plate for him. 'Edwyn, whoever,' she says, needing for him only to eat.

At the sound of that name he almost runs across the room. He sits neatly in the chair and takes a small bite of the toast, chewing it politely, his feet side-by-side on the floor.

'Edwyn?' Auntie whispers, so quietly that Stephen doesn't seem to hear as he looks at the morning through the window. She perches on the end of his bed, her hands clasped in her lap. There's an absurd look of wonder spread on her face.

'Do you remember when we went on the boat?' Stephen asks, not turning to look at her.

'Yes,' Auntie says.

Stephen drinks from his glass, big glugs of water until it's half gone.

'Our feet got wet getting into it,' he continues. 'We were so cold.'

'Yes,' Auntie says. Her mind seems to have disappeared, sunk low into the mud on the shores of the loch.

'And I thought we'd fall overboard.'

'Yes. I remember,' Auntie says.

Madness is steeping around them. It's found a way in.

Stephen turns to Auntie. 'I'm here again now.'

'Yes,' she answers, her voice barely more than a murmur.

Clara touches her hand on her brother's arm, but he doesn't even flinch. 'Stephen?'

He chews his last bit of toast quickly, swallowing the mouthful before he speaks. 'Can we bake a cake together?' His smile matches Auntie's.

'Yes. Yes, we can.'

'You know he's just pretending, don't you?' Clara is convinced. 'He thinks that if he says this, you'll let him out.'

But when Stephen looks at Clara his eyes are different. He's not her brother.

'Do you want to come?' he asks her.

'No,' Clara says. She wants him to say that he won't go, then, that he'll stay with her.

'You can wait here,' Auntie tells her as she stands up and takes the boy's hand in hers. She doesn't even remember the tray. Nothing else matters.

'Stephen?' Clara says, but the sound may as well be dust. It feels like her heart fractures as they go from her, the bedroom door closing behind them.

Clara curls onto the bed and pulls the blanket over her face so no one can hear her tears. There's darkness behind her eyes and a headache is creeping in. It feels like Auntie has peeled back her skull and cut thin slices from her brain. It makes her thoughts bleed into each other. There's just the grinding of a blade, twisting enough to scar.

* * *

*A*untie barely takes her eyes from him. He held her hand as they walked down the stairs and she can still feel it now, his innocent skin pressed into hers, his fingers curled around her own.

It's healed her. She feels herself pushing up through the ground, a new shoot of a plant unfurling her leaves, her petals, in the glow of this boy. Before, she was buried, but now she's alive and it makes her want to laugh and dance, throw open the kitchen window and sing to the clouds.

'What's so funny?' Stephen asks from where he sits on the worktop, his hands in the flour in the bowl.

'I'm just happy that you're here,' Auntie says. She reaches over to push his sleeves higher, past his elbows. 'We don't want your clothes getting mucky.'

Already there's flour sprinkled outside the bowl and on his skin, a smear on his cheek and she has to try hard not to let it irritate her. She doesn't want to upset him by making him leave the room to get clean.

When she pours oil instead of eggs into the mixture, he sticks his finger into the golden liquid as it trickles from the bottle. She flinches, but manages not to stop him. And at the end, when all is done, she cups her hands under his arms to lift him down and she wants to hold this moment, stop time so that she can keep this feeling forever.

He hugs her when she puts him gently onto the floor, nestles his head into her stomach. He's here. And the knowledge whittles away those empty, yearning years. Her loss, once a gaping hole, has been filled with the blood, the breath, the bones of this boy. Her hand hovers before she puts it on him, stroking his hair. She is complete.

15

It's a long time before Clara's headache begins to ebb away. The rest of the house is silent. She doesn't want to imagine Stephen with Auntie, standing together, pouring flour onto the weighing scales, their heads touching. Instead, she reaches under her pillow for the little boy doll and rests him on her knee.

'Hello, Clara,' she makes the toy say.

'Hello, Stevie. What shall we do today?'

'What would you like to do?'

'We could run away.'

'Run away?'

'Yes.'

'Where to?'

'I haven't figured that out yet,' Clara says. 'We just need to get away from here.'

She tries to hold his hand, but his fingers won't move properly.

'I like it here,' he says.

'But it's a bad place, Stephen. Don't you know that?'

He doesn't answer and she knows that she can't leave him here alone with Uncle Warren and Auntie. She's been forced into a helpless corner where anger rumbles in her bones. Clara pokes him in the face to get him to react, but he doesn't even blink. She doesn't hear him scream as he should as she forces him back under the pillow, where he won't be able to breathe.

* * *

Clara puts down her book when she hears the door unlock. The clock says that it's midday. No one comes in. Instead, a tray is pushed along the floor and all Clara sees of Auntie is her hand.

'Aren't you going to take away the breakfast things?' Clara asks loudly. But the door just closes quickly. 'I thought you didn't like mess,' she calls out. There's no reply, no response at all. Clara waits to hear footsteps leaving, but there's nothing. 'Are you still there?'

On the tray there's a plate of congealing food and next to it is a small slice of cake. It has white icing and one dried cherry sitting on the top. Has Stephen forgotten that she hates them? She picks it off and throws it hard at the door, where it drops down with barely a noise.

She's glad of the water. The viscid thirst in her mouth hasn't left her since this morning, but for now she can wash it away. Clara doesn't drink all of it. She wants to pour the rest of it over the cake, but then she thinks of Stephen concentrating as he helped to make it, the tip of his tongue peeking from the corner of his mouth, his hand holding the wooden spoon. He'll be so proud.

Clara aches to have seen his face as the cake came out of the oven. She missed it all.

* * *

It's evening and Stephen hasn't come back. Clara has heard him through the day, darting from one room to the next downstairs, his laughter jumping around but stopping short of this room. She knows he's played with the train track and she hopes he's happy. She thinks he is.

Darkness comes up to the window, but Clara won't let it in. She closes the curtains and keeps on the light. She hears her brother in the bathroom with Auntie. There's a silence where maybe she's brushing his teeth. The tap turning, the rush of water. The flush of the toilet.

Clara is only half-here, half-real without him.

But still he doesn't come back. Clara doesn't know where Auntie puts him, but he doesn't return to the bedroom. She balances Walrus on her brother's pillow, tucking it just under the blanket, before she steps across the floor and taps at the door.

'Stephen, are you there?' She turns the handle, but of course it's locked. 'Stephen?' She should slam it hard with her fists and scream and shout his name so that even the moon hears, but she knows that would frighten him. She realises too that she's got to get on the good side of Auntie. She's got to behave so that she'll be let out.

Clara doesn't want to sleep, not yet; not without her brother safe in here. Instead, she takes out the second drawer, piles his clothes neatly on his bed, before she turns it over and starts to carve his name. *Stephen*. The wood gives way to the scissors and it isn't too difficult. She cuts in a picture of his truck. It isn't very good, but he'll be able to tell what it is when she shows him.

'You're not Edwyn,' Clara says, as she traces the letters of his name with her finger. 'You're Stephen.'

She slips the drawer back in and gets into Stephen's bed. The sheets are cold and unwelcoming, but his pillow smells of him and it makes her feel safe. She holds Walrus close, inhaling the memories he must have inside him. Somewhere, buried in Walrus, is their real home. Clara closes her eyes and believes that she's there.

* * *

In the morning, the dirty plates have all been taken away. The chamber pot has been emptied. But Clara is still alone.

She gets out of Stephen's bed and reaches under her pillow for the doll.

'Good morning,' she says, but it just fills her with missing him. She puts the doll on the windowsill and sits opposite at the table. 'Well, if she's going to lock me in here, I'm going to have to find a way out.'

She peers down towards the garden, to the patio below. If she could get the lock on the window loose, perhaps two sheets tied together would reach the ground. Hope whispers inside her as she gets the scissors from the curtain's hem and steps up onto the table. Clara crouches, her knee brushing the doll as she opens the blades and, using only one half, begins to chip away at the wood around the window lock. It's not as easy as she'd hoped. In her mind, the scissors sliced as if through skin, but the frame makes it difficult for her. Clara niggles the tip of the blade deeper, wriggles it through the layers, making tiny wounds.

She's so determined, unaware of the door opening, of Auntie standing behind her, holding breakfast on a tray.

'What are you doing?' Auntie's voice is soft, but Clara swings around in terror, knowing enough to grab the little boy doll and tuck him in the palm of her hand.

'You locked me in here.'

Auntie studies the girl's face, her own head tipped to the side.

'But it's for your own good.'

'You've taken Stephen from me. How can that be for my own good?'

'I have to protect him.'

Clara laughs. 'You're mad if you think he'll want to stay with you.'

'We both know that he does,' she says.

'You think so?'

'What I think,' Auntie says as she puts down the tray on the table where Clara still crouches, 'is that you're a danger to

yourself and your brother. And I don't trust you with scissors.'
She holds out her hand.

'I'm not giving them to you,' Clara says.

'Aren't you?'

'No.' Yet certainty is a slippery beast.

'But I'm looking after Stephen for you,' Auntie says.

Clara feels her heart against her ribs. She has no choice but to
hold out the scissors.

'There's a good girl.' Auntie beams. 'And there has to be a
punishment too, don't you think?' She goes to the wardrobe and,
from the back of it, takes the satchel.

Clara's futile rage flares and is smothered. 'Don't take it,'
she pleads.

'Don't you worry,' Auntie says, her thumb stroking the buckle.
'It'll be safe with me.'

* * *

There's too much time to think, with the soft ticking of the clock
eating into Clara. Hours and minutes and seconds turn her
inside out.

Tick, tock.

Tick, tock, tick.

She counts them.

She checks under the bed in case someone is hiding there. There's
nothing, no one, but when she lies back down she can feel them.

Something is waiting. If she lets her arm hang down, her fingertips touching the floor, she knows they'll be able to feel her skin.

She pulls up her arm, not brave enough.

Clara wants to hide under the blankets, make the day go away, but she knows it'll make her brain too muggy. She'll get confused with night and then she'll be wide-awake in the dark, with the clock ticking.

From here, she can see the soul catcher. But he can't see her, with his scratched-out eyes. She sits up, as quietly as she can. First one foot on the floor, then the other, the tiniest exhalation from the bed as it stops holding her.

The boy doesn't move, he doesn't try to run before she picks him up, her fingers curling tight around his clothes. What would happen if she squeezed too hard? She feels for a beating heart, but there's none.

She wants to bring him close, but she's scared her lips will touch him. If she keeps her arms straight, he'll still be able to hear.

'I don't want you to take my mother's soul,' she says.

The little boy doesn't move.

'She's not ready to die.'

He doesn't even breathe.

'Please, if you leave her alone, I promise I won't tell anyone about you.'

He doesn't answer. There's only silence.

'If you go near her, I might hurt you.' She squeezes him harder. 'But if you promise me you won't, then I'll let you go.'

She waits. But the soul catcher doesn't promise. There's only the sound of the clock.

Tick tock tick tock.

Clara holds the boy close enough now that there's no pretending he can't hear. 'You're useless,' she whispers. 'You're pointless and worthless and I hate you.' When she throws him onto the floor he doesn't break, so she stamps on him and feels him crack under her bare foot. She stamps down again, crushing his bones.

Clara kneels next to his remains. Maybe he's kept the souls he's gathered over the years and now she's let them free. She doesn't move, just observes so carefully.

Watches and waits.

There's nothing. There are no souls reaching out for her to drag them back to the living.

She feels a pain in her foot and sits back so she can look at it, but it makes her start to cry. Her tears are muddy and fierce so it's difficult to see the blood. She tries to pick out the china splinters scratched through her skin, the little boy's fingernails that cling to the sole of her foot.

Her chest hurts with crying. She doesn't know how to clean the cuts. She needs to go to the bathroom and rinse them under running water, but she's locked in. Clara wants her mother. She wants her to clean it and bandage it and heal it, but she's not here. She's not here to save her. To save them.

There are only her tears, ice-sharp against her throat. Clara buries her face into the pillow, screaming into its softness, suffocating the sound so that it ripples back into her, fills her up and makes her scream again.

*　*　*

When the tray is slipped in, Clara jumps towards the door. She's not quick enough to grab it open.

'I'm not eating until you give Stephen back to me,' she says. There's a silence. 'It's true. I won't eat another scrap until he's with me again.'

Footsteps disappear down the stairs.

Clara is so hungry, but she leaves the food sitting on the floor. It teases her, watching. She takes one of the dresses from the wardrobe and throws it over the top of the plate. The thought of the material sinking into the juices of the food makes Clara feel sick, so she takes it and pushes it under the bed and pretends that it's not there.

The skeleton of the china boy still lies scattered on the floor. Clara picks up the biggest of the shards and hides them in the hem of the curtain. The rest she sweeps into a corner, where she hopes Auntie won't see.

*　*　*

The day creeps by. Creeps up and around and under her skin.

Clara reads, until she's too full with the printed world. She listens, obsessively, for Stephen. He sounds happy, which is good, but it sears her too.

The door opens a crack, enough to push in the wooden toy, the maze with the ball. Clara doesn't want to even touch it, because she knows that Auntie's hands have been there. But she thinks Stephen must have asked her to put it here. And she's bored and the game will help chip away at the blankness.

So she plays it on her own. There's no one but Clara to pick up the ball when it drops and rolls away. There's no hand on her shoulder, no eyes to share the space with hers. But still she plays it. And it's fun.

* * *

The evening comes and Stephen isn't here.

* * *

Clara doesn't eat the next meal that she's given, instead pushing it under the bed. But when she tries to sleep, she knows it's there, sticky and cold. Her stomach cramps as she kneels down and pulls out the tray.

She drinks the water.

And eats one slice of bread, its crusts dried hard.

* * *

It's during the night when Clara is woken by the sound of banging.

'Stephen?'

But it's too loud to be someone knocking on the door.

She's disorientated, thinking for a moment that it's coming from somewhere above her.

'Auntie?'

Clara doesn't want to sit up, scared that the noise will touch her, that her skin will bruise. She lies still. Through her nightdress, she taps each of her ribs in turn, in time with the thudding, convinced that it will make it stop.

It's coming from outside the window. Clara moves her head, sees nothing but thick darkness. She wants to reach for the switch on the lamp, but daren't. Can only listen to the banging, each knock hammering on her lungs, making it hard to breathe.

She knows without doubt that someone is shutting her in.

* * *

For Auntie, it is a miracle that her world has found its way out of the shadows. She's emerged from the cruel, harsh state of hibernation, blinking in wonder at the colours she sees everywhere, realising that for too long her life has been steeped in sepia. Now it unfolds, one bud at a time. She has a son, named in honour of her brother and it is this that eases her grief at losing him to the grains.

The simple act of taking her son's hand in her own awakens her pulse, beating in rhythm with his, and sometimes she can only laugh at the wonder of not knowing where her skin ends and his begins.

There's a brief, cruel reminder of the obstacle. But she has the girl's scissors now and Uncle Warren has sorted it so that she can't get out. Auntie has a sense of satisfaction that her instincts were right – there's a dangerous quality in Clara, a definite need to destroy and she can't risk such a person anywhere near her son. What kind of mother would it make her, if she put someone so precious in the eye of the storm?

Edwyn sleeps in the attic now. He is safe at the top of the house, in the room that has been patiently waiting. He'd seemed frightened as she'd led him up the stairs too narrow to fit them both, so she'd gone ahead, the familiar scent of childhood almost moving her to tears. How had the smell of bread crusts and bottled leaves lasted so long? Maybe her children have been playing here all along. For all these years she's been downstairs with Warren, so close, but they hadn't known.

There was the familiar greeting from the stairs, leading to the room where once she hid for hide-and-seek, the trunk's lid closed tight all through that lunch until a tearful Jane found her. Perhaps she and Edwyn can play again, although she'll have to limit where he can roam.

The attic isn't as pretty as the east room, but the bed in the corner is comfortable and Auntie has placed one of her tapestry cushions on the chair against the wall. The window is a bit small, but it's one she's always liked, circular and tucked into the roof. She *thinks of Edwyn sleeping there now, the starlight trickling through to touch his dreaming eyelids.*

Auntie knows she cannot remain outside the door to the attic stairs all night, but she'd like to stay on the landing for just a few moments more. The three dolls on the windowsill watch her and she has to fight the urge to turn and talk to them, her excitement straining to engage them in her joy.

When she is too tired to stand, Auntie reaches out to pat the dolls' hands. They're colder than she'd expected, the night creeping in to lay claim. They stare at Edwyn's door, as Auntie hoped they might.

'Keep an eye,' she whispers. 'You know where I am if you need me.'

She kisses her palm and places it flat on the wooden door, before she almost skips back to her own bedroom, hampered only by the age in her bones.

16

There are boards outside the window; Clara can tell from the thick lines of sunlight alternating with dark. They make the room smaller and she's sure more than ever that she'll run out of air. She opens the curtains and finds the wooden planks hammered all the way across. Through the gaps, the garden squints at her. She reaches her hand towards it, but the glass stops her, filling her with a desolation that strips her bare.

Clara curls back onto the bed, the scratch of the blanket battling with her hunger in the semi-darkness. She waits for Uncle Warren to take away the boards and make the sun shine again, but there's only a terrifying stillness beyond the window now.

* * *

Loneliness sits on her lungs. It also gets its finger into her brain and starts itching and itching until she wants to hit her head against a wall. Finally, it empties her, scooping out her real self and stuffing her full with nothing.

She tries the handle on the bedroom door again and again, just in case, but it's always locked. She turns on the light, sees the stack of white paper on the desk and takes the top sheet. It's on her fourth attempt that she manages to cut a girl from it, scrunching up the failed ones and dropping their skin-thin limbs into the bin.

She stands on the bed to pull the painting from the wall, rubbing the dust gathered on the back of it.

'Not so clean now, are you?' Clara finds the shard of the china boy in the hem of the curtain and starts to cut into the picture, taking care to trace around the trees with the blade and not slice into the hills. She puts all of the pieces onto the table, tips back on the chair and reaches for the doll under her pillow. She has to lean the cut-out hill against the window to stand it up straight, so that Stephen and the cut-out paper girl can scramble over the top of it.

'Where are we going?' Stephen asks as he treks after her. He doesn't see the planks that have trapped him inside.

'Over the hills and far away.' Clara holds them both in one hand so she can pick up the sun, moving its yellow circle high above them. 'It's a beautiful day.'

'Yes,' Stephen says. And she wants to make them skip, so she has to put down the sun so that the doll and the paper girl can run down the hill, side-by-side.

'It's nice that we're together again,' she tells Stephen.

'You're my favourite person in the world,' Stephen says and he hugs her.

There's a noise outside the window and they peer through a

gap in the planks of wood. Auntie and Stephen are in the garden holding hands, both their coats buttoned up to their chins, a new woollen hat pulled almost to Stephen's eyebrows, even though the sun is shining.

Clara puts her hand to the glass. 'I'm here,' she says, but he doesn't look up.

They turn and stroll across the lawn, their backs to her now. When they go through the arch in the hedge they vanish, so Clara stands on the table and from the top of the window she can see them. How Stephen runs towards the swing, calling back to Auntie. How when she gets to him, she holds it steady and waits for him to sit straight. She says something and he laughs, pulling on the ropes.

She pushes him, but Clara knows it's not strong enough.

'You're doing it wrong,' she says. 'He won't like that.'

Stephen talks to Auntie over his shoulder and she steps forward to push harder. It's still not enough, he'll want to go higher, but he only kicks his legs and laughs.

Look up, Stephen. I'm here. If you just look up, you'll remember me.

He closes his eyes, leans back into Auntie's hands and she glows as she pushes him.

'He's not Edwyn!' Clara shouts. 'He's not Edwyn!' And she slams her palm into the glass, rattling the pane. 'Let him go.'

Clara sinks down onto the table and curls her body into the window, lashing out at the chair with her feet so that it tumbles pathetically against the bed. 'Give him back.'

She jumps up and kicks at the chest of drawers. She pulls out one and smashes it onto the floor, scattering Stephen's vests and underwear.

'Give him back,' she shouts again as she picks up the blade, stands on his bed and starts to slash at the other painting. Again and again, scraping through the trees until they bleed. Broken, like she is, like Auntie should be.

Clara picks up the pillow and cuts a dark scar into it, shaking it until the room is filled with feathers. She hears Nancy's voice telling her how white feathers mean a dead person is visiting. And here they are. Hundreds of them.

'So is this where you kept their souls?' Clara's tears turn into laughter as she scoops up handfuls and throws them into the air, watches them spin and fall. 'You came back,' she laughs, the feathers soft and spiky as she scatters them over the bed, over the floor. She kicks through them like autumn leaves, picking up a handful to hold them to her cheek. 'See?' she tells the doll and cut-out girl watching from the window. 'Our souls never really go.'

The door suddenly opens. Clara stands and stares at Auntie, whose eyes flash anger at the chaos, her hand gripping the handle tight. She looks from the walls, to the bed, to the floor, and rage begins to shake her, forcing Clara to step away to the corner of the room.

'You're determined to destroy everything, aren't you?' Auntie says.

Clara wants to speak, but fear has taken her voice and hidden it inside her skin. Auntie moves towards her, just as Clara hears Stephen singing in the hallway downstairs, his childish voice drifting up to them.

Auntie steps back. She stares at Clara with a hatred that rocks her bones, before she closes the door, the key turning in her fingers.

* * *

Clara tries to pick up every last feather and puts them in the bottom drawer. It takes time to find them all. There are some tucked behind the bed, pushed under the table, hidden in the corner. She starts to name every one, to help the day move faster. To make her forget the fear she felt when Auntie was here.

She names the feathers and fills the drawer, tucking the broken pillowcase on top, before she shuts them away from the world.

* * *

At night, Clara leaves on the light.

'I'm hungry,' she tells Walrus. He looks so sad. He misses Stephen too.

She feels the hunger in her throat, stretching in a line all the way to her stomach, an ache that goes through her veins so that no part of her can forget. Clara closes her eyes and opens them, but the hunger is still there, like a storm, breaking her body.

'She'll bring him back tomorrow,' she tells Walrus and he believes her.

* * *

In the room's silence, Clara hears the voices. They're quiet, muffled, and she knows they're the souls of the dead people, coming from inside the drawer. She wants to pull the blanket over her head, but she can't move, terrified that they'll know she's here.

Stay still, Walrus, then they won't see you.

The voices get louder, blurring as they scratch to get out of the drawer.

Clara curls into a foetus and presses her palms into her head.

'Mummy,' she says. But her mother doesn't come.

Only a smell of smoke seeps into the room. Acrid, sharp against her skin, pushing inside. Clara's eyes hurt too much to open.

'Stephen,' she tries to call. She has to save him. She doesn't want him to burn.

She hears her mother crying, pitiful sounds looped tight with the fire. The smoke struggling into her, pulling out a scream as she crawls in circles, the boiling wood cracking and crumbling around her.

Clara hides now in the sheets, shaking her head to make the visions fall away. But her mother hangs there, clinging to her mind, until Clara can't tell which screams are her own.

* * *

There's something in Clara's bed in the morning, small pieces digging into her arm. She pulls back the blanket to find four doll's fingers lying next to her. She doesn't move, as the hollow fingers stare back. Can think only of their snapped skin that wants to scrape at her lungs.

Clara jumps back when the door opens. Stephen. He's here. He scurries in, the shine on his face fading when he sees what's on the sheet.

'They belong to the dolls,' he whispers.

Clara just stares at him, wanting him to change it. He picks up one of the fingers and tries to crush it, grimacing as he forces it with his thumb. Finally, the finger cracks, leaving only a stubborn pink nail like a paralysed rosebud.

Stephen does the same to the other three. Clara's eyes follow him as he gets a book from beside the toadstool lamp and clumsily brushes the doll's remains between the pages, before putting it under the bed.

'Now she'll never know.' His voice is still altered.

'Where is she?' Clara asks.

'I made you this,' Stephen says. From his pocket he takes a cardboard heart, coloured to the edges with a red pencil.

'It's beautiful,' Clara says, with no energy left to cry. She wants to have it in her hands, but he puts it on the table.

'You must eat your breakfast,' he says, pointing to the tray with a plate of food, a glass of water.

'Will you stay with me if I eat?' Clara asks.

Stephen glances towards the door, before he nods. He knows that she is different now and he'll have to help her, so he pulls back the sheet and blanket for her to step out.

'Are you cold?' he asks.

'A bit.'

He gets her cardigan and holds it for her so she can slip in her arms.

'We're making a kite,' he says as he sits next to her.

'That's good.' Clara is feeling dizzy and drinks too quickly.

'I'm allowed to choose the colours, so it's going to be black and with a green and purple tail.'

'Will you show me when it's finished?' Clara asks.

'If she lets me.'

'Is she looking after you well?' Clara asks.

Stephen tips his head slightly to the side. 'Of course.'

'Where are you sleeping?'

'In my old room.'

'Your old room?'

'The one I was in when I was born.'

A pain gnaws at Clara's head. She feels her brain being picked apart as it's taken from her skull.

'It's in the attic,' she hears him say. 'With my name painted above the bed.'

'But you're Stephen,' she says.

He feels little flushes of anger stamp across his cheeks. 'No,' he says. 'I'm not.'

'We can still live here if you want,' Clara says. 'But you have to stop pretending to be someone else.'

'I'm not pretending,' he shouts. 'I'm Edwyn. You know I am.'

'Fine.' She needs him to calm, so that he'll stay with her. 'It's all right.'

'You're just jealous because she loves me more.'

'No, it's not that.'

There's a sound in the doorway and they both look up to see Auntie standing there. She looks transformed, as though real happiness has found its way into her being.

'Edwyn?' she asks, but she doesn't step into the room. 'Why are you in here?'

'I don't know,' he says, his chair scraping the floor as he stands up. He needs to leave this girl he doesn't recognise, this girl made of sticks. He picks up the painted cardboard heart and takes it to Auntie.

'I made this for you,' he says.

Her face glows as she takes it. 'It's perfect.'

She puts her arm over his shoulder, pulling him from the room and neither of them looks back.

* * *

Clara eats the toast, every last crumb.

She eats the lunch when it's pushed through.

And supper too.

279

* * *

The next day, Clara hears voices outside the window. Stephen and Auntie carry the kite between them. It's black, as Stephen promised, with a rainbow tail. Clara pretends she's down there with them, stepping through the window glass, past the nailed-in wood and floating to the ground; they don't see her as she holds the kite too. The material is rougher than she'd expected – from the bedroom it looked like silk.

Stephen holds the string as Auntie keeps the kite from the ground. She tells him that he must run as fast as he can, and the wind will catch it and it will fly.

'Ready?' she asks, and he nods. 'Go!' And as he runs the wind seems to catch underneath the kite so Auntie lets go. Stephen looks behind him as it crashes to the grass.

Clara can feel his disappointment as if it were her own.

'Not to worry,' Auntie says. 'We'll try again.'

This time Stephen runs faster, his face determined. He daren't glance back, but knows when it fails again, the string tugging heavy against the ground.

Auntie's composure tips slightly, her smile not quite so sturdy anymore.

'Let's try again,' she says.

Clara recognises the scowl on Stephen's face, the one that precedes an outburst. She's seen his hands balled into fists too many times, but Auntie hasn't.

When he runs again, his feet stamp more heavily. He looks back, pulling at the string, and in desperation Auntie throws the kite. It slams into the ground as Stephen falls too, mud smearing up his clothes. Auntie watches him, her arms by her sides. When he struggles to his feet, his face spilling red, she lifts her hand towards him.

Stephen runs to the flightless kite and stamps on it, twisting his whole body so that underneath his feet it rams and breaks into the earth. He yanks at the colours of the tail, but can't rip them free, anger shaking him as Auntie hesitates. When she reaches him, Stephen turns and pushes her so hard that she nearly falls.

The only word that Clara clearly hears is *hate*, as Stephen's wildness drags him furiously from the garden. There's a hanging silence, before Clara hears the front door open and slam, the banging of his feet on the stairs, the turn of the key and he rushes in, throwing himself into his sister, where he's held tight.

'Shh,' she says, stroking his hair, his anger shuddering in gulps beneath her palms. 'You can try the kite another day.'

'It didn't work,' he says.

'It will.'

'It won't,' he says, and his wail winds its way around them.

'It'll be all right, Bean. We'll make it better.'

Clara holds him until he quietens, her heart hurting at the feel of him in her arms. If she stays like this then no one will be able to take him. If she keeps her hands clasped firm, then Auntie will have to leave him with her.

'I saw daddy's car,' Stephen says.

'Daddy's here?' Clara lets go of him, sitting back to get a clear look at his face. She sees only truth there. 'Where is he?'

'It was just his car. In the garage.'

'In the garage?'

'I was exploring and I found it.'

'But where's daddy?'

'I don't know.'

'Did you ask her?' She thinks her grip on his arm might be too hard, but she doesn't let go. 'Tell me, Stevie.'

'I'm not Stephen,' he shouts, kicking Clara hard enough to make her cry out. 'He's dead.' And he runs from her.

She stares after him, thinking only that their father's car is here, but he is not. There's a thought somewhere, a loop of reason just out of reach. When she glances out of the window, Auntie stands in the middle of the broken kite, its string wrapped around her wrists. Clara imagines twisting it tighter, sees the lost expression turn to surprise as the kite lifts and is carried by the wind. Auntie's arms are pulled into the air as her feet leave the ground, the kite gathering speed to take her over the hedge, the forest now far below. She watches the gaping hole of Auntie's mouth suck in the shock as she's taken to the clouds, the greyness stepping over her, covering her knees, her stomach, her neck, until her face is washed away.

Clara turns back to the bedroom and she sees the wide-open door and from here she can just see the key jutting out from its metal hole. She knows it's waiting for her. It isn't difficult to pull it from its place. In her palm, it looks harmless – she could almost swallow it whole. Clara's mind is muddled as she heads across the landing, the only sense she knows is that she must get away from the bedroom and find her father, but first she must hide the key. She thinks of burying it underneath the crosses in the garden, or among the forgotten feathers of the dead chickens.

There are people speaking, in the hallway below. The strange sound of Edwyn laid over her brother's voice.

'I'm sorry.'

And Clara's reality blurs and smudges as she leans back against the wall.

'If you pop into the dining room I'll bring some milk to make everything better,' she hears Auntie say and then the soft touch of footsteps across the floor, the opening and closing of a door.

There's a pause, pregnant with the unknown, pressing Clara further into the painted wood-panelling. Someone is coming up the stairs. Clara can't go back into the bedroom and risk being locked in again, so she rushes towards the room next to the bathroom and barely hears herself step inside.

She knows instantly that it's Auntie and Uncle Warren's room. She has to cover her mouth to stop herself from swallowing the smell of ashen skin. It's dark in here, the curtains only open a crack, but it's light enough to see the carved headboard behind the bed, the two bedside tables with silent lamps. The dent in one pillow where a head has rested.

There are footsteps on the landing outside. Clara thinks they're moving away and she should hide under the bed, but she's scared that too much of Auntie will be there. She catches sight of something in the mirror and turns to see the little stitched boy sitting on a chair in the corner, one arm hanging down, the other laying his leather hand across his lap.

'Help me,' she whispers. But the sewn mouth stays closed as footsteps turn and come closer. Clara hurries towards the boy, lifts the cover of his pocket and slips in the key.

The only place to hide is the wardrobe. Clara opens the thick wooden door and curls inside, the hems of dresses like webs on her face as she closes away the bedroom.

'Clara?' she hears Auntie say. 'Clara?' There's the sound of the bathroom door opening, closing. 'Where are you?'

Clara is too close to Auntie's clothes, to the dust of her. She moves her head lower into her knees so that the dress above her only rests against the back of her neck.

'Clara?' Auntie is in the room. 'Are you here?'

She mustn't move, she mustn't breathe.

'Come out, come out wherever you are,' Auntie's voice sings, so quietly.

There's the sound of a drawer opening and another. Stockinged feet coming closer across the floor, stopping next to the wardrobe door. A gentle tap tapping.

'Is anyone in there?'

No. I'm not here. I'm far away.

A hand brushing against the wood, the handle turning.

And Auntie is looking down at her, at the girl twisted terrified among her dresses.

'What are you doing there?' A stretch of pale neck showing as she tilts her head to the side.

'Go away,' Clara says.

'Go where?' Auntie says. 'I live here.'

'But I don't want to. I want to go home.'

'That's not for you to decide,' Auntie says, pushing the hangers aside so that her clothes part enough to see Clara in full.

'Stephen will come up any minute,' Clara says. 'He'll see what you're really like.'

These words make Auntie lunge forward, undignified as she sinks her fingers into Clara's wrist and pulls the child from the wardrobe.

'Where's my daddy?' Clara shouts. 'He's been here. Where is he?'

'Your father didn't want to visit. It's too far to travel,' Auntie says.

'His car is here. It's in the garage.'

Auntie stares at her, stunned for a moment, before she holds her head straight.

'That's not your father's car. I've told you, he doesn't want to see you.'

'That's not true.'

'Isn't it?'

Clara is barely able to stand, but she has something else.

'I've hidden the key. You can't lock me in that room again.'

'It's not the only room in this house.'

Another sound, smaller footsteps.

'What's wrong, mummy?' It's Stephen's voice.

'Clara has got out,' Auntie says. She slaps her own cheek suddenly, shocking Clara to stillness. 'She's hurt me, Stephen. You mustn't come too close.'

'I didn't touch you,' Clara says, as Stephen hesitates into the room, where he sees Auntie's cheek with its reddening stain, the tears brought stinging into her eyes.

'Why did you?' Stephen accuses Clara.

Auntie lifts a key from a hook by the door.

'Come with me,' Auntie tells her.

'I won't,' Clara says, but Auntie grabs her arm again and pulls with a strength that terrifies her.

'She wants to take you from me,' Auntie tells Stephen. 'But I won't have it.'

Clara starts to scream, the noise ripping through the painted walls, scratching its path along the banisters, forcing Stephen to fall huddled onto the floor, his arms clasped tight over his head. He doesn't like how the girl's bones stick through her skin, her hips awkward, lips cracked.

'Stevie!'

But he won't hear it, doesn't see Auntie drag her the length of the landing to the door that's always been locked. Clara kicks out as Auntie struggles to fit the key into its place; she manages to break free, running towards the stairs. But Auntie's determined grip is on her and she hauls her back, past the dolls that sit staring.

'Mummy!' Clara screams as Auntie turns the handle and opens the door onto a room that stalls her. In front of them is a crib, the pink bows crusted with dust.

'You can't put me in there!' Clara writhes in the grasp of a lonely person made steel from despair. They both battle different demons as they're forced into the room, where the only cries should be a distant newborn.

Clara feels herself pushed slippery from Auntie, separated with a grotesque groan that shrinks her aunt up to the wall before she gathers her skirt and staggers empty from the room. The little key perfectly placed, twisting. And now Clara hears the voices speaking, just the other side of the door and she knows that Auntie kneels with her brother, cradling him in her arms.

'You're safe now,' is whispered. 'We're both safe.'

Clara thinks she mustn't scream anymore, mustn't scare Stephen further from her. There'll be a way to bring him back and she'll work it out when her mind has enough space to settle in this place cluttered with emptiness.

It's a long time before she hears Stephen and Auntie stand up, the soles of their feet soft on the landing. She's sure they must be hand-in-hand as they disappear away from her, down the stairs.

* * *

*A*untie can admit to herself that it hasn't been an easy day. Edwyn's outburst took her quite by surprise. The kite had been such a treat and although she realises now that maybe their hopes had been too high, there had been no need for such devastation from her son. She was only glad that Warren had been at work and unable to see.

And the girl's peculiar attempt at hide-and-seek. Perhaps if she'd asked, then they all could have played, but to take a lead like that and even venture into a room that she must have known was out of bounds. It had made Auntie uncomfortable, seeing the girl crouched among her dresses like that, an intrusion of some kind. But Auntie is pleased that she masked her own discomfort well. And she's found a solution so that it won't happen again.

There's a sharp pain in Auntie's chest. The ribbons were still there on the crib, the blanket tucked neatly into the tiny mattress. She remembers the feeling of the wool in her hands as she crocheted the stalks and petals of daffodils. Now those knitting needles are being pressed through her chest, have found their way to her heart where they move back and forth, tearing through her fragile tissue, breaking the walls of chambers, the pain so extreme that it's blinding.

17

Clara rips the wallpaper in long strips, finding a gash in its papery skin, peeling it slowly to reveal the white bones underneath.

'Daddy,' she whispers, over and over, but there's never a reply.

Early on day three, she puts her palm flat to the weeping plaster and can feel its heartbeat ticking there against the lines of her hand. Beating slower and slower as the day moves by with no food or water, until her mouth sticks and her tongue slips lolling and desperate. When it rains beyond the window, Clara crawls under the empty crib, curls tight into a foetus and she's back in her mother's womb, getting all she needs from that twisted cord that binds them together.

Slipping momentarily into consciousness, Clara licks the floor, sure of the water collected there, but finding only grains of Auntie's bitter dreams that scratch against her gums.

When the door unlocks, Clara opens her eyes enough to see the gash of it exposing the landing outside and Auntie's feet dipped in flesh-coloured tights, the hem of her skirt brushing her calves.

'I brought you food.' Auntie must see the wallpaper shredded in mounds of faded-rose confetti. She must smell the stench of defecation. 'Ham and just a few potatoes, so as not to upset your stomach.'

There she is, her knees, her hands coming into view, until all Clara can see is Auntie's face peeking under the crib, so close to her own.

'And I've made you cocoa.'

Clara feels herself unfurl, a blossoming as she drags herself out, sharp knees and shoulders as she finds a way to sit.

'I'll bring a table next time,' the smiling lips say. 'But for now the floor will have to do.'

Clara reaches out for the warm mug. She doesn't hesitate at the taste of too many crushed pills, swallowing the liquid back before a spoonful of food hovers near her lips. And she swallows.

'Good girl. There'll be pudding later. Would you like that?'

But Clara doesn't answer. She doesn't even lift her eyes.

* * *

Auntie watches Stephen as he sleeps and thinks she's never seen anything more beautiful. The soft touch of his hair on his forehead, curling slightly on the top of his cheeks. It frames a face she feels she's always known. Finally, she belongs in this world.

The book is open on his lap, one from when she was young. She'd carried on reading after his eyes were closed, held the rhythm of the language to his breathing and linked it in turn with her own. Now he's fallen asleep with his hand in hers and she's reluctant to go. She wants to stay by his side all of the time, a gaping emptiness appearing in the moments when they're apart.

The corridor is so familiar to her, yet now the walls seem softer, swollen with new life, as she enters her own bedroom. Her exhaustion is unfamiliar, made heavier by the knowledge of that girl, tucked in a corner where she doesn't belong.

When Auntie turns to see the stitched boy behind the door, he's watching her with pity in his eyes. She hadn't been expecting that – she'd thought instead she'd be singed in the glare of his disapproval.

'What shall I do, Warren?' she asks, reaching out to touch the long-dried skin of his cheek.

'Make it better,' he whispers, his voice coming from Auntie's mouth.

And she understands. Because maybe she's known all along.

* * *

The darkness of the night carries her in its silence. She hesitates outside the bedroom door, startled in the knowledge that the breath of something living mists up the window behind it. She feels the rub of her heart beating as she lets herself in.

The room is empty, Auntie is sure of it. Her eyes flicker about, too aware of the desertion, until she sees a hand reaching out from under the crib, tipped up, catching the air.

'Clara?'

The hand doesn't move. Auntie walks forward, a bit at a time, to where Clara is lying still, her leg twisted ugly beneath her. Auntie wants to leave the room, to lock the door and pretend that she hasn't seen, but she hesitates forward and touches Clara's arm. It's surprisingly cold. So she reaches over into the crib and picks up the small pink blanket she folded all those years ago. The touch of it stalls her and she has to hold tight to her babies' bed to find her way back into the room.

It takes a lot of effort to move the girl, sliding her out across the floor.

'This will warm you,' Auntie says, wrapping the blanket over Clara, leaving her head out of the end so she can breathe. Because she is breathing. Bird-like breaths so shallow that her chest barely rises.

The girl looks so peaceful that Auntie wonders now how she ever managed to stir her mind into chaos. She's so young, so pretty. They should have been very happy, if only Clara had given her a chance.

She's surprisingly light, although a little bit awkward to carry. Auntie has to balance her almost entirely on her leg as she opens the door. Stephen sleeps soundly in his room in the attic and she knows that he won't wake as she carries Clara down the stairs. Auntie has to put the girl onto the hallway floor so she can slip on her shoes. She feels Warren place his coat on her shoulders.

'That'll keep away the night's chill,' her husband's low voice speaks from her mouth.

She unlocks the front door and Clara seems heavier this time as she picks her up. Silently around the edge of the house, Auntie barely noticing the cold nipping at her legs. She carries Clara across her two arms, one of the girl's elbows pressing against her chest, the fingers of the other hand drifting towards the ground, her head falling backwards, rolling in the air like the pheasants that sometimes Uncle Warren is lucky enough to catch.

They walk down the lawn, through the arch in the hedge and past the hushed blackberry bushes. The moon is distant, hiding, but Auntie could find this way in her sleep. She pauses at the edge of the loch, at the thick slick of tar-black water yawning into the distance.

'You want to play in the boat, don't you?' she whispers into Clara's ear. She doesn't want to look at the girl but she can't help herself, and when she sees her daughter's body hanging in her arms she starts to shake. A wail forms, just one high note stretching from her lips, running fast towards the mountains.

'Pull yourself together,' Warren tells her, the sudden downturn of Auntie's mouth twisting with the effort. 'This needs to be done.' And she has to pull her pain back in. 'Give the girl to me.'

But Auntie can't, not yet. She's not ready. And so Warren yanks the sleeping child from her, separating her skin from Clara. The boat is far away, but still Warren wades towards it, the mud sucking at his ankles as he grinds his teeth, chews his lip, moves forward with the girl useless in his arms. Auntie watches as he struggles. She won't take her eyes from them, needing every last glimpse of her daughter. Her beautiful daughter. It would have worked, if they'd had more time.

Warren doesn't reach the boat. Instead, he lifts Clara above his head and throws her with all his strength. Her arms, her legs, her head form such aberrant shapes, before she lands twisted and heavy on the mud that's been waiting. And now it welcomes her, touching her toes, her palms, her face. Sweeping over Clara's eyes, drinking the tips of her ears, filling her mouth.

Auntie watches as her daughter disappears, until no sign remains. She hangs her head low as Warren storms past her, trailing the swathe of his anger. And it's only when she knows he's gone, the red scorch of his fury leaving no trace, that Auntie hurries alone back through the trees, across the lawn with only the moon and scattered stars to show the way.

She climbs the stairs with the loch's saliva slick on the hem of her dress. She needs more than ever to see the living force of her surviving son and goes quietly up to his room. He lies on his back, one hand resting on Walrus. She wonders where he is in his dreams, and whether she's there with him. Panic nips at her when she thinks that maybe she's not.

Auntie's shadow spills over Stephen as she leans forward, covering half of his face. It's the germs lifting from the walrus, drifting too close to her boy, that make her reach over and lift his arm. His skin feels cold in her hand and she wants to hold it, mix his blood with the warmth of her own. He moves, shifting to a different position, and she knows she must be quick.

'I'll only take it for a bit,' she whispers, before she lowers Stephen's arm and reluctantly lets him go, stepping away from the bed, the *dirt-encrusted animal hanging from the tips of her fingers.*

In the kitchen, she puts on her rubber gloves, runs a sink of scalding water and sprinkles in white powder that dissolves before she dunks in Walrus. She holds him under the surface, watching bubbles wheeze and pop around him. Through the suds, his brown eyes stare up at her, so she turns him over and starts to scrub at his fur, cleaning out the years of muck, making it safe for her son.

When she's satisfied, she holds it under the tap until the water runs completely clean. The walrus is difficult to squeeze, and Auntie has to hold each section of its body, twisting until it's dry enough to carry outside without dripping on her floor.

The lights from the house spread enough into the garden to show her the way to the washing line strung by the edge of the vegetable patch. Auntie takes two pegs from her apron, clipping the toy's legs so that he hangs in the darkness. It's cold and Auntie knows that he won't dry until tomorrow's sun, but at least it's a start.

She's pleased as she returns to the house, humming a faint tune in the night air. Behind her, clean drops of water fall from Walrus, but there's no one to hear them as they're gathered by the earth.

* * *

Stephen is sleeping when a sticky hand wraps so tight around his neck that he can no longer breathe. He's gasping, shaken awake, confused as the room regains focus and becomes his own, the bad dream gone. There's a figure sat next to him, the warmth of Auntie adding weight to the mattress.

'Hush now. I'm here,' she says, as she brushes his hair from his forehead, slick now with childish sweat. 'No one can hurt you.'

He puts his thumb in his mouth, as Edwyn would, until his terror fades completely. He grins up at Auntie in the almost-darkness, his thumb still wedged against his tongue, before he closes his eyes to sleep again.

* * *

In the morning, Stephen is alone as he registers the absence of Walrus.

'Clara?' he whispers, a hint of longing bound tight to the accusation. But there's no reply.

He's able to dress himself and fix all the fiddly buttons, to pull his socks straight and fold the collar. And he doesn't need help down the stairs, to go into the dining room where he knows his clean breakfast bowl will be.

He sits in his chair, feet just touching the ground as he pulls at one sleeve of his suit jacket and then the other, hiding the cuffs of his shirt. He gets bored, waiting with his back rod-straight and so he picks up his spoon and starts tapping it against the edge of the china and his glass, hearing the different sounds ringing out, the strange singing filling the room. He tries to whistle to himself as he hits against the leather place mat, unaware that it's his Uncle

Warren's dried skin adding its own dull grunt to the air.

He stops the instant Auntie comes in, but her face shows only delight to see him sitting there.

'We can eat together,' she says, her voice painstakingly childlike as he smiles at her, at the butter-smothered toast she carries, the jug of milk she pours.

'What shall we do today?' he asks, eager for the morning to start, for the adventure to be found.

'I could teach you to sew?' Auntie wants to stay inside, to keep the loch at a distance for a while.

'We'll go exploring,' Stephen tells her. 'Into the woods.'

The keys in her pocket rub slightly as she moves, reminding Stephen of his fingers on the key at home, the one that used to sit tight in the door of the shed. The powerful chill of it as he turned it in the lock, the hammering of his mother's fists. He'd covered his ears but not his eyes as he'd watched the flames build and grow, a fascinating monster with burning teeth to take his mother away.

'Maybe we could make something for the train track?' Auntie tries.

Stephen looks at her. 'No,' he says. 'We'll play outside.'

And Auntie knows they will.

ACKNOWLEDGEMENTS

To my brave and beautiful mum, always with me.

To Veronique Baxter - thank you for being an incredible agent, even during such a challenging year. Thank you also to Sara Langham and all at David Higham.

To my truly brilliant editor, George Sandison – this book wouldn't be a pinch of what it is without you. And thank you to all at Titan, in particular Davi Lancett, Lydia Gittins, Polly Grice and a special mention to Julia Lloyd for creating such a strikingly perfect cover.

Thank you, Ali Dougal for your much-valued input into this book.

I live with the best people - thank you Miles, Albert, Arthur and Frank for a home filled with chaos and love.

I wrote so much of this book with our beautiful cat, Panda, curled up on my lap - I miss you, sweetest girl.

To Philip, Lara, Emma and Flan and my extended family and friends – especially my Rolle alumni, NCT family, the Howes, my Book Group, the Whinneys (welcoming Kai and Skye to the world!) and the Cameroons.

To my lovely writing group - Allie, Deb, Lucy, Nikki, Sandi and Suzanna, you always inspire me to be better. To Samala Bernstein, for your encouragement after reading an early draft. And thank you to Jules Bryant for always finding time to read chunks of this book when I needed advice.

To all the booksellers, librarians and bloggers around the world – thank you. Special mention to Ness, Jules, Lara, Naomi and Carmen at The Book Nook.

To the inspirational staff and students at the school where I work, in particular Raven, Archie, Ashley, Callum, Jamie, Lauran, Sam and Tyler – keep shining.

And finally, to my writing spirit – this was a strange and dark book, but it was so much fun to write. Thank you for bringing it to me.

ABOUT THE AUTHOR

Lisa Heathfield is the award-winning author of *Paper Butterflies*, *Seed*, *Flight of a Starling* and *I Am Not A Number*. She has been shortlisted twice for the Waterstones Children's Book Prize and her young adult novels have won the North-East Teen Book Award, the Southern Schools Book Award, the Fab Award, the GDST Award and the Concorde Award. *Such Pretty Things* is her first novel for adults. Lisa works as a literacy coordinator and teaching-assistant in a secondary school for students with social, emotional and mental health challenges. She lives by the sea in Brighton, UK, with her husband and their three sons.

For more fantastic fiction, author events,
exclusive excerpts, competitions, limited editions and more

VISIT OUR WEBSITE
titanbooks.com

LIKE US ON FACEBOOK
facebook.com/titanbooks

FOLLOW US ON TWITTER AND INSTAGRAM
@TitanBooks

EMAIL US
readerfeedback@titanemail.com